I0777637

MUFFIN BUT TROUBLE

A DONNER BAKERY NOVEL

TALIA HUNTER

WWW.SMARTYPANTSROMANCE.COM

COPYRIGHT

CHAPTER 1

MAGDALENA

reen Valley was not the kind of place I was used to. That became especially clear to me when I discovered my sister Carla had left her front door key under her doormat.

I mean, why go to the trouble of hiding the key if you're going to put it in the most obvious place? Why not just leave the front door open and provide sacks for burglars to carry off your valuables?

Okay, so I'll admit I couldn't see any potential burglars. The quiet rural street wasn't exactly teeming with criminal activity. Or any activity. There were practically tumbleweeds. Still, my sister may as well have changed her computer password to PASSWORD while she was at it. Sheesh!

I'd just unlocked Carla's front door and pulled my suitcase into her hallway when my phone rang. It was a video call from my sister, and when I accepted it, Carla appeared on the screen. Judging from the beige wall behind her, she was in a hotel room.

"Hi, brat," she said with a smile. "Are you there yet?"

"The shuttle dropped me off two minutes ago, and I just stepped through your front door. Do you have a spy camera set up in here?" I pretended to peer into the corners of the hallway.

"Just a lucky guess. But listen, Mags, are you completely sure you're going to be okay staying there on your own?" Carla leaned closer to the camera, her brow furrowed and her expression intent, as though we hadn't had this exact conversation before I left New York.

My sister liked to overanalyze things, which usually made her my opposite. But this time, I was secretly more worried than she was about staying at her place in rural Tennessee while she and Noah were away.

"Stop worrying, nerd," I told her, trying to force a smile. "I'll be fine."

No point in telling her that I was so far from fine, I'd lost sight of it completely.

The truth was, I hated being alone. I was used to living in a noisy sea of people. And I liked New York people, with all their blunt, impatient assertiveness. I liked watching bands play in grungy dive bars, hunting for bargains in tiny boutiques, and seeing graffiti artists creating rough masterpieces as I walked home from work. And I was going to miss my favorite taco truck with its delicious quesabirria and hilariously rude server. From what I'd seen so far, Green Valley was basically an expanse of barely populated nothingness.

"Okay." Carla's frown eased. "I'm still surprised that you wanted to do this, but the countryside is beautiful, isn't it? And don't you love the fresh country air?"

"Hmm." I tilted my head, pretending to think about it. "Is it the animals crapping everywhere that makes it smell so fresh?"

My sister laughed. "Give it a few days, and you'll start to love it. Our bedroom's on the right. Yours is on the left."

I peered into their bedroom first. Sunshine was streaming in, and a fluffy black-and-white cat was lying on its back in the middle of their bed, fast asleep on the white cover.

Wheeling my suitcase further down the hallway, I found the guest bedroom. It was twice the size of my tiny, shared-bathroom studio apartment in Brooklyn, and instead of buildings, the window looked out onto green fields and trees.

"What do you think?" asked Carla. "Nice, right?"

"A view of open space with no people for miles. What's not to like?" I made my voice light, as though I was joking, but if I let myself dwell on the solitude, I was going to freak out.

"I left you a note on the kitchen counter with all the information about feeding the cat and chickens." Some doubt crept into her tone. "You *can* feed the chickens, right? And Freud, my cat?"

"That's why I'm here. Cat and chickens. Wait, the chickens are the ones with the feathers, right?"

"Very funny, brat."

"Chill out, already." I rolled my eyes. "It's only a few weeks. There's a better-than-even chance your animals will survive."

"I wish we could have been there when you arrived," my sister said. "I would have loved to see you."

"When do you start your medical trial?"

"Tomorrow. But I'm trying not to get my hopes up. It might come to nothing, lots of things have."

Despite her caution, I could sense her excitement. She'd been sick for a long time and the new drug she was going to get to test sounded promising. When she discovered she could be included in the trial, she and Noah had dropped everything and taken a last-minute flight. And it had been perfect timing for me.

"Wait," Carla said. "Here's Noah."

My sister's fiancé appeared next to her. Noah was dark haired and handsome, and though I didn't know him that well yet, I liked him a lot. Mostly because he was so obviously in love with her.

"Hey, Mags." Noah flashed me his white teeth. "I spoke to Jennifer. She's expecting you at the bakery at six o'clock tomorrow morning. Is that too soon?"

"No, it's perfect. Thanks for setting me up with a job at such short notice."

"Jennifer's happy for you to work there for as long as you're in town." Noah's Southern drawl made it sound like he was speaking at half speed. If time was money, everything he said would cost about twice as much as it should.

"The folks in the bakery are real nice," he added. "Like a family. We won't have to worry about you, seeing as they'll look out for you. Anything you need, just ask Jennifer or Joy."

I nodded. Though I'd never worked in a bakery before, I wasn't nervous. For the last few years I'd been the star salesperson at a fashion boutique, so being behind the counter in a bakery should be . . . well, a piece of cake. Pun intended.

The only thing I didn't want was for my new co-workers to ask too many questions. My sole experience with small towns was from watching *Virgin River* and *Hart of Dixie,* and in those shows, everyone knew each other's business. I didn't even want to tell my eldest sister what I was really doing in Green Valley, and we were close. I wasn't about to share my problems with a bunch of strangers and have them judge me for my mistakes.

"Well, we'd better get to the medical center," said Noah. "You enjoy yourself, okay?"

"Have fun, brat!" Carla waved and hung up.

I shrugged off my jacket, dumping it and my phone onto the bed. Leaving my suitcase, I walked past a room that was clearly a home office, and found the kitchen at the end of the hallway. Thank goodness there was a coffee machine on the kitchen counter. An essential, seeing how far it was to the closest café.

Poking my head into the living room next, I figured the colorful cushions on the leather couches had to have been chosen by Carla, and the pop-art paintings were probably Noah's. The house was roomy, comfortable, and just as tidy as I'd expected.

But the silence was already pressing in on me. I couldn't hear cars, or shouting, or sirens.

In Brooklyn, I'd never been alone. Between my friends, boyfriend, job, and loud neighbors, there'd been no such thing as spare time. Or silence.

Wandering back to Carla's bedroom, I found the cat still asleep on the bed. As far as I knew, the cat and the chickens were the only other living things for miles around.

Maybe if I woke the cat up, I wouldn't feel so alone.

"It's you and me now, cat." I petted his back, but the cat didn't stir, except maybe to press his eyes more tightly closed.

It was just me and my thoughts.

And my thoughts *sucked*.

"I won't be here for long," I said to the cat. "I'll be leaving as soon as I can get a scary drug dealer off my back."

The cat didn't seem to care either way.

And I can only imagine how Carla and Noah would have reacted if I'd told them the truth about why I'd volunteered to look after their farmhouse.

"By the way, what do you do for fun around here?" I asked the cat.

Silence.

"Yeah. That's what I figured."

Wandering back to the kitchen, I found a stack of paper on the counter. It was covered in my sister's obsessively neat handwriting. Carla had said she'd left me a note, only her so-called *note* was longer than the entire Harry Potter series.

Still, I felt a little less glum when I saw Carla had also left me some car keys. "At least I won't have to rely on Ubers now, if there even are any this far in the middle of nowheresville." I said it out loud, because apparently the Tennessee version of me liked to talk to herself, as well as to animals.

My only answer was the sound of my stomach rumbling. I was starving. And hopefully everything would seem less terrible once I'd eaten.

There were some apples in a bowl on the counter, but my last meal had been hours ago, and I needed something more substantial. Opening the fridge, I found only vegetables and condiments.

The cupboards and pantry proved equally bare. Oh sure, there were plenty of herbs and spices. Dried beans, lentils, rice, and seeds. Different flours and baking supplies. But there were no Hot Pockets or Pop-Tarts. No snack foods, or candy, or even breakfast cereals.

"I'll have to get takeout delivered," I said. Though I was woefully short of funds, I had enough money for a decent meal, at least.

Fetching my phone from the bedroom, I searched for all the pizza places that delivered to my current location.

Nothing came up. Weird. Was it a glitch?

I retyped my search, this time looking for any type of food delivery.

Still nothing.

"You've got to be kidding me," I muttered. "This must be some kind of joke, right?"

Could there really be no takeout delivery? Sure, Carla and Noah's farmhouse was half an hour from the nearest store, but could *nobody* drive out here to bring me something to eat?

"First the silence, then the starvation." I sighed. "Guess I'd better drive into town to pick up supplies."

But first, I took an apple from the bowl on the counter and bit into it. I had to admit it was delicious, crisp and fresh. But nowhere near as good as a bacon-egg-and-cheese from my local bodega.

My phone rang, making me jump. I turned to where I'd left it on the counter.

The name on the screen read *Scary Drug Dealer*.

My stomach churned. Feeling suddenly sick, I spat remnants of apple from my mouth into the sink.

The drug dealer's name was Spike. I'd come here to get away from him. And he'd totally ruined *Buffy the Vampire Slayer* for me, seeing as I used to have a huge crush on the Spike character in the TV series, and now I couldn't even hear the name without my nipples retracting all the way into my body.

There was no way I was going to answer Spike's call. I let it ring out and go to voicemail while I wiped apple juice off my hands with one of Carla's dishcloths.

As soon as the ringing stopped, I called Eric. My boyfriend's phone rang for a while before he answered.

"Babe." His voice was croaky. "You know what time it is here? It's way early, and we played last night."

Eric and his band were on tour in Japan, and I hadn't stopped to check the time difference. Not that I could bring myself to care. Too bad if I'd woken him.

"Spike just called me again." I tried not to sound angry, seeing as yelling wasn't the way to get Eric to do anything. "When will you pay the money you owe him?"

Eric groaned. "I'll get a bonus once the tour ends."

"Three weeks?" I huffed out my breath. "No, I can't wait that long. I'll have to go to the police."

"You can't!" Eric's voice rose with alarm. "Promise me, babe. If you do, I'll be the one in trouble."

"But Spike's relentless. He's so scary, I had to leave town! I gave up my apartment, and moved my stuff into storage, and—"

"Can't you just pay him? Lend me the money until I get back?"

I clenched my jaw, barely keeping hold of my temper. Eric's ability to forget any fact he didn't like had to be his least likeable trait, though right now, there was stiff competition for top spot on my list.

"Remember how you already talked me into that?" I hissed the words through my teeth. "Well, like I've already told you, I gave him all my savings. I have nothing left, and you still owe him another ten grand!"

"Don't get snippy, babe. I'm under pressure here too, you know. Once the tour's over, I'll deal with it. But I gotta go now, okay?"

"Wait!" I gripped the phone harder, silently reminding myself that yelling would only make him hang up faster. "At least call Spike and tell him to stop harassing me. Please, Eric!"

"Sure, babe. Love you." The call disconnected.

I wanted to scream. Considering how Eric had been acting lately, how could I believe he'd keep his promise? Most likely, he'd go back to sleep and forget about it. He hadn't even cared that I'd uprooted my entire life and fled New York.

Snatching up the car keys Carla had left for me, I strode outside. Once on the front porch, I blinked in the bright sunshine for a moment, then squinted up into the enormous blue sky. It was almost as quiet outside as it was inside. All I could hear was Carla's chickens, clucking in their run.

All this silence wasn't natural. It wasn't *right*.

And my stomach was growling. On top of everything else, I was getting hangry. I urgently needed to eat something substantial before I turned into a monster.

Car keys in hand, I strode down the porch steps. There was a pickup truck parked by the house, but no other cars. So the keys I was holding had to be for the truck. And it had vivid gold-and-red flames painted down its sides and across its hood.

Flames!

"You've got to be shitting me," I muttered. "I have nothing to drive but a flame-painted pickup truck? What is this, an episode of *Pimp My Ride*?"

Sucking in a deep breath, I lifted my face to the sky and yelled as loud as I could.

"FUCK FUCKITY FUCK FUCK FUCK!"

An ancient rust-colored pickup rattled around the bend in the road. Whoever was driving it must have heard me bellow, because he slowed right down.

Straightening my back, I glared at the windshield. It was streaked with dirt, so I could only make out a blurry impression of a man's face. But even if the driver happened to be a gorgeous billionaire who wanted to take me to a fancy restaurant and treat me to the best bacon-egg-and-cheese of my entire life, I'd still order him to drive right by.

I was DONE with men. Romance was a con! Men were the source of all evil!

The truck made a loud grinding noise as it changed gear. And as the rusty old pickup got closer, I got a better look at the driver. He had a wild shock of long black hair and a full beard that stuck out in all directions. So much hair, he seemed more animal than man.

To make things worse, his elbow was resting on his open window, and he was wearing the worst of all fashion crimes, a plaid flannel shirt in shades of vomit green.

I wrinkled my nose, and he gaped back at me with his lips parted. Judging from his shocked expression, he'd never before seen a woman yelling at the sky while wearing a black leather miniskirt, an asymmetric one-sleeved crop top, and thigh-length lace-up boots.

His truck engine coughed as it slowed even more.

Wait, was he planning to stop?

Oh, no. No way. I might be the only woman in a ten-mile radius, but I wouldn't even be interested in talking to a bacon-offering billionaire right now, let alone a country bumpkin with a beard like a toilet brush.

"Keep driving!" I yelled at the pickup. "This isn't *Deliverance*. There are no banjos here!"

CHAPTER 2

CY

I squinted at the woman who was standing outside the Malones' farmhouse, yelling at the top of her lungs. What in the devil was she hollering about? Was she having some kind of emergency?

Did she need help?

At the thought, I pulled to the side of the road, slowing my pickup to turn into her driveway.

I knew the house, of course, and not just because I'd driven past it every day since arriving back in Green Valley. I'd gone to the same school as Noah Malone, and I used to say hello to his momma when I bicycled past the house as a boy. But this woman was new to me.

She gestured at me, making a waving motion with her palm as though telling me to keep driving. Maybe she didn't need help after all. Only I was too caught up in gazing at her to drive by right away.

She was extremely pretty, with long dark hair and olive skin. She was wearing a shirt with only one sleeve, and a very short skirt. Instead of the cowboy boots I was used to seeing around here, she had on boots that went all the way past her knees, almost up to the hem of her skirt. Her thighs were on display. Accentuated, even. And they were such fine-looking thighs, it was no hardship to let my eyes drop to them.

No way was the woman from around here. I'd never seen her or her thighs before. A stunning woman like that, I'd be sure to remember. And if I didn't know her, that meant she didn't know who I was, either. She might not recoil at the mere mention of my last name. That realization alone made me want to stop.

An image flashed through my mind of having those delectable thighs wrapped around me, though it wasn't at all like me to have sexual fantasies about strangers. I'd seen plenty of thighs before, but hers were exceptionally shapely.

The woman put her fists on her hips. Now I was closer, I could see she was glaring at me. Though it had to be said, the expression on her face didn't dim her beauty any. In fact, the closer I got, the more beautiful I realized she was. Her face was perfectly heart shaped, and she had the cutest upturned nose I'd ever seen. But it was the way she tossed her hair back from her face that was most attractive of all. From just that gesture, I could tell she was no wallflower.

When she hollered again, I was finally close enough to make out what she was saying over the racket of my engine.

"Don't you dare stop, Deliverance!" she yelled. Her tone was so caustic, it burned my eardrums like acid. "Just keep on driving!"

Deliverance?

Did she just call me Deliverance? What in the devil?

Deliverance was the name of an old movie about some big-city hikers who go rafting down a river in Georgia and are set upon by some hillbilly villains with very few teeth and features that imply inbreeding. No need to wonder which of the characters she was comparing me to.

Forget my sexual fantasies. The woman was a judgmental bigot, and that was not at all sexy. Could she be any more offensive?

I gaped at her in shock for a moment longer before coming to my senses and putting my foot back on the accelerator. As pretty as she was, there was clearly a lot wrong with the woman, and I wasn't planning on sticking around to find out exactly why she was pitching a fit. She didn't want me to stop, and now I knew how abrasive she was, I had no wish to meet her.

My pickup coughed a couple of times, then reluctantly sped up, passing the woman by. In the rearview, I saw her holler again, but whatever she yelled was drowned out by my engine's clanking.

"Deliverance," I muttered to myself in disgust. "That woman's cheese has slipped right off her cracker."

The rest of the way home, I thought about how rude she was. Annoyingly, my thoughts kept straying to her thighs as well. But when I pulled up to the ramshackle farmhouse I'd inherited from my daddy, I decided to push her right out of my head.

Picking up the cupcakes I'd bought from the bakery, I went into the old house. The door hinges made a rusty creak, and my shoes clomped over the once-lustrous floorboards, long since dulled and scarred by years of my daddy's dropped cigarette butts.

"Gemma!" I called. "I have cake."

No answer. The house was eerily silent, my niece's bedroom door closed.

With the box of cupcakes in hand, I rapped on her door. "Gemma?"

Still no answer.

"May I come in?" As uncomfortable as I was at the idea of opening her door uninvited, I needed to know she was in there. The alternative was that she may have run off. And that thought halted my hesitation. "I'm coming in," I called loudly, then pushed the door open.

Gemma was sitting on her bed, propped up against her pillows, so at least she hadn't run away. She was fifteen years old and had an ultra-short haircut, her momma's blue eyes, and a nose piercing I still thought she was too young to wear.

She was staring at her phone. A glimpse of plastic in her ears told me why she hadn't answered my knock. She was wearing earbuds, most likely listening to that awful rock music she liked.

When she saw me, her expression darkened. Reaching up, she pulled one of the earbuds out. "What?" she demanded.

Safe to say, my niece wasn't in danger of starting a fan club for me anytime soon.

Before she'd arrived, I'd struggled with the idea of looking after her when I knew nothing whatsoever about parenting. I hadn't seen her in several years, we barely knew each other, and I'd been worried I'd do everything wrong.

But now she was here, I didn't have to worry about that anymore, because I *knew* I was doing everything wrong. Mostly because she told me I was, every day.

"I have cupcakes." I showed her the box. "You want some?"

A flicker of interest crossed her face, and I silently cheered. Maybe I'd finally done something that she wouldn't call annoying or embarrassing.

But I must have made the mistake of letting my hope show, because her expression instantly closed back down.

"I'm not hungry." Her tone was curt.

"I got three different flavors. And if you come into the kitchen to eat, I'll even fix you a cherry cola to go with the cake."

Her lip curled. "I said no."

"You're so unwilling to share a kitchen with me that you won't do it, even for cake?"

The look she gave me was pure disdain. "You're keeping me here against my will, which makes you my *kidnapper*. And no, I don't feel like eating cupcakes and drinking cherry cola with my kidnapper. That's sick." Her glower went back to her phone.

"You can't keep ignoring me, Gem."

"Oh yeah? Watch me." She lifted the earbud, clearly intending to reinsert it and shut me back out.

I sighed, wishing for the thousandth time that Gemma had arrived with some kind of technical documentation to explain how she worked. I had no data. Nothing about her made logical sense. Without an instruction manual, how was I supposed to figure her out?

"I'll eat all the cake myself if you don't come out," I warned.

The earbud hovered over her ear. "Go ahead."

"When are you going to talk to me?" Frustration made my tone rougher than I meant it to be.

"When you let me go home."

"You know I can't do that." I made an effort to gentle my voice. "And you won't be here forever, so why not make the best of it in the meantime?"

She screwed up her nose. "Because I hate this horrible, stinking, ugly house, and I hate this boring town. All my friends are hundreds of miles away, and all the cake in the world won't make being here any better!"

"Not even if the cake is delicious? With thick frosting?" I drew back the lid of the box to show her the treats inside.

"Go away!"

I silently counted to three, then made my tone as sweet as I could manage. "How can I make this better for you, Gem?"

She rolled her eyes. "You're supposed to be some kind of math genius, and you can't figure it out? The only way you could make it better is if you let me go back to Nashville."

Without waiting for me to answer, she shoved the earbud back into her ear and her gaze went pointedly back to her phone. Presumably, she could no longer hear me.

With a sigh, I shut her door and took the cakes into the kitchen, setting the box on the counter. I'd barely put it down when my phone rang. The number that flashed up told me it was the facility where my sister was staying. It could be Ruth calling, though she usually called Gemma first. Or perhaps it was Ruth's doctor. Seeing as I was Ruth's next of kin, her doctor gave me regular updates. And of course, my phone rang when bills needed to be paid.

"Hello?" I said, answering the call.

"Cy, it's me." The flat monotone of my sister's voice made my chest contract, but I made sure my reply was cheerful.

"Hey, Ruth. How are you? Are you doing okay?"

My sister hesitated, as though she wasn't sure whether to brush off my question with a platitude, or whether to be honest. After a moment she said, "It's not easy. Every day is a struggle."

I leaned heavily against the counter, wishing there was something I could do or say to make things easier for her. "Last time I spoke to your doctor, she said you're doing great." I tried to sound encouraging.

"Cy, I need to talk to you about Gemma."

Shit. I'd asked Gemma not to complain to her mother about being here, seeing as Ruth didn't need any added stress. But maybe she'd ignored my request.

"Don't worry about Gemma," I said. "She's taking some time to settle in, but she'll grow to love it here. By the time you're feeling better, she'll most likely be so happy, she won't want to leave."

"That's the thing. I might be here for a long time, and I thought Gemma should go to school."

"School? In Green Valley?" The idea triggered a rush of dread. "I don't think that's a good idea."

"Well, it'd be better than falling behind. And at least she's not a Baxter. She's got that going for her."

That was true. Gemma's last name wasn't Baxter. Her father—Ruth's ex— was a good-for-nothing asshole, but he'd given his daughter his surname. And if the other kids didn't know she was a member of one of the most notorious families in Green Valley, maybe Gemma would be spared the bullying Ruth and I had gone through.

"Okay," I said on an exhale of breath. "I'll see about getting her enrolled. And if anyone shit-talks her, they'll need to deal with me."

"Thanks, Cy. We're lucky to have you looking out for us." Maybe it was wishful thinking, but her voice seemed to get a little brighter.

"It's good to be finally getting to know my niece," I said. "And she'll be okay here for as long as you need. You just concentrate on working things out so you can start feeling better."

"I still can't understand why you're back in that house."

My gaze went to the big window over the kitchen sink, where I could see past the barn to the woods. "It's not so bad here now," I said. I meant that it wasn't so bad now that our daddy was dead, but I knew she'd get what I was saying without having to spell it out.

"There are too many awful memories there." Ruth's voice held something like a shudder.

"Not all our memories are bad. Remember how we used to catch fish? And how we'd skim stones, only I always won?"

"I remember that time I did eight jumps, and your best was only six." There was definitely a trace of amusement in her voice now. It wasn't just wishful thinking.

"You made that up. If I didn't see the throw, it doesn't count."

"Eight jumps, Cy!"

It was an ancient, good-natured argument, as well-worn as the stones we'd skimmed across the surface of the river. But it made me grin to myself. Not so much because of what she was saying, but because I was so glad to hear a spark of the old, feisty Ruth, instead of the flat, emotionless version of my sister I'd been speaking to for the last few weeks.

"We'll have a rematch," I promised. "You'll get to prove it. Or more likely, I'll get to prove it never happened."

"I love you, Cy," Ruth said. "And thank you."

"No need to thank me."

"Yes, there is. Thank you for everything. For being there for me and Gemma, and for not giving up on me."

"Give up on you? Of course not! Never." I made a *pfft* sound to emphasize how ridiculous the idea was. "And you never have to thank me, Ruthie." I walked toward the closed door of Ruth's old bedroom where Gemma was staying. "You want to speak to Gem now?" I asked, already sure she would.

"Yes, please."

I rapped on the closed door of Gemma's room again before remembering about her earbuds. When I opened the door, Gemma yanked her earbud out of her ear with an angry "what now" expression.

"Your momma's on the line. She wants to say hi."

Gemma's expression changed at once, her face lighting up. She couldn't wait for her momma to feel better so the two of them could go home.

As I handed her my phone, I noticed Gemma had pinned a poster over the hole my daddy had once punched in the bedroom wall. It was a band poster. Three young people dressed all in black, with makeup, piercings, and tattoos to match. One glance told me how wince-inducing their music would likely be, but I was just glad Gemma had covered the hole.

Come to think of it, I should have covered it myself.

Walking back into the living room, I vowed to start making the house nicer for my niece. And to find a way to bridge the gulf between Gemma and me.

Somehow.

CHAPTER 3

MAGDALENA

The next morning, I started work at the Donner Bakery. My expectations of Green Valley's inhabitants had been lowered by the hillbilly who'd driven past the house in his rattly old pickup yesterday, so I was pleasantly surprised when I met my new co-workers.

The owner of the bakery was a short, confident woman called Jennifer, and it was clear all the bakers looked up to her. It was easy to see why. The place was obviously well run, the kitchen humming with efficient activity. The aroma of baked goods made me drool, and all the food in the cabinets out front looked delicious.

After showing me around, Jennifer introduced me to two women. Joy was given the job of teaching me how to work the counter, and Amber was going to be working beside me. Both women welcomed me with enough warmth to bowl me over.

"We're happy you're joining us!" Joy exclaimed with so much enthusiasm, I let out a laugh.

"I've never had anyone be this pleased to meet me before," I told her.

"Noah used to work here, so we're great friends," Joy explained. "And I just love Carla. I'm excited to meet her sister." She had a naturally bubbly personality, and looked to be around my age, with brown hair and more freckles than I'd had tequila shots. It was impossible not to like her.

"I'll be glad to have your help at the register," said Amber. "It can be such a rush when we're busy." She looked several years younger than me, around nineteen or so, and she was very pretty. She had hair that was blacker than mine, and darker skin than my own olive complexion, except for what looked like a patch of vitiligo just above her jawline.

Both women had their clothes protected with aprons, and I tied on an apron as well, covering my retro David Bowie T-shirt and skinny jeans. At Joy's request, I also secured my hair in a ponytail so customers wouldn't be in danger of discovering any stray hairs in their food. Then Joy gave me a quick tutorial on using the register.

"Are you ready?" Amber asked, heading to the front door. "I'm about to open up, and our first customers are already waiting outside."

I took in a steadying breath, then gave her a nod. "Ready."

Amber flipped the Closed sign on the door so it said Open, and our first customer came in right away. He was a red-haired man with blue eyes, who was handsome even though he had a beard. He held the door open for a stunning, tall woman with light brown, almost blonde hair.

"Hey y'all," Joy said to them, her delight obvious. She turned to me. "Magdalena, this is Beau and Shelly." Then back to them. "You know Carla, who's engaged to Noah Malone? Well, this here's Carla's sister, visiting from New York and helping us out for a few weeks."

Her detailed introduction surprised me. How small *was* this town? Did every single person know everyone else?

"Please call me Mags," I said.

Beau returned my smile. "Welcome to Green Valley, Mags."

His manner was easy, but Shelly's striking eyes held a hint of coolness. She assessed me for a long moment before giving me a nod. She didn't say anything, and the door was already opening behind her for another customer to come in. I busied myself ringing up Beau and Shelly's order and bagging the muffins they wanted. When I said goodbye, Joy introduced me to the next person in line.

After I'd served a few more customers, Amber greeted a young woman called Wren who asked for a piece of banana cake. While I got her cake, Amber explained who I was. *Carla's sister who's visiting for a few weeks.* How often was I going to hear those words?

But when Amber kept talking to Wren, asking her about her weekend despite the fact we had a line of customers waiting, Joy nudged me. She tilted her head at Amber, then gave me a secretive smile, clearly wanting me to notice how the two of them were gazing at each other.

Wren looked to be around Amber's age, with short hair and a curvy build. She was leaning a little too casually against the counter as she spoke to Amber, her attention solely focused on Amber's face. Judging from the animation in both their expressions, they had a crush on each other.

"Don't say anything," Joy whispered while I was pulling an order of lemon custard cakes out of the cabinet, and she was reaching for cookies. "Amber's hoping Wren will ask her out."

"Why doesn't Amber ask Wren out?" I whispered back.

"It's complicated. They've been friends for a while, and Amber thinks Wren might not want to take things to a new level. She's afraid of risking their friendship."

"Well, my lips are sealed," I promised.

Admittedly, it was only early in my first day, but I was starting to relax. I'd half expected my co-workers to pepper me with questions, curious about why I'd come all this way to look after my sister's house and pets, when Carla could have asked a neighbor to do it. But so far, they'd seemed to accept it.

"Are all our customers going to be so friendly?" I asked Joy after she'd introduced me to several more of them.

"Sure, while it's nice and quiet," she said. "When it gets busy, we don't talk much. Then we're all business."

"Nice and *quiet*?" I glanced at the line of people who were waiting to choose their baked goods from the bakery's extensive selection. Then I smiled to myself. It wasn't exactly the lifeless country town I'd been afraid of. While I was at work, at least, I wouldn't have to worry about getting lonely or bored.

As busy as it was, it wasn't until an hour or so later that we had a small lull between customers. "Are you feeling confident enough for me to head back into the kitchen for a while?" Joy asked me. I nodded, and she added, "Do you like to bake, Mags? If you'd like to learn how things work in the kitchen, I could take you back there and show you—"

I raised a hand to stop her. "I may as well tell you now that I've never baked anything."

"What, never?" Joy's eyes widened. "But you must have!"

"My apartment in Brooklyn didn't have an oven."

"Then what did you use to cook your food?" Amber moved next to her. Both women's eyebrows were climbing.

"There was a hot plate—"

Amber's gasp cut me off. "You only used one hot plate to cook your meals?"

I couldn't help but grin at how incredulous they both were. "I was about to say that I never actually used the hot plate. I don't cook."

"You don't . . . ?" Joy's voice trailed off and she looked at Amber. Amber shook her head helplessly, spreading her hands.

"It might be weird here, but not so strange where I live," I assured them with a laugh.

"Do you want to learn how to cook?" asked Amber.

"I don't know. I've never needed to."

"Well, being behind the counter's fun," Joy said, as though she needed to try to make me feel better about my lack of cooking skills. "You get to talk to people all day long. And you're single, aren't you?"

I screwed up my nose. "Not really. Well, technically I have a boyfriend, but not for much longer."

Both their faces fell.

"I'm sorry," said Joy, her eyes kind.

"Are you okay?" Amber put a comforting hand on my arm.

They were so nice! I'd known them less than a day, but they seemed genuinely upset for me.

"Don't be sorry," I told them. "Men are awful. I'm always attracted to the worst kind."

"What kind is that?" Amber asked.

"Rebels and bad boys. My boyfriend's in a rock band, and they had a song that did really well, so he suddenly got famous. It's gone to his head, and he's been acting like a jerk."

Amber looked interested. "Is it a band I might know?"

"Storm Front." I winced, bracing for her reaction.

"No!" She clapped her hands to her heart. "Are you serious? Storm Front as in *the* Storm Front?"

I nodded, then glanced at Joy who gave me an apologetic shrug. She clearly didn't know the band.

"Tell me you're not dating the lead singer," Amber exclaimed. "He's gorgeous!"

I grimaced. "Eric Storm," I confirmed. "But he's been acting so selfish lately, I'd rather be single."

Her excitement turned to sympathy, her brow wrinkling. "That's a shame. I'm sorry."

"I really need to get the cakes out of the oven," said Joy. "Give me fifteen minutes, then I want to hear all about it!"

As she bustled through the door that separated the kitchen from the service area, I remembered how I'd been determined not to tell my new co-workers about my problems. Dammit, I'd already shared more than I'd meant to. And it's not like they'd pressed me for information about Eric, either. They were so easy to talk to that I'd volunteered it.

At least I hadn't blurted out anything about Spike. They'd think a whole lot less of me if they knew I'd gotten tangled up with a drug dealer. I'd made some serious mistakes when I was a teenager, and sometimes when I was with my family, I still felt the shadow of those misdeeds hanging over me. I didn't need that happening here.

Amber patted me on the back. "Never mind," she said. "You might meet someone nice in Green Valley."

I shuddered, remembering the scruffy redneck who'd driven his rusty pickup past the house yesterday. I'd only seen him for a few seconds, but he'd made quite an impression. Not in a good way.

"I'd rather give birth to a porcupine," I muttered.

Amber's brow creased. "What's wrong with the local men?"

"Nothing. They're just not my type."

"Why not?"

"Well they're so *country*. Beards, jeans, and cowboy boots." I spread my hands helplessly, not sure how else to phrase it.

I didn't mean to offend her, but Amber drew back, folding her arms. "I'm proud of where I live. We might not dress like New Yorkers, but we have our own style."

Damn. I'd hurt her feelings.

"And it's a good style," I said, backtracking. "There's nothing wrong with it, even if it's not my thing."

She tipped her chin down. "Plenty of sophisticated, intelligent women happen to like the men around here. Like Shelly, the woman you met earlier, who's a world-famous sculptor. And some movie stars have moved here, including—"

"I know." I put my hand on her arm. "Amber, I'm sorry, I didn't mean to sound critical. And it's not really that I don't want to date a local man. But a lot of the bad stuff that's happened to me has been thanks to some awful guy. When Eric and I split up, I won't be dating again for a very long time. If ever."

The hard line of Amber's mouth softened. "He's that bad, huh?"

"He really is," I said wholeheartedly.

"I'm sorry he's been such a jerk to you."

"Thank you. I'm sorry too." I offered her an apologetic smile. "Friends?"

I was glad when she smiled back. "Friends. Of course." Then she pulled her apron off. "Will you be okay here on your own for a minute, Mags? I need to use the restroom while it's quiet."

"Go ahead. I'm fine."

But no sooner had she left me alone when the bakery's front door opened and a man with long black hair and an even wilder beard strode in.

"Deliverance!" Before I could stop myself, I'd exclaimed the word out loud.

Unless the man had an equally scruffy twin, it was the country bumpkin who'd almost stopped outside the house in his decrepit truck yesterday. He was like Hagrid from the Harry Potter movies, only his unkempt explosion of hair was pure black, with no gray. He was wearing a plaid flannel shirt again, this time in a hideous shade of brown.

It seemed an awfully big coincidence to see him again so soon. This town had to be even smaller than I'd thought. Either that, or he was stalking me like a creep.

Hagrid folded his arms. "Why do you keep insulting me?" He spoke in a rumbly Southern drawl, even slower than Noah's, each word like liquid honey.

It wasn't until he spoke that I dragged my gaze away from his ugly clothing and hair for long enough to notice his eyes. His irises were the lightest shade of blue imaginable. So light, they were luminous. Framed by his dark lashes, his eyes were breathtaking. I mean, literally. The air was snatched from my lungs and for a moment, I couldn't breathe.

I swallowed, trying to work some moisture back into my throat. He was right. Calling him Deliverance had been mean. First I'd insulted Amber, and now a complete stranger. I should apologize.

Only, it was difficult to concentrate with his eyes focused on me. I found myself staring into them, mesmerized by them. They were like ice water infused with a single drop of blue food coloring. And though they were lighter than I had known blue eyes could be, there was no gray in them at all.

"Do you know how offensive it is to call someone Deliverance?" he demanded.

I was searching for the words to tell him I was sorry when he added, "The way you were screeching yesterday, I figured you must need help. That's the only reason I was about to stop my truck."

The mockery in his tone filtered through my semi-mesmerized brain.

"I didn't screech," I protested.

"You were hollering at clouds, wearing a crazy outfit with only one sleeve. Looked like your roof wasn't nailed on tight."

What the hell? The man who looked like he'd fished his clothes out of a dumpster was insulting the way I dressed?

Suddenly, I had no problem getting words out.

"Perhaps I should have asked for your fashion advice." I used a sweet tone, nodding at his shirt. "What do you call that shade of brown? Is it *feces*, or *regurgitation*?"

"I call it being fully dressed. Two sleeves. One for each arm."

"Congratulations on counting to two. Keep working on three. You'll get there."

His hand went up to rub at one side of his ugly beard. "That must be a New York accent. Explains the rudeness."

"Brooklyn, actually." I gestured to the vast array of food in the bakery's cabinets, still mad. "Are you going to buy something, or did you just come in to chew on a hay stalk and spit tobacco?"

"I'll take some chocolate cake, *Brooklyn*. Two slices."

"Brooklyn is a place, not my name."

"*Brooklyn* sums up your bad manners. And *Deliverance* is an insult that perpetuates harmful stereotypes."

I was so surprised by the number of syllables he'd uttered, I accidentally settled my focus back on his eyes, and their luminous beauty almost stole my outrage.

"Big words," I remarked, forcing my gaze away. As I bent to the cabinet, I muttered, "Guess you're smarter than you look."

I'd meant to say it under my breath, not to escalate our argument. But he must have heard me.

"Every word out of your mouth has been an insult." He sounded annoyed. "Customer service isn't the occupation you're suited to. You should be a lighthouse keeper on a remote island."

Scooping up two slices of cake, I maneuvered them into a bag. And this time, I made sure to mutter my retort quietly enough for him not to hear it. "If 'remote' means away from you, sign me up."

Another customer came in, a middle-aged woman. As I glanced up, juggling cake, I nodded a greeting. But she was busy staring at Hagrid's back with narrow eyes and pursed lips. Stopping behind him, she clutched her handbag close to her body, holding it with both hands as though he might turn and try to snatch it away from her.

When Hagrid glanced at her, the woman glared back.

"Cy Baxter," she snapped. "Back in town and making trouble, no doubt." The sharpness of her tone surprised me.

"No, ma'am. No trouble here." Though his voice stayed even, when he looked back at me, his frown was heavy. He stayed silent while I took his money and made change. When he left, he gave the woman a wide berth.

The woman glowered after him, her nostrils flared, before turning to me. She had lines around her mouth as though she spent a lot of time with her lips pinched. Her wrinkles spoke of more frowns than smiles, which made me want to limit the amount of time I spent in her company.

"You're Carla's sister, aren't you?" she said. "I'm Karen Smith."

"I'm Magdalena. Everyone calls me Mags."

She nodded at the door. "That was Cy Baxter. Be careful of him. He comes from a long line of criminals." The gleam in her eyes suggested she enjoyed spreading spiteful gossip.

"What can I get for you, Mrs. Smith?" I forced a smile.

"Baxters have never been anything but trouble for this town. The son is as bad as his daddy was, growing drugs in that derelict old house. Make sure you stay clear of him, y'hear?"

Usually, such a mean-spirited order would make me want to do the exact opposite. But I wasn't about to make friends with Hagrid, especially if what she said was true. There'd be no more thugs with drugs for me. Not ever.

I waved my hand at the cabinet as more customers came into the bakery. "What would you like today?"

Mrs. Smith leaned over the counter to eyeball me, dropping her voice as though sharing a confidence. "I wonder if the sheriff has gone up to the Baxter house to see what he's up to? I should give him a call to find out."

"Go ahead," I said. "But first, please tell me what you came in for so I can get it for you."

She sniffed disapprovingly, and I figured my impatient tone might have landed me onto the list of people she had a problem with. Not that I cared. As soon as I fixed my Spike problem and could go back to New York, I'd never have to see this sourpuss nor Hagrid ever again.

CHAPTER 4

CY

With her high ponytail and cute nose, the Donner Bakery's newest employee had to be one of the most attractive women I'd ever seen. But she was also, hands down, the rudest. Every insult that had tumbled from her full lips had been worse than the last.

If I were never forced to endure another moment of her company, that would be just fine by me. She could take her abrasive Brooklyn attitude and disappear back to where she came from.

And as for Karen Smith, well I didn't care what she or anyone else in this town thought of me. The only thing I cared about was that they left Gemma alone.

In a black mood, I got into my truck and drove home, speeding up as I passed the farmhouse where the Brooklyn she-devil was staying. The house I'd grown up in was a further five minutes' drive up the same road, on a stretch that was lined with forest. The gravel driveway was rutted, and my ancient truck bumped over the rough surface.

The house had been both comfortable and attractive once, more than a decade ago, when my momma had still been alive. I'd moved to Boston a few months after her death, taking my sister with me. With our brother in prison, our daddy had lived alone in the house for years, and he'd let it fall into disrepair.

Now my father was dead too, and waist-high weeds choked what had once been my momma's front garden. The weeds stretched all the way to the woods,

"

though the trees still made for a picturesque backdrop. The house's weathered clapboard siding had faded to a dull gray, with paint peeling off around the windows and porch.

I'd done little to fix the place up since I'd arrived. I'd meant to. But returning to Green Valley and seeing the house again had been so overwhelming, it had sent me spiraling. Days had gone by, then weeks and months, without me doing much of anything. And though I was back in a functioning state, lately I'd been too busy setting up my new business in the large barn out back to do much about the way the house looked.

Sliding out of my truck with the bag of chocolate cake, I made a mental list of all the things that needed to be done to bring the place back to its former glory. Now that my niece was staying with me, I couldn't keep putting it off.

"Gemma, I'm home!" I called when I got inside. There was no answer, so I put the chocolate cake on the kitchen counter. Yesterday, after leaving the cupcakes on the counter, I'd discovered the chocolate ones had disappeared. She must have crept out and eaten them. I'd counted it as a win and hoped to double down on my success with more cake today.

I rapped softly on her bedroom door, and when I still got no answer, I opened it.

Gemma was sitting at the little desk next to her bed, watching something on her phone with her earbuds in place. Turning her face to me, she pulled one from her ear. "What?"

"We need to talk." Leaving her door open, I moved toward the kitchen. "Please come out here a moment."

She emerged from the bedroom dragging her feet, and flopped onto the couch with a loud sigh. "What is it?"

"I have chocolate cake." I put the slices onto plates. "We can eat while we talk."

She said nothing for a moment, and I could feel the weight of her gaze on me. She was frowning, as though she was mulling over something serious. And when I carried the plates into the living room, she said, "You were yelling in your sleep again last night."

"Bad dreams. Sorry if I woke you." I handed her a plate.

Her eyes lit up as she ate a bite of cake. She even made a small *mmm* sound as she chewed. They made excellent cake at the Donner Bakery. I'd hoped it might help smooth a path between us, and maybe it was working a little.

"Good?" I asked.

She nodded. "Good," she said with her mouth full.

At least I was making some kind of progress. Maybe bribing her with cake was cheating, but I needed all the help I could get, as this was sure to be a tricky conversation. While I ate my cake, I tried to think of how to approach the matter of her schooling.

"What do you dream about?" Gemma asked. "Last night it sounded pretty bad."

I took my time swallowing, not sure how to answer. I wasn't sure if I wanted to reveal the bleakness of my nightmares. But we were having an actual conversation, and they'd been few and far between in the weeks since she'd arrived. My privacy seemed less important than keeping the conversation going.

"Your momma and I had a difficult childhood," I said. "She told you about your granddaddy, didn't she?"

Gemma nodded.

"He was a violent man. And he sold drugs to other violent people. Your mother and I spent most of our childhood feeling afraid, and it's a hard feeling to shake. Sometimes I dream about it. That's why I yell in my sleep."

"If growing up here was so bad, why are you still living here?"

"I came here to fix the house up and sell it. You know that."

She screwed up her nose, looking around. "But you haven't done anything."

"Not yet." My own glance around was rueful. The wallpaper was peeling, the curtains were faded, the kitchen hadn't been updated for at least thirty years, and I'd contributed to the ugliness by piling a huge stack of moving boxes in the living room. I hadn't even carted away my father's old, broken-down furniture yet, though my own, much nicer furniture was stacked in one end of the barn.

"This place needs a bulldozer." Gemma scooped the last of the cake into her mouth.

"It's structurally sound. You'd be surprised at how good it could look. I've been meaning to paint, and maybe it's something we could work on together. You could pick all the colors. It'd be fun." As I spoke, the idea was growing on me. Why hadn't I thought about getting her involved in the renovation before? It could take her mind off being away from her friends.

She set her plate on the coffee table. "I hate it here. Why can't I go back to Nashville?"

"Because I've been setting up a business here."

"I could go back without you and stay with one of my friends. They wouldn't mind."

We'd had this argument before, but I made sure to keep my tone kind. "Your momma would rather you stay with me, and you don't want to give her something else to worry about, do you? She's trying her hardest to feel better, and once she does, you can go home."

"It could be *months* until she's better."

"It might be. But if you make the best of things and try to settle in, your perception of time will change. It'll pass more quickly." I braced myself for her reaction. "Gem, I spoke to Green Valley High School's principal."

"What? Why?" Jerking her head back, she narrowed her eyes. "I don't want to go to school here."

"It's the law. You have to go to school, and it won't be so bad. You'll make friends and enjoy yourself." It was all I could do to say it as though I had no doubts. But Gemma wasn't a Baxter. I had to believe she'd be okay.

"I won't!" Her voice rose. "I don't want to go! I'm going to hate it!"

"Moping around here is making you miserable. Going to school will help."

She leapt to her feet, fists clenched. "I won't go!"

"I'm sorry, Gem, it's already organized. They want you to go in on Friday to get shown around and sort out the books you'll need, then start classes on Monday."

Her glare of furious betrayal made my heart ache, but what could I do? I'd promised Ruth I'd send her to school.

Gemma stormed to her bedroom. "I hate you!" Her door slammed behind her.

I sighed into the empty living room, then got up and walked over to her closed door.

"Tomorrow I'll pick up some test pots of paint so we can start choosing colors to make the house look nicer," I called through the door.

She didn't reply.

I thought about asking if she wanted to come with me, but if folks saw the two of us together, they'd know she was a Baxter. It'd be better if she started school without having that hanging over her head.

"On my way back, I could get us more cake," I added.

My suggestion was met with sullen silence, and I had a feeling I'd be in for a whole lot more of it over the next few days. All I wanted was to connect with her, but now we were further apart than ever.

CHAPTER 5

MAGDALENA

I was tired after working at the bakery all day, and my stomach was rumbling. But before I could sit down and eat, I had chores to do. Carla had filled the chicken feeder up before she left, but now it was almost empty.

There was a bucket next to the chicken run. I pulled the lid off to find it was full of grain, with a scoop for dishing it out. I scooped some up, and when I turned to the run, three large birds were lined up against the wire, staring at me with their beady black eyes.

"Eeep!" I flinched backward. "You birds don't bite, do you?"

Carla had written down every detail about feeding them, but hadn't said whether they were dangerous. The only birds I had any experience with were the pigeons that swooped down on dropped crumbs at the park. Compared to them, the chickens were giants. Practically dinosaur sized.

"Back up. Don't stand so close to the door." I approached nervously. The feeder was a little way inside, which meant that for me to pour the corn into it, I'd need to expose my tender flesh to their sharp-looking beaks.

Nope. Not going to happen.

"Here's your dinner," I said to the danger birds, pouring the grain through the wire onto the ground. They started gobbling it up right away, not seeming to care that I hadn't put it into their feeder.

"Job done." I dropped the scoop back into the bucket of grain. "That wasn't so hard. If I feed you more often, it won't matter if I don't fill your feeder. You'll have full stomachs just the same."

But my moment of self-congratulation was over quickly, because when I went back inside, the house reeked of smoke. Rushing to the oven, I yanked it open and groaned. The frozen pizza that was supposed to be my dinner was black and smoking.

Cursing, I grabbed a dishcloth to yank it out of the oven and dumped the charred mess onto the counter. As I waved the dishcloth over it to waft the smoke away, I wanted to howl.

The oven had bamboozled me. The only options on the dial were incomprehensible pictures. Why couldn't it have a simple on-off switch?

At least I'd managed to get music playing out of Carla's stereo. I picked the least-burned bits off the top of the pizza, put them on a plate, and plonked myself onto the couch to eat them. My feet were sore. I was used to standing all day, but the bakery was several times busier than the fashion boutique had ever been, even on sale days.

My phone rang.

When I glanced at it, my stomach twisted. The screen said *Scary Drug Dealer*.

Spike was calling. *Again.*

I let the call ring out, then tried Eric's number. It rang for ages, then clicked to voicemail when he didn't answer, so I left him a message.

"Eric, it's me." Though I wanted to yell and curse, I kept my tone calm. "Call me back right away, okay? Spike's still calling me, and you promised you'd speak to him. I'm afraid of the guy, Eric. You can't leave me to deal with him alone. Please call as soon as you get this message."

I hung up with a frustrated huff of breath, wishing I'd thought to buy a bottle of wine. All I had was water, burned pizza toppings, and singed cheese. None of those things tasted good.

After finishing my unappetizing dinner, I dumped the rest of the pizza into the trash and took myself off to bed. The cat was already there, curled on top of the covers, presumably waiting for me. He'd had his dinner, and if last night was any indication, he wouldn't move again until it was time for breakfast.

I brushed my teeth, put on pajamas, and climbed into bed next to Freud, deciding to call a friend from home, then watch *Project Runway* on my phone until I fell asleep. After a long day, it wouldn't take long to nod off.

But after chatting to my friend, I'd barely hung up when my phone rang again. *Scary Drug Dealer* flashed on the screen and my stomach took another dive. This was getting ridiculous. Spike was relentless.

Acting on impulse, I snatched my phone up and answered his call.

"Hello, Spike," I said in as cool a tone as I could muster.

"Where's my money?" Spike snarled the question, kicking my heart rate up.

"You mean the money that Eric owes you? You should check with him seeing as he's the one who borrowed it in the first place."

"Eric left the country. You're here. I'm asking you."

"Actually, I've had to leave town for a few weeks. Eric's going to get back into the city before I will, so if you—"

"I don't care where you are. You'll give me my money."

My mouth went dry. At the same time, I realized I was sweating. Fear was somehow expelling all the moisture from my body through my skin.

It took an effort to swallow. "Eric will pay you as soon as he gets home," I croaked. "He's the one who owes you the money, not me."

"If I don't get my money, shit's going to get messy. That'll be bad for you. Consider this a warning."

He hung up.

I whooshed out my breath, then wiped my damp face on the bed sheet and took a sip of water.

"That was intense," I muttered.

Without much hope he'd pick up, I called Eric's phone again. Sure enough, I had to leave another message.

Needing the reassurance, I put my arm around Freud and cuddled into his small body. "Don't worry," I murmured. "We'll be okay. Eric will come through for us. He has to."

The cat didn't say anything.

"You don't believe me?" I asked. Then I sighed. "That's smart. I'm not sure I believe me, either."

Switching my light off, I lay in the dark. It wasn't silent anymore, but there weren't any of the sounds I was used to hearing. There were no sirens. There were no voices, car engines, or thumps of distant music. Instead there were chirps and croaks, and a creepy chatter like a thousand tiny insects all talking at once.

A loud screech made me jump. What the hell was that? An owl?

Freud was curled in a ball with his head tucked in, and I tried to cuddle closer. He was warm, but still. Sound asleep, despite all the unsettling noises coming from outside.

"Don't you hear those sounds, Freud?" I asked. "Want to tell me what they are?"

It'd be a lot more comforting having him with me if he wasn't practically an inanimate object.

A loud scraping sound came from the outside porch.

Heart jumping, I flicked on the light switch.

Could it be Spike outside? No, there was no way. He had no idea where I was.

Did he?

Another noise came from the wooden porch, like someone scraping the edge of their shoe over the boards.

I grabbed my phone off the nightstand and keyed in 911. But I wasn't sure whether to hit the green button. Before I connected the call, I needed to be sure what was out there, whether it really was a person creeping around, or a false alarm.

In horror movies, the first scary noises always turned out to be tree branches scratching on a windowpane. It was only after the victim relaxed that the serial killer came leaping out.

Clutching the phone, I jumped out of bed, edged out of the bedroom, then crept down the dark hallway. Scratching sounds came from the front door. Definitely not tree branches. It sounded like fingernails on wood, as though someone was taunting me.

"The cops are on their way!" I yelled at the top of my lungs. "You'll hear the sirens any minute!"

The scratching sound stopped. Then it started again, getting louder and a lot faster, as though whoever was out there was giving it his all, in a weird, only-using-his-fingernails way.

I searched frantically around for a weapon. The hallway was bare, apart from a coatrack and a couple of jackets. Maybe I could hit him with an umbrella? Ugh, no! I wasn't thinking straight.

Scratch, scratch, scratch.

Dashing into the kitchen, I fumbled the biggest knife out of the drawer then crept back down the dark hallway. With one hand, I brandished the knife in front of me. With the other, I clutched my phone. The light shone from my bedroom, casting creepy shadows. My chest was so tight, my heart could hardly beat.

"I have a rifle pointed at you, and my finger is on the trigger." My voice was loud, but a little too shrill, betraying my fear.

Scratch, scratch, scratch, scratch, scratch.

I lifted the knife. My hand was shaking, but maybe I could scare away whoever was out there.

With the knife held high, I flung the door open.

A dog stood frozen, staring at me with frightened eyes. It was tall, but skinny, and a patchy shade of brown. Its tail was between its legs, and it looked like it was about to bound away.

I lowered the knife.

"Well, hello." I let out a nervous bray of laughter, suddenly feeling in urgent need of a chair. "What are you doing here, besides giving me heart failure and almost getting yourself turned into a dog meat skewer?"

The dog backed up, its tail even lower, as though it found the high, trembling tone of my voice disturbing.

Well, me too, Dog. Me too.

"Okay." I pulled myself together. "You'd better come in. I don't want to keep standing here with the door wide open."

I went into the kitchen, opened a tin of cat food, and dumped it into a bowl. By the time I was done, the dog was standing next to me in the kitchen, gazing up at the bowl with hopeful eyes. It was a big dog, as tall as a full-grown Labrador, but a lot skinnier. Close up, I could see it was dirty. Some of its darker brown patches looked like dried mud, and the smell of damp dog hair was strong.

I put the bowl down and watched the dog gobble up the food for a moment, then went to shut and lock the front door. By the time I came back into the kitchen, the dog was licking the bowl clean. Though I knew nothing about dogs, judging from my view of what was between its hind legs, my late-night visitor had to be male.

"Don't make yourself sick," I told him, dumping another tin of Freud's cat food into the bowl. "That's all you're getting for now, so slow down."

The dog didn't listen to me. He gulped that tin as fast as the first one, then looked up at me hopefully, his tail punctuating the look with a slow wag.

"Nope," I told him. "No more food. And you stink. I'll try to clean you up, then I'm going back to bed. You can have some breakfast in the morning, before we look for your owner."

When I padded into the bathroom, the dog followed me. I wiped as much dirt off as I could with a wet washcloth, then rubbed him down with a towel. Finally, I padded back into the bedroom, the dog at my heels. Freud stayed curled up, but lifted his head to stare at the intruder with an impressive level of disdain.

"Mr. Cat, meet Mr. Dog," I said. "Don't worry, it's only for tonight. The dog will be leaving in the morning."

Come to think of it, I needed a photo of the dog to post online. Grabbing my phone, I lowered myself to his eye level. "Say cheese!" The dog's tongue lolled out as I snapped his picture.

After searching online for the local lost-and-found pets page, I posted the dog's photo with my contact details. Once that was done, I spread a towel on the floor. "You can sleep on that," I told the dog, clambering back into bed next to Freud.

The words were barely out of my mouth before the dog jumped onto the bed, landing squarely on my legs.

"Hey! Get down!"

The dog sniffed Freud, who lifted a paw in warning. Wisely, the dog retreated to my other side. He collapsed beside me on the bed with a sigh so loud it was comical. It was the kind of sigh you'd make after a very long and trying night, once you'd finally clambered into bed and were looking forward to getting some sleep.

Now I was sandwiched between the two animals. Strangely enough, it was comforting. Neither of them seemed bothered by the strange croaks, chirps, and chattering sounds coming from outside. And if anybody tried to break in, the dog would probably bark, right? Maybe even attack?

I tried hard to convince myself the dog would protect me, and I had nothing to fear. But sleep was still a long time coming.

CHAPTER 6

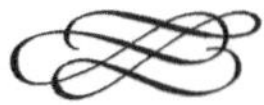

MAGDALENA

"He has no microchip or registration," the vet told me the next morning. She was about my age, and her name tag said Kat Barker, which had to be the coolest name for a vet I'd ever seen. "And he's underweight. I'd say he's been on his own for a while. But other than that, he seems in good health."

The dog moved his gaze from her to me as though he was following our conversation. He was sitting on her examination table, his tail gently wagging back and forth across the metal surface. He looked like he was grinning.

"I posted on the lost-and-found page, but nobody's claimed him yet."

"Hmm." The vet took another look at his teeth. "I know most of the local dogs. He could have been dumped by someone passing through. It happens sometimes."

"Who'd do that? Man, some people suck!"

She nodded with feeling, and we shared a silent moment of disgust for dog-abandoners.

"What type of dog is he?" I asked.

Doctor Barker scratched him behind the ears and made his tail wag faster. "A mixed breed, but they often have the best temperament. He seems like a sweetie." She pushed back the dog's shaggy bangs to get a better look at his friendly black eyes. Under all that matted hair, the dog was cute. And it seemed like I was leaving him in great hands. The vet would take good care of him.

"Okay," I said, checking the time on my phone. Thankfully, I was on a later shift today, starting at eight and finishing at four. But the dog's examination had taken longer than I expected, and I was barely going to make it. "Well, if he isn't sick or anything, that's good, right? So thanks a lot, Doctor. And goodbye, Dog. It was nice knowing you." I started toward the door.

"Wait!" she called. "Where are you going? You can't leave your dog here."

I stopped reluctantly, my heart sinking. "But he's not my dog. His owner's likely to come here to find him, but if not, you must know lots of people looking for a dog just like him." I gave her a hopeful smile.

She shook her head. "I'll ask around. But in the meantime, you'll need to take him with you."

"I'm only in town for a few weeks. Then I'm going back to New York to look for a new apartment. And I don't know the first thing about taking care of a dog. The only animals I've ever owned are my kitten heels."

Lifting a foot, I showed her my shoes. I'd hesitated about wearing them to work, but convinced myself the heels were low enough to be practical, seeing as they went so well with my red pants and made my legs look longer.

"You could take him to the animal shelter," she suggested. "The closest one is in Knoxville."

"Could I leave him here for the day while I go to work? I'm supposed to start in ten minutes."

She looked apologetic, and I already knew what she was going to say before she started in on a long explanation as to why they didn't have the room to keep him, even for the day.

Fifteen minutes later, I pulled Noah's flame-painted truck into the parking lot outside the Donner Bakery. The dog was sitting next to me, staring happily out of the window as though he hadn't made me late for work.

"What am I going to do with you, Dog?" I asked as I cut off the engine. "Will you be okay waiting in the truck? I can't take you into the bakery with me, can I?"

The dog grinned at me, sitting up in the passenger seat like an inconvenient doofus.

I hesitated with my hand on the door handle. "Today's shift is eight hours long," I told him. "I'll have a few breaks when I can let you out, but will that be enough?"

Would it be cruel to leave him in the pickup that long? Would it get too hot? He'd need water, wouldn't he?

Wait. Were there any laws against this?

The last thing I needed was for a cop to come into the bakery looking for the inhumane monster who'd left a dog in their truck.

"Shit." I puffed out a sigh. "Okay. I'll take you back to Carla's house so you can stay there for the day. But you'll have to wait here while I go in and explain how I'm going to be an hour late for work—*on my second day*—because I have to drive all the way home to drop you off."

I emphasized the "second day" part, even though it was clear the dog didn't care. We'd already established he didn't have much of a social conscience. He would have eaten Freud's breakfast as well as his own this morning if I'd let him.

"Wait here," I repeated, and slid out of the truck.

Apparently, the dog hadn't been to obedience school, because he ignored my order. He catapulted out of the door before I could close it, then bounced around me excitedly, not paying any attention to my commands to get back into the truck.

Then I heard a familiar rattle and grinding of gears. Turning, I recognized the old pickup truck that was pulling into a parking spot near the bakery's front door. With a final wheeze, the clanking engine shut off, then the driver's door opened.

Hagrid slid out, wearing what looked like the *same* hideous flannel shirt as yesterday. Only now it had to be a day dirtier.

I could not shudder hard enough.

But come to think of it, could Hagrid be an answer to my problem? There was no dog in his pickup truck, and didn't dogs and country bumpkins go together like Jack Daniel's and Coke? Even criminals could be kind to animals, right? And the fact he didn't already have a dog with him had to be a misdemeanor in the state of Tennessee.

Hagrid started walking to the bakery door. With his back to me, all I could see was his too-long tangle of black hair and his oversized shirt. What was his real name again? Dammit, I was usually good with names, but all I could think of was the Harry Potter character.

"Hey, Hagrid!" I strode toward him, the dog bouncing around near my feet.

He turned to face me, and his gaze landed on mine. The air whooshed out of my lungs. Those *eyes*! How could a backwater bumpkin like him have eyes like that? And now I was looking, had I ever seen a man with such sharp cheekbones? Under all that unruly hair, he must have an angular, masculine face.

"What did you call me this time?" Hagrid asked in his low, rumbly voice, an annoyed frown weighing heavily over his eyes. "My name is Cy. It's only two letters. C. Y. That's not too complicated for you, is it? It could hardly get any easier."

The dog ran over to him, sniffing his ankles with interest, and Cy bent to pet him. Judging by the easy way he stroked down his side, the bumpkin must like dogs. That was an excellent sign.

"Okay," I said, trying to arrange my features into a pleasant expression. "You've got yourself a deal. I'll call you by your name if you take the dog with you. What do you say?"

He straightened. "Take the dog? What does that mean?"

"I'm late for work and if I have to drop the dog off at my place, I'll be even later. I mean, I never wanted a dog in the first place, and you seem like a dog person. So you can take him, right?" I dug deep to force out one more word. "Please?"

"You'd hand your dog over to a stranger?" His tone was disapproving. Another good sign. He was definitely an animal lover.

"He's not my dog. He just showed up, and then I couldn't get rid of him."

"Get *rid* of him?" Cy recoiled.

I blinked at his shocked tone. Maybe I'd used the wrong phrase. Did he think I'd tried to kill the dog?

Before I could clarify that I'd only intended to leave the dog with the vet until his owner showed up, Cy crouched by the dog's side. There was something so protective in the way his big hands stroked the dog's head that the explanation dried in my throat. His icy gaze bored into me, his eyes narrow. And for some reason, I was suddenly flustered.

"Um." I cleared my throat. "So will you take him?"

"What do you mean the dog just showed up? He's a stray?"

I nodded. "His real owner will probably be looking for him, and the vet has my phone number. By tonight, he's likely to be claimed."

Cy frowned at me as he stood. Then he ran his hand over the rat's nest of his beard, not managing to smooth it, but somehow messing it up even more. He was clearly thinking my request over, but I could imagine how his thoughts must run as slowly as syrup. I didn't have time to let him ruminate.

"My shift started five minutes ago." I waved a desperate hand at the dog. "Look how cute he is. And he's smart. Probably a great guard dog. He could guard your crop, or whatever."

Cy's eyebrows jerked up. They were surprisingly tidy considering the rest of his hair was a scruffy nightmare.

"My crop?" He growled the words as though I'd pissed him off.

Whoops.

"I just meant the dog can help you with whatever it is you do all day." Trying to backpedal, I took a wild stab at other options. "Maybe he could chase raccoons out of your cornfield. Or, I don't know . . . keep intruders away from your moonshine distillery."

"Stop talking." He folded his arms across his wide chest. "You haven't uttered a single thing that isn't offensive. I'd rather listen to a field of roosters at four in the morning than hear another word from you."

Ugh. I was making a mess of this.

"How about I promise to stop talking if you take the dog?" I asked.

"Tempting."

I pressed my lips together and lifted a hand to mime turning a key over them. Then I threw the key away over my shoulder.

He studied me silently for what felt like forever. Meanwhile, I shifted from one foot to the other, widening my eyes to look imploring. Though I was very conscious of time ticking by as I got even later for work, I managed to resist the urge to break the silence.

"Some people can't be trusted with animals," he finally grumbled under his breath.

"Right?" I exclaimed. "I was going to shut him in my truck all day."

His brow drew down. "You can't do that."

"Exactly. The poor dog deserves better than me."

He grunted. "No argument. What's his name?"

Yes! I gave him a relieved grin and a farewell wave. "It's whatever you want it to be. I need to run." Then I dashed toward the bakery's staff entrance as fast as my kitten heels would carry me.

"Wait!"

I turned reluctantly, walking backward to show how much of a hurry I was in. "Yeah?"

"You don't have a collar for him, or a leash, or—?"

"Nope. None of that."

"What's *your* name?" He projected his voice across the widening gap between us.

I stared at him a moment. Karen Smith's warning to stay away from him was ringing in my ears. Making a quick decision, I shook my head. "You don't need to know my name," I called back.

His brow drew down in a puzzled frown, and his eyes narrowed as though he was trying to understand why I didn't want to tell him. Then I guess he figured it out because his expression hardened.

Whistling for the dog to follow, he turned and strode stiffly away.

CHAPTER 7

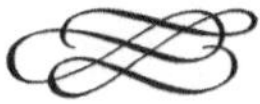

CY

I may not have known the dog's real name, but I enjoyed having him for company that afternoon as I harvested mushrooms. Unlike the woman who'd asked me to look after him, he was a good-natured, likeable dog. I christened him Duke.

Brooklyn had rushed off without arranging to pick the dog back up, so I took Duke back to the Donner Bakery around the time I figured she'd finish work. Sure enough, the bakery's back door opened just after four o'clock, and she was backlit by the warm glow inside. As she stepped out, she was still looking behind her and calling out a goodbye to whoever was in there. Then she let the door close with a loud sigh, as though relieved.

She was wearing the same tight dark-red pants, leather jacket, and shiny black shoes as this morning, but her hair was in a ponytail and her shoulders were slumped. As she walked toward me, I could tell she'd had a long day. Her posture seemed tired, the light gait she'd had this morning gone. Now her steps were heavy, and she was favoring one leg.

I didn't want to talk to her or interact in any way. I was only there to give the dog back and wasn't asking for more insults. But she was limping, and no matter how much I disliked her, I was still a gentleman.

"You hurt your foot?" I asked. "Do you need help?"

She waved a hand, dismissing my offer. "Wore heels today, that's all. I thought they'd be comfortable enough." She didn't stop, but limped determinedly past me, heading toward one of the pickup trucks in the parking lot.

She was getting around town in Noah Malone's distinctive truck with flames painted on its sides and over the hood. Hard to miss.

"Here's the dog." I went after her, holding the end of the leash out for her to take. We'd had two dogs when I was a kid, and I'd searched through the junk in my daddy's attic until I found an old collar and leash that were serviceable enough to use.

"He's not my dog." She pulled her jacket tighter around her, not looking me in the eyes. "He's better off with you."

"Wait." I caught her arm to stop her forward momentum, turning her to face me. "You haven't found his owner yet?" From the way she was acting, I knew the answer before she shook her head. "I only said I'd take him for the day," I reminded her. "Now he's yours again."

Brooklyn let out another sigh. Her eyes looked as tired as her gait, and despite what a terrible person she was, I felt sorry for her. How exhausting had her day been? Hadn't she gotten any breaks?

"I can't have a dog," she said. "And I don't know the first thing about them. You obviously do."

"Now, wait a minute . . ." I stopped talking when a muffled ringing sound came from her jacket pocket.

Tugging her phone out, she looked down at the screen and drew in a ragged breath. She bit her lip, staring at the phone for a moment, and her face lost its color. Whoever it was, she seemed uncertain about talking to them. Then she squared her shoulders. "I need to take this," she said. Turning her back to me, she brought the phone to her ear. "Yes, Spike?"

I frowned. Spike was an unusual name. Was she talking to her boyfriend?

"I'm sorry, but I can't do more than I'm already doing. I'm trying to arrange for—"

The person on the other end cut her off, and she listened for a moment, shaking her head. "No," she said. "There's no point in threatening me. I can't give you what I don't have."

Brooklyn's tone was matter-of-fact, but her words made me stiffen. She was being threatened?

"That kind of talk won't get you anywhere," she added. "Scare me as much as you like, but I can't get you the money any faster. All I can do is my best." She listened a moment longer, then hung up.

"What's going on?" I asked.

She clenched her jaw, lifting her chin. Her eyes had lost their tired look, and they flashed as though she was angry. But her cheeks were pale and there was a deep furrow in her forehead. I was pretty sure she was fighting against being afraid.

I used to see a look like that in Ruth's eyes when my daddy's biker friends would turn up at our house. Though I'd done my best to shield my sister from them, I'd been a boy, and they'd been grown men. As far as I knew, they'd never actually hurt her. But the threat of it had been as strong as the stench of sweat and dirty leather.

My gut roiled at the memory.

"I'll take the dog," Brooklyn said, putting out her hand for the leash I was holding. "Thanks for looking after him today."

"You've changed your mind?"

As I wasn't giving it to her, she stepped forward to take the leash from me. I didn't miss her wince as she took the step to reach me.

"I might as well keep him overnight." She looked down at Duke, and I had a feeling she was weighing up his guard dog potential. Did she expect to be in physical danger?

"Who was on the phone?" I asked, my tone rougher than it should be seeing as I hardly knew her. Not that I could help the way I sounded when my throat had gone dry and my muscles were tense. Though Brooklyn wasn't anything like my sister, my reaction to a potential threat had been triggered as though Ruth were the one in danger.

As a boy, I'd lived in fear. And when fear keeps hold of you for long enough, its dark fingerprints on your thoughts can become a permanent stain.

"It's personal." With her chin lifted, she gave me another of her defiant looks. Or maybe that was her normal look, and anything softer was unusual.

"It sounded like you need help."

"Nope." She walked toward her pickup, the dog trotting at her side.

"I'll stop at your place to check everything's okay there," I said as she reached her truck. "I live past your place, further up the mountain, so it's on my way."

The glare she gave me was impressive. "No, thank you. My husband is twice your size. He's there right now with his gun collection and an itchy trigger finger. So drive right past, and don't even slow down."

She wasn't wearing a wedding ring. Maybe I was wrong, but I suspected she was making up a husband to keep me away. And who could blame her? I was a big man with a bad reputation.

"I understand you might be afraid of me," I said. "But I'm—"

"I'm not afraid of you." She opened her truck door and the dog jumped in. "By all means, stop by. The last creep to follow me home is still alive. Mostly.

Apparently, having to be fed through a tube isn't *so* bad. And the chance of a bullet going through one of your major organs is only fifty-fifty. Why not risk it?"

The woman was infuriating. Still, I had to admire her quick tongue. She didn't give an inch.

"All I'm suggesting is that I take a quick look to make sure everything's as it should be," I said. "No need for me to come inside."

Maybe nobody in Green Valley would want a Baxter hanging around, but I couldn't leave her to fend for herself.

She slid into her driver's seat. "I might have let you borrow the dog, but that doesn't make us friends."

"You *let* me borrow—?" The slam of her truck door cut off the rest of my incredulous question.

She didn't turn the truck on right away, but bent over in the driver's seat. It wasn't until she pulled them off that I realized she had been fiddling with her shoes. She probably had blisters.

I got into my truck, and when she pulled out of the parking lot, I followed her all the way up to the Malones' farmhouse. It was a pretty house, neat and tidy, with a vegetable garden and a chicken run. It was close to what my own family home had looked like once, before my momma's death and the house's subsequent years of neglect.

When Brooklyn slid out of her truck, she was in bare feet with her shoes in one hand. She'd taken her hair out of its ponytail so it was loose around her shoulders. Duke leapt out with her, bouncing around like he was overjoyed to be there. Probably knew he was likely to get fed.

She glared at me as I got out of my pickup. "What don't you understand about the words *go* and *away*? Do you need me to spell them for you? Shall I write them on flash cards?"

I held up both hands. "I don't mean you any harm. But if someone you'd rather not see is fixing on paying you a visit, maybe you should let me—"

"*You're* the person I'd rather not see."

"Good grief. You're impossible." Shaking my head, I gave up. "I'll be on my way then, ma'am. Have a pleasant evening. Or not. I can't bring myself to care much either way."

Getting back in my truck, I tried to start it. The engine turned over but didn't catch. I tried it again. Same thing.

I held in a curse. The battery needed replacing, and I should have done it already, when it first showed signs of giving out. Getting a new battery put in would make me late, and Gemma was waiting at home for me. Not that she'd miss me much, seeing as she wasn't currently speaking to me.

Sliding out, I opened the truck's hood.

Brooklyn hadn't gone inside but was watching from the porch with narrowed eyes. "Your truck's broken down, huh?" She made quotation marks with her fingers around the "broken down" part, as though I might have somehow faked the death of my battery. "I suppose now you think I'll invite you in?"

I scratched my beard, thinking about what to do next. "Now we have two choices," I said. "First option is that you pull your truck up to mine so I can use jumper cables to start my engine."

She folded her arms. "Option two?"

"I could call Winston Auto Shop, see if Cletus or Beau will come out to switch out the old battery with a new one." She was still glaring with her arms folded, so I added, "Seems like that's the best option. I'll stay out here and make the call. You can go inside and carry on with your regular business. Sharpen your fangs, or cook up some small children for your dinner. Don't worry about me."

Brooklyn pushed her lips to the side, looking me up and down. Then she gave an impatient huff of breath. "I'll move my truck closer. It'll get you out of here faster."

"A highly desirable outcome for both of us," I agreed.

She positioned her pickup so its hood was almost touching mine. While I hooked up one end of the cables, she did the other. She was in bare feet and walked gingerly, still favoring one leg.

"You've done this before," I remarked as she deftly attached her end of the cables to the right battery terminals.

Her gaze jerked up to mine. "You sound surprised. You think a woman can't know how to start an engine?" Her tone held a note of challenge.

I shrugged. "There's a woman working at Winston Auto Shop who seems like a great mechanic. But you don't look much like a car person."

She tossed her long hair back from her face, the gesture full of that fiery attitude I'd been so attracted to when I'd first seen her, before the insults had started.

"What exactly does a car person look like?" she demanded.

"Dirtier." I cast a meaningful look at her red pants. Though I couldn't help but admire the way they hugged her shapely legs and bottom, they clearly hadn't been designed with greasy engines in mind.

She waved a dismissive hand. "I've done this plenty of times. When my boyfriend's band was playing in small venues, they used to haul their gear around in a van that broke down all the time." She pressed her lips together as though the memory wasn't a good one. "I was the sap who always helped out."

It seemed like it was a sore point with her, so I didn't comment. Besides, the word *boyfriend* had started a number of questions circling in my mind, like sharks in a small pool. Was she still dating him? Had he been the man threatening her on the phone? And why was I wondering about the dating habits of the rudest, most unlikeable woman I'd ever had the misfortune to meet?

I got into my pickup to start it up. When I turned the key, it roared to life. Leaving it idling, I got out to retrieve my jumper cables.

"Thank you," I told her, stowing them away. "And goodbye. Hopefully forever."

She chewed her lower lip, frowning at me like she was trying to figure something out. "You're really leaving," she said, as though she hadn't been sure.

"As fast as my truck will take me." I walked to my driver's side door.

"So you just stopped to check I wasn't in danger?"

"My mistake. Won't happen again." I slid behind the wheel and swiveled to look out the back window, ready to reverse out of there.

She rapped on my window, the sharp sound of her knuckles on the glass startling me.

I stomped on the brakes and wound down the window. "Did you forget something?"

"Do you know how to work an oven?"

I turned the sentence over in my head, looking for a hidden meaning. Didn't everyone know how to work an oven?

"You having trouble getting Hansel and Gretel up to roasting temperature?" I asked.

She shot me a withering look, but turned away so quickly, I half suspected she'd had to stifle a laugh. Then she motioned to the house. "Would you come in for a moment?"

"Why?"

"I need help deciphering the symbols on the oven. Please. It'll only take a second, and believe me, I wouldn't ask if I wasn't desperate. I can't eat burned cheese again."

She walked toward her porch, as though hoping I'd follow. But I just sat there, debating whether I should. Why suffer through more time with her when I could just drive away?

As I watched her climb the steps to her porch, I noticed she was still limping. And dammit, if she needed help, it was all but impossible for me to refuse. I just wasn't wired that way.

Still, I cursed out loud before I got back out of my idling truck and followed her inside, sure I was going to regret it. Duke rushed down the hallway in front of us, his tail wagging furiously. I'd never seen a bouncier dog. He was practically on springs.

The farmhouse was as nice inside as out. As I walked down the hallway to the kitchen, I noticed the things that made it seem homey. Like how well the color of the curtains complemented the walls. And the fresh herbs on the kitchen windowsill that were in cheerful pots. Although when I took a closer look, the plants were limper than they should be, as though deprived of water.

But on the whole, the place had a stylish yet comfortable feel. And the difference between this place and my daddy's—*my*—neglected old house reminded me how I'd let Gemma down by letting her live somewhere that was so rundown. I should be working harder to fix it up.

Once in the kitchen, Brooklyn shrugged off her leather jacket. My thoughts about how I could make my house look more like hers screeched to an abrupt halt. Underneath, she was wearing a black shirt that hugged her top half just as well as her red pants hugged her bottom half. Which was to say, very well indeed.

That proved the old saying about not judging books. She might have a deceptively pretty cover, but inside she read like a horror story.

Moving to Brooklyn's oven, I peered at the dial. "That symbol there, with the line on top? That's for broiling. The one with two lines is for baking. The one with the fan—"

"Which one for pizza?" Brooklyn interrupted. She moved next to me, and I became sharply aware of the soft line of her cheek as she peered at the dial. The scent of the bakery was on her, and the hint of baked goods was delicious. But underneath that was another scent. Something feminine and sexy.

How could someone so abrasive be so beautiful? It didn't seem right. But my body was reacting to her, my blood pumping faster. My biology didn't care that she called me rude names. It was more interested in the sensational curves under her clothes.

"Frozen pizza?" I gave myself a mental shake. If a flower was poisonous, did it really matter how good it looked?

She nodded. "That's what I want to cook for dinner."

"This symbol here. Set it like this, then turn this knob to four hundred. And see how the rack's at the top? Put it in the middle." I slid the rack into place for her.

"Four hundred. Okay, got it. Thank you."

Next to my bulk, she seemed small. She only came up to my shoulder. Her size reminded me of the conversation I'd overheard. If someone was threatening her, how could she protect herself?

"You're staying here by yourself?" I asked.

She narrowed her eyes, suspicion returning to her expression. "Of course not. My husband's out back, wiring up some of his explosives."

I lifted both hands, motioning for her to simmer down. "You're in no danger from me, ma'am. That phone call made me concerned for your safety, but I can see you're already fully armed. Your tongue is sharp enough to be lethal."

"Did you miss the part where I said my phone call was none of your business? And don't call me ma'am. It makes me feel like I'm starring in a Western."

Turning my back on her, I headed toward the door. "Well, I sure hope Noah and his girlfriend come back soon," I said over my shoulder. "I liked it better when they were living here."

"Wait. You know Noah?"

Stepping outside, I glanced back at her and nodded. "I grew up here. I know lots of folks, and lots of folks know me. At least, they think they do." I tried not to sound bitter, but it wasn't easy. I hadn't cared what people said when I was here by myself, but having to expose Gemma to the town's gossip mill didn't sit well with me. "Ask me, they're overly interested in things that don't concern them."

"Ugh," Brooklyn muttered as she moved to shut the door behind me, "that's what I was afraid of."

CHAPTER 8

MAGDALENA

The next day, I told the dog to be good and not to annoy the cat, and left the two of them behind when I went to the bakery. I got there on time, wearing comfortable sneakers instead of yesterday's kitten heels, and a practical T-shirt and jeans, ready for my third day of work.

The bakery was busy with lots of customers all morning, as I was coming to expect. Amber and I worked on the counter, while Joy and the other bakers were busy out back. There was often a line of customers waiting to be served that stretched all the way out the door.

When I worked in the fashion boutique, customers didn't usually introduce themselves. Here, lots of them did, especially the ones who came in every day. It was weird, but kind of nice to keep seeing the same faces. I tried to remember everyone's name and what they liked to order. They seemed to enjoy it when I greeted them as though I'd known them for longer than a few days.

We had a short lull just after lunchtime, and Amber grabbed the chance to take a break out the back. She'd only just left me alone when a short older woman with gray curls and pronounced laugh lines around her eyes came into the bakery. She introduced herself as Mary Malone, the mother of Carla's fiancé, Noah. I'd never actually met her, though Carla had raved to me about how nice she was.

"Oh my goodness, look at you," she gushed, her smile bright. "You're just as lovely as your sister!"

"Thank you, Mrs. Malone." I smiled back at her, liking the woman immediately. And not just because of the compliment. She had a warm, open manner, as though we were instantly friends. Maybe it was a small-town trait, because I'd gotten a similar feeling when I'd met Joy and Amber.

"How are you enjoying yourself here in Green Valley?" she asked.

"Well, I've only been here a few days, but . . ." Just in time, I stopped myself from telling her it wasn't nearly as bad as I'd expected. "It's nicer than I thought it'd be," I said instead, framing the thought more positively.

"And you're staying at the farmhouse all alone? You're not lonely?"

"I'm doing okay, thank you."

"You must come and visit me often, you hear?" She shot me a wink. "And we'll see if we can find you a nice romantic partner so you can have some company."

I wrinkled my nose. "No, thanks. I don't want any more men in my life. They're nothing but trouble."

"Not my Noah. I wish I had another one just like him for you."

"I have to admit, Noah is sweet," I told her, smiling at her enthusiastic nod of agreement. "He's perfect for my sister."

"He sure is! Now, Magdalena, I'll take a slice of banana cake, if you please."

I was putting a slice in a bag for her when the door opened and two more women came into the bakery. They were both around Mrs. Malone's age, and greeted her with hellos. But neither woman had the same instantly likeable warmth that she did. One of them was the unpleasant, sharp-tongued woman who'd come into the bakery while Cy was buying chocolate cake.

"Oh, hello." Mrs. Malone's tone got noticeably cooler, but she turned and introduced me. "This is Magdalena, Carla's sister. Magdalena, this is Karen Smith and Bonnie Linton."

"Nice to meet you, Mrs. Linton." I said politely. "I met Mrs. Smith the other day."

"Cy Baxter was in the bakery when I was here last," announced Mrs. Smith.

"Ike Baxter's son?" Mrs. Linton's eyes sharpened on me. "You be careful of that Baxter boy. The whole family's rotten."

"That's what I told her," Mrs. Smith said. "But she seemed like she didn't want to listen."

"Why do you call him a boy?" I asked Mrs. Linton, keeping my tone pleasant. "He must be in his early thirties, right?"

"Come now, ladies," Noah's mother said to the other two women. "Let's not gossip."

I was pretty sure that was like telling water not to be wet. And sure enough, the two of them kept right on talking.

"I heard not a single soul turned up to Ike Baxter's funeral," Mrs. Linton said. "None of his children went. Of course, one of them is dead, and one's in prison. But the other two simply didn't bother. So why is Cy Baxter back in town now, up in that old house of his daddy's?"

Mrs. Smith leaned in. "He's back to sell his daddy's drugs, of course."

"Why would you say something like that when you don't know it for a fact?" chided Noah's mother.

"Well, why else would he be holed up there? That old house is little more than bare boards, termites, and marijuana plants. How is he earning a living if he's not selling drugs?"

I'd already heard Karen Smith's theories about Cy. His unkempt look made those theories easy to believe, though Cy had acted offended when I'd said the dog could guard his crop. If the rumors weren't true, I could only feel bad about the way she was slandering him. Especially seeing as I had some idea of how much it sucked to have a bad reputation.

"Don't jump to conclusions." Mrs. Malone echoed my thoughts. "Could be any number of ways he might be getting by."

Mrs. Linton sniffed. "Those Baxters have always been bad, and the apple doesn't fall far, does it? We all know Cy's mother didn't take an accidental tumble down any stairs. Cy covered up her killing, and it wouldn't surprise me if he played a part in murdering her, too."

I froze, stunned by the turn the conversation had taken. Bonnie Linton thought Cy was a *murderer*?

Noah's mother tsked. "That's enough of that kind of talk." She turned back to me, murmuring under her breath so quietly that only I could hear. "If gossip were gravy, that woman's biscuits would never be dry."

I gave her a secret eye roll, silently agreeing, and we shared a smile like co-conspirators.

Still, as awful as the town gossips were, it was safest to keep well away from Cy in future. It was hard to believe he was a murderer, but his involvement in drugs was bad enough. I already had one scary drug dealer in my life. And it wasn't like I was Cy's biggest fan, though I had to admit he'd been kind enough to help with the dog. And with my oven. He'd been nicer than I'd probably deserved after our terrible introduction, and some of his comebacks had been funny. Biting the inside of my cheek had been the only way to keep from laughing at his "Hansel and Gretel" crack.

"Here's your cake, Mrs. Malone." I slid it across the counter to her. "It really was a pleasure to meet you."

"You too, Magdalena."

"Please call me Mags. Everyone does."

"Mags, I'd like you to come to lunch with me sometime soon. Maybe next weekend, if you have some time off work?"

"I'd love to," I said honestly. With a mother like his, no wonder Noah was so sweet.

As she was leaving, and the other two women were mulling over the items in the cabinet, Amber emerged from the kitchen into the service area.

"Are you ready to take a break?" Amber asked, smoothing her apron. "You must be hungry."

"I'm starving. Thanks."

I left her with Mrs. Linton and Mrs. Smith, and went to the breakroom to enjoy some delicious baked goods. After eating, I tried calling Eric. It was around three o'clock in the morning in Japan, which meant I might catch him before he crashed for the night, seeing as he was usually awake late after performing.

Sure enough, he picked up on the third ring.

"Hey, babe." There was hip-hop music in the background, and I could hear the murmur of other voices. "We played so well tonight. Wish you were here to celebrate with me." His voice was a little slurred as though he was either drunk or high, and my heart sank. Now clearly wasn't the best time to talk sense into him. Still, I had to try.

"Eric, have you spoken to Spike about the money yet?"

"Is that all you're calling for?" He sounded disappointed, as though he'd been expecting me to congratulate him. Did he care so little about the mess he'd left me in?

"I told you Spike's been threatening me, didn't I? I've had to go to Carla's place to get away from him."

"Oh yeah? She lives in Green Hills, right?"

"Green Valley."

"Right. Yeah, I remember. It's in . . . Alabama?"

"Tennessee."

"Right, that's it. Green Hills, Tennessee. When I get back, let's visit your sister together. Would you like that, babe?"

I let out a long, slow breath through my nose. I felt like a pot of water coming to a boil and starting to leak steam.

"The money, Eric." I snapped the words. "When are you sending it to Spike? Focus on what I'm saying and give me an answer. This is *important*!"

"Yeah, okay. The money, right? You're giving it to him?" There was a shout of laughter in the background that almost drowned Eric out. Wherever he was, at least four or five other people were in the room with him. Probably more.

"No, I'm not. I *can't*! Eric, that bonus you said you were going to get at the end of the tour. Can you ask Sullivan for it now, and—"

Another burst of shouting and laughter came over the line, so loud it cut me off. Someone was calling Eric's name. It sounded like the other people in the room had surrounded him.

"Listen, babe, I need to go," Eric shouted over the noise. "Jonesy has poured shots. Let's talk later, okay?"

The line went dead.

I drew the phone from my ear so I could check the screen, not quite able to believe the call had ended so abruptly. But it was true. Eric had hung up on me.

I wanted to scream.

I wanted to wring his selfish neck.

Jumping up, I paced up and down the length of the breakroom for a few minutes, clenching and unclenching my fists while I took several deep breaths.

Then I sent a text message to Eric.

Mags: *Spike is threatening me and I'm afraid. Please call him NOW. Tell him to leave me alone. Promise you'll send him the money. Then ask Sullivan if you can have your bonus, and give it to Spike.*

The plan was simple. It was clear. Surely the message would get through to Eric and he'd realize how badly his actions were hurting me. We'd been dating for two whole years, and though the better his band had been doing, the more self-absorbed and thoughtless he'd seemed to get, he'd never been cruel. Not until recently.

Throwing my phone back onto the table, I tried taking more deep breaths. My anger was still red hot. I wanted to scream or punch something, and I couldn't go back out to do my job when I was in danger of snarling at the bakery's customers. In New York, I'd been the best salesperson in the boutique. And even though I was now selling baked goods instead of thousand-dollar outfits, I was still a professional. Nobody wanted to buy anything from a grouch.

Fetching myself a plate piled high with banana cake, I sat back at the table and put my earbuds in. For starters, I chose the song 'Bite Me' by Avril Lavigne. Next was 'The Best Thing' by We Are The In Crowd. Then 'Stronger' by Kelly Clarkson. By the time the last note faded, I'd power-eaten the entire plate.

Hey, whatever worked, right? I needed the sugar high and the empowerment songs to counteract Eric's toxicity. Besides, it was by far the best banana cake I'd ever eaten, and it'd be a crime not to finish it.

Once my plate was clean, I switched the soundtrack to something softer to recalibrate my mood. 'Watch Me While I Bloom' by Hayley Williams did the trick. When the song finished, I felt in control again and ready to get back to work.

The bakery was busy all afternoon, and Amber and I worked together serving customers. I kept my manner friendly and my smile switched on, and by the end of the day, I was exhausted and looking forward to getting home and flopping onto the couch. When we switched the sign on the door from Open to Closed, I wanted to cheer.

Amber had to rush to an appointment, so Joy helped me clear the leftover food out of the cabinet, getting it ready for the cleaning staff who'd come in overnight. She started chatting about some of the customers, and I took the opportunity to ask, "Do you know Cy Baxter?"

"I haven't spoken a handful of words to him, but I know who he is." Joy straightened, holding a plate full of crumbs. "His daddy was notorious. And when I was just a kid, I saw Cy's brother getting arrested in the Piggly Wiggly. He was yelling and breaking things. He was only around fourteen or fifteen, but it took two grown men to hold him down while they called the sheriff."

"Bonnie Linton said Cy's a drug dealer who killed his own mother."

She snorted. "Bonnie Linton likes to sweeten her tea with scandal."

"So you don't think there's any truth to it?"

Joy wrinkled her freckled nose, her eyes thoughtful. "I'm not sure what to think about Cy."

She was usually so kind and positive, hearing her sound doubtful about him hit hard. And I felt strangely disappointed. Some part of me had been hoping Mrs. Linton and Mrs. Smith were wrong about Cy.

I'd been ready to admit I'd made some unfair assumptions based on his scruffy appearance. But maybe my first negative impression of him had been the right one.

"How likely is it that he's a drug dealer?" I asked, stacking the dirty food trays to carry out back.

Joy shrugged. "Folks say his daddy grew marijuana behind his house. Cy's moved in there, and Flo McClure saw him at the hardware store buying a lot of straw. Why would he need straw if he wasn't growing something?"

I picked up some of the trays, and she grabbed the others. "He doesn't seem like a bad person," I mused as we carried them into the kitchen. "At least he didn't last night."

"Last night?" She raised her eyebrows, putting the trays by the sink.

"I gave him a dog and he insisted on bringing it back."

Her surprise turned into a puzzled frown. "I don't know what that means."

"It doesn't matter." I put my trays next to hers. "I'll tell you tomorrow. Right now, I'm beat."

"Me too." She took off her apron. "Hey, if you want to know more about the people here, why don't you come to the jam session on Friday night? It's at the community center, and lots of folks go. There'll be some good bluegrass. It's fun!"

Bluegrass? I considered myself pretty open-minded when it came to music. I mean, I liked indie rock, alternative rock, punk rock, *and* pop rock. But there was no bluegrass on my playlist.

I shook my head, pulling my own apron off with relief. "My first week at a new job, and I'm exhausted. Thanks anyway, but I don't think I'm up for a party."

"Next week, then." Her smile reassured me that she wasn't hurt by my refusal.

"Sure." It was easier to agree to that, seeing as anything could happen in the meantime.

After saying goodbye, I drove Noah's pickup back to the farmhouse. By the time I parked out front, I was looking forward to putting my feet up and watching some TV while I ate pizza. And when I opened the door, I was greeted by an excited dog, tail wagging, body wriggling, tongue lolling, clearly overjoyed to see me.

Behind the dog was a scene of devastation.

The couch cushions had been dragged from the living room into the hallway and ripped open. Their stuffing was spread everywhere, white clumps scattered over the floor. The empty cushions were limp, drained carcasses with nothing left to give.

I let out a horrified wail. "What did you do, Dog?"

He sat, gazing up at me with a smile. His tail wagged across the floor, sending tufts of cushion stuffing flying.

"Right." Tugging my phone out of my pocket, I gave him a stern look.

"Let's see if your owner's seen my lost-and-found post. Then you can go to your real home and stop destroying my sister's place."

Standing in the hallway with white puffs at my feet, I scrolled to the post. The dog watched, surrounded by the evidence of his crime.

There was no response to my post. Nobody was claiming ownership of the dog.

Weirdly, I found myself letting out a relieved breath, as though a deep part of me was happy about that. But no, it wasn't that weird, seeing as a goofy, cushion-killing guard dog was better than no guard dog at all. And he was good company. It was more reassuring to have him with me at night than the cute-but-lazy cat who slept all the time and would be useless in an emergency.

"You can stick around a little longer," I told the dog. "Just don't kill any more cushions, okay? Tomorrow, I'll need to put everything you can destroy out of reach."

He barked and bounded past me, disappearing out of the front door before I could stop him.

"Dog!" I yelled after him. "Don't get into any more trouble!"

I was still holding my phone, so when it rang, I jumped and let out a little squeak of surprise.

The screen said *Scary Drug Dealer*.

Heart thumping, I pressed the Reject button to send the call to voicemail. More threats were the last thing I needed.

Moments later, a text message flashed onto my screen.

Scary Drug Dealer: *Spoke to your boyfriend. Call me.*

I stared at the message, a rush of relief flooding through me. But confusion was hot on its heels. If Eric had finally called Spike, did that mean he'd sorted everything out? In that case, why would Spike still need to talk to me?

With a muttered curse, I dialed Spike's number.

"You spoke to Eric?" I asked when the scary drug dealer answered.

"Yeah, the rock star finally answered his phone." Spike sounded as surly as ever.

"And he arranged to pay you the money he owes you?"

"He said you'd pay."

"What?" I gasped the word. "No! He can't have! It's Eric's bill, and I had nothing to do with it. I don't take drugs! I'm not the one who borrowed the money."

"Yeah, but you're the one who's still in the country. You're in Green Hills, right?"

Green Hills? That's what Eric always called it instead of Green Valley. A bitter surge of bile rose from my gut, threatening to choke me. Eric may have been getting progressively more insufferable, but this was unforgivable.

"Tennessee isn't so far away that I couldn't pay you a visit," Spike added. "You're staying at your sister's place, and you have another sister who lives right here in the city. Her name's Josephina." His tone grew smug. "Your boyfriend likes to talk when he's stoned. He can be real chatty."

Fucking Eric! I was going to kill him.

"Eric's tour finishes in three weeks, then he'll be back with your money." I tried hard to keep my cool. "I don't have any money to give you, so you need to wait for him."

"I've waited long enough. If you don't pay up, I'll visit your sister. See if she'll give me my money."

My heart launched itself into my throat. I strode out to the porch. "Don't you dare! Leave her out of it!"

"Then pay me."

"Okay, yes. I will. I'll go to the bank and see if I can borrow the money. It might take me a day or two, but I'll get it to you as fast as I can." My heart was beating out of my chest. There was no way I could raise ten thousand dollars in a day or two, but all I needed was enough time to get Josephina to safety.

"You do that." He hung up.

Sinking onto the steps that led from the porch to the driveway, I called Josephina. My hand was sweating, and my legs felt weak. "Pick up," I muttered while it rang. "Pick up, Josie. Please pick up."

"Hi, Mags." My sister's voice filled me with relief. I couldn't see her, as unlike Carla, Josie was a technophobe who preferred regular phone calls instead of video calls. But she sounded just as cheerful as ever.

"Josie, listen. Could you leave town for a few days? Is that possible?"

"What?" she asked. "What's wrong? You're not in trouble again?" She chuckled as she asked the question, her tone affectionate rather than accusing. But even in my frantic state, the "again" she tacked on to the end of her question had a barb that stung a little.

"Eric's the one in trouble. He owes money to a drug dealer called Spike." I didn't try to sugarcoat it. "Problem is, Spike thinks I'm going to pay Eric's debt. I'm staying at Carla's place for a few weeks, but Eric told Spike about you."

I still couldn't believe he'd done that, stoned or not. The Eric I'd started dating two years ago had been charismatic and driven, more focused on his music career than partying. Back then, he'd been a whole lot nicer.

"Eric can't pay what he owes?" asked my sister.

"No, and he's gone to Japan."

"You're telling me that Eric left you to pay his bill?" Josie was usually a ray of walking sunshine, and this was the sharpest I'd ever heard her tone go. "Why would he do that?"

"He's let the rock-star thing go to his head. Lately, he only thinks of himself."

"Is the drug dealer dangerous? He won't try to hurt you, will he?"

"I think I'm safe, but I'm worried about you. Would you be willing to leave town for a few days, while I sort this out? Come to Tennessee if you want. Stay at Carla's with me."

She let out a sigh. "I'd love to hang out with you, only I'm going to New Haven for a yoga retreat this weekend. It's already arranged."

"At least you'll be out of town. Could you leave early? Maybe tomorrow?" I held my breath, hoping she'd be her normal easygoing self and agree.

"Sure."

The breath rushed from my lungs in a relieved whoosh. That had been even easier than I'd hoped.

Thank goodness it was Josie and not Carla I'd had to convince. Josie was laid back, while Carla would have asked more questions. Though I loved both my sisters fiercely, sometimes Carla could be intimidating. Josie's impulsive, free-spirited nature was working in my favor.

"Will you go first thing?" I asked.

"If you want. I love the New Haven countryside. Fresh air and birdsong. I could take a tent and find somewhere to pitch it."

"Thanks, Josie. I'm really glad I won't have to worry about you."

We chatted for a while longer, and when I hung up, I was filled with fresh determination. Time to stop expecting Eric to do the right thing, and time to fix his mess myself. After all, I'd been helping Eric's band out for so long that his manager and I had become friends. Sullivan's number was right there in my phone, so why not call him? It would be close to eight o'clock in the morning in Japan. Eric would be fast asleep, but Sullivan wasn't the partying type. He'd probably be up, ready to start work.

Leaning my shoulder against the porch railing with the last rays of the setting sun on my arms, I dialed Sullivan's number. Sure enough, he answered.

"Hi, Mags." His voice was bright. "It's nice to hear from you."

"Hey, Sullivan. How are you enjoying Japan?"

"It's very different. A great experience. Shame you couldn't make it."

What?

"Um. We've got a bad line," I said, thinking fast. "Would you repeat what you just said?"

"I said it's a shame you couldn't get enough time off work to come on tour. Setting up for our shows isn't the same without you."

"Such a shame." I tried to sound casual, as though his words hadn't been a punch in the gut.

Eric hadn't asked me to go on tour with him. He'd never suggested it as a possibility. And as for taking time off work, I'd had plenty of leave accrued. Besides, Eric knew I'd decided to leave my job and look for something else. We'd talked about how I wanted a change at least a dozen times. I could easily have gone with him.

Though I was breathless at the extent of his betrayal, I managed to keep talking. "Anyway, the reason I'm calling is because Eric wanted me to ask you about putting some of his bonus into my account, so I can pay a bill that he—"

"Bonus? What bonus?" Sullivan's confused tone made my stomach turn over. Could Eric have been lying about that, too?

"Eric said he was getting a bonus at the end of the tour."

"Not at the end of the tour, at the beginning. He was paid a signing bonus a few weeks ago. That's the only one, I'm afraid."

"Oh right. That must have been it. My mistake." My voice was getting croaky and tears pricked at my eyes.

"Mags, are you okay?"

"Thanks, I'm fine." I stared down at the porch step I was sitting on and did my best to sound normal.

"Hey, I'm sorry." Sullivan's voice had gone soft and regretful. "If it's Eric who's upset you, please understand that sudden fame can be hard to deal with. He doesn't seem to be handling it all that well, but he'll have to come back down to earth soon. I really do wish you were here, you know. We all do. He's a better person when you're around. And whatever he's done wrong, he's a fool who's bound to regret it."

I fought for composure. "Thanks, Sullivan."

"We miss you. Next tour, you have to come. No excuses."

"Sure. Hey, I need to run. I'll catch you later, okay?"

"See you in a few weeks, Mags."

Hanging up, I dragged a hand over my eyes. "It's okay," I said aloud. "Maybe I blew all my savings, but Spike wouldn't really hurt Josie or come all the way to Tennessee to collect his money. He's just trying to scare me. And even if he wants to come here, there's no such place as Green Hills. So his threats are empty. Josie's going to be fine. She'll leave town, and nothing will go wrong. Everything's . . ."

I couldn't keep talking. My throat was closing up and tears were springing free, rolling fatly down my cheeks. But as I sunk my face into my hands, I heard a familiar sound: the roar of a poorly maintained engine, punctuated by the rattling of parts that were threatening to fall off it.

It was the distinctive racket of Cy's pickup truck.

CHAPTER 9

CY

"*A*re you crying?" I asked Brooklyn.

As soon as the words left my mouth, I silently cursed myself for asking such a ridiculous question. I was standing in front of Brooklyn, and she was sitting on the bottom step that led up to her porch, glaring at me.

I was impressed she *could* glare, seeing as her eyes were bloodshot and traces of tears still glistened on her cheeks. Her makeup had run, putting black smudges around her eyes that made her look no less beautiful than before. If a makeup artist had created the smudges for her, they couldn't have been more flattering.

"Of course I'm not crying." Her tone was as caustic as I'd come to expect. "Why would I be crying when everything's so freakin' fantastic? I'm so happy, I'm sitting here singing show tunes."

"What's wrong?"

A miniature teardrop trembled on one of her eyelashes. "Why exactly are you here?" she asked. "Are you a stalker? Are you obsessed with me?" She sniffed, wiping her nose on the back of her hand.

Tugging a handkerchief out of my pocket, I offered it to her. "Saw your dog running around by the road back there." I hooked my head back the way I'd come. "Thought I'd be neighborly and let you know he was out."

I'd been worried about Duke straying onto the road, but that wasn't the only reason I'd stopped. It was mostly because she was sitting on the step with her head in her hands and her shoulders shaking. It didn't matter how much I disliked her, I couldn't drive past if she was crying now, could I?

She ignored the handkerchief, instead craning her head the way I'd indicated. "He's on the road? Where?"

"In that muddy bit. Pretty sure he's rolling in puddles."

"Dog!" she yelled.

"You haven't given him a name?" Taking her hand, I put the handkerchief into it so she had no choice but to accept it.

She stared at it a moment, then used it to wipe her eyes, smearing more black stuff around. "Dog!" she shouted again, ignoring my question.

"I'll get him." Walking back down her driveway a little, I put my fingers in the corners of my mouth and let out a piercing whistle.

A few moments later, Duke came bounding up, covered in mud. He jumped around me, then rushed off to see Brooklyn. By the time I reached the house, Brooklyn had gotten up from the step and moved inside, trying to coax the excited dog to come in after her.

I followed Brooklyn, intending to get my handkerchief back and make sure she was okay before leaving. But I froze just inside the entrance. Her hallway was in a shambles. White tufts of cushion filler were all over the floor like a polyester snowstorm.

"What happened?" I asked.

"I'm redecorating. What, you don't like it?"

Her sarcasm was reassuring. If she could muster some bite to her words, she couldn't be too miserable, could she?

"You left the dog inside all day," I guessed. "He didn't pee anywhere, did he?"

She flinched at the suggestion, then moved further down the hallway, peering into corners. Her pained expression made me regret the question. Especially when her shoulders rose as though she was bracing for a fresh blow.

"Hey." I only realized I'd gone in without being invited once I was striding toward her. "It's okay," I said. "He can't have peed or we'd have smelled it by now."

Just then, Duke came bounding in from outside, his muddy paws leaving a trail behind him.

"Stop right there, boy." Scooping him up, I held him in front of me, away from my body. "I only washed you yesterday, and now you're filthy again."

"You washed him?" Brooklyn's brow was still furrowed, and she was squeezing my balled-up handkerchief in one fist.

"Yesterday. You didn't notice?"

"He did seem less smelly, but I thought he might have decided to roll in some flowers for a change."

"Well, do you want to grab a towel to wipe him down, or should I put him straight into the bathtub?"

"I don't know. I know nothing about dogs."

Her shoulders slumped. The sharpness had drained from her tone, and her sarcasm seemed to have gone with it. That was worrying. Something really had shaken her. Could it have to do with the phone call I'd overheard?

I bit back the urge to ask her again whether she was in any danger, keeping my tone casual instead. "For this level of filth, bathtub would be best," I suggested.

"It's down the hall." She pointed at a door.

I carried the dog into the well-appointed bathroom, plonked him in the tub, then ran the water. While the tub was filling, Brooklyn came in with a towel. I splashed some water over the dog while he tried his best to jump at me and lick my face.

"Would you hold him?" I asked Brooklyn.

She knelt next to me, close enough that our shoulders were touching. As she grabbed him, the dog wagged his tail through the water that was cascading from the faucet, spraying us both.

Brooklyn yelped and I let out a surprised laugh, then cursed when the dog did it again, covering us with water. "Sit!" I ordered. "Sit, boy. Go on. Sit!"

He backed up as he sat, managing to position himself right under the faucet so more water sprayed at us. By the time we maneuvered him away from the stream and turned the faucet off, I was so wet, water was trickling down my face.

When I turned to Brooklyn, she was laughing softly instead of crying, and my heart turned over. She was soaked, her hair clinging around her face in damp strands, and her cheeks were wet from bathwater rather than tears. Her T-shirt was clinging to her too, though I tried to be a gentleman and not look down.

She seemed to have fought back from her despair. Whatever it was that had knocked her down hadn't been able to keep her there, which didn't surprise me. She seemed like a fighter.

And she was achingly beautiful. Her full lips were higher on one side than the other. With her hair slicked down, her delicate features stood out. Her olive skin seemed to glow, and the smudged makeup around her eyes only high-lighted their warmth.

My admiring gaze stayed on her a little too long, and her laughter died, though her lips stayed tugged up on one side.

"What?" she asked. "Do I have something on my face?" She licked a drop of water that fell onto her lip from her wet hair, then grinned.

I didn't want to respond to that smile. I tried to remind myself that she was rude and unlikeable. But somehow, I found myself grinning back at her. "I think you have a little something"—I lifted a hand and dragged a soft finger over her wet cheek—"right here."

I meant it as a joke, but with the tip of my finger touching her face, a shock of awareness shot through me. Her eyes widened, and her lips parted as though she was surprised. Maybe she'd felt that sensation too.

The water glistened on her lips, and I realized I was staring at them, my breath hitching with a rush of desire. And her eyes darkened as though she was as conscious of how close we were as I was.

We sat frozen, the moment stretching out for a beat longer than I'd meant it to. Then Brooklyn pulled back, turning her face away from me.

"I think the dog's clean enough now," she said.

Grabbing the towel, I rubbed the dog dry while I pushed that spike of unwelcome desire out of my mind. "Two baths in two days," I grumbled to him. "You'd better stay out of the mud from now on."

Brooklyn fetched some towels for us, handing one to me, and I dried my face and hair while she did the same.

"Why haven't you given the dog a name?" I asked when I was mostly dry.

"He's not my dog. Nobody's claimed him yet, but I can't keep him. If I can't find his owner, I'll have to take him to the shelter."

That was a shame. Despite his attraction to mud, Duke was a nice dog. Brooklyn seemed to like him. And the dog clearly liked her, though that had to be because he didn't understand English, so he had no idea how rude she could be.

"At least give him a name in the meantime," I suggested.

She tilted her head, thinking. "His name could be . . . Zeppelin."

"Like Led Zeppelin, the band?"

"Exactly. They had a reputation for trashing hotel rooms, and John Bonham once drove his Harley through a swanky hotel on Sunset." She gave her hair a last rub with the towel. "But the band was less destructive than the dog has been since he's been staying with me. So maybe the name will be a good influence. Encourage him to clean up his act." Hanging her towel over the edge of the bath, she smiled.

Maybe I didn't like her, but I sure liked her smile. I liked the slight crookedness of it, and its warmth. The way it had reappeared so easily, despite the way she'd been crying. One look at that smile, and I decided not to tell her that I'd been calling the dog Duke. Zeppelin suited him better anyway. His nature was too boisterous to be a Duke.

"Anyway, thanks for helping to wash him," she said, combing her damp hair with her fingers. "I appreciate it. Really. But I'm okay now."

It sounded like an invitation to leave, and she probably wanted to clean up. Collecting my handkerchief from where she'd left it on the bathroom counter, I headed to the door.

She walked behind me, and when I got to her front porch, I turned to face her. She was standing inside the door, waiting to shut it behind me. Her T-shirt was still damp, clinging to her, highlighting her generous curves. She really was something. That face and body combined with her quick tongue and biting sarcasm. Had Green Valley ever seen the likes of her? I certainly hadn't.

"I'll look after Zeppelin tomorrow while you're at work," I found myself saying. "Then he won't rip any more of your cushions."

She blinked at me. "You'd do that?"

I shrugged, not entirely sure why I'd offered. "He's good company."

"Carla doesn't even know about Zeppelin yet," she confessed. "If he destroys any more of her stuff, she might disown me."

"I'll pick him up in the morning."

"Could you come at seven, before I have to leave for work?"

"Okay," I agreed, though it was earlier than I'd expected.

It wasn't until after I left that I questioned why I was so willing to go out of my way to help her. Was it because she could be in danger? Or was it simply because we'd had an entire conversation in which she'd managed not to insult me?

CHAPTER 10

MAGDALENA

The next morning, there was a knock on my door at seven o'clock sharp. Zeppelin raced to the door, barking excitedly. I followed, telling him to pipe down. I had a coffee in one hand and stuffed a Pop-Tart into my mouth with the other so I could open the door. When it swung open, I was still chewing.

Cy was on my doorstep, and the beauty of his eyes struck me full force with such strength that I had trouble swallowing the last of the Pop-Tart. His long black hair was neatly combed this morning, which was a definite improvement.

His unruly beard still stuck out in all directions, but maybe I was getting used to it seeing as I found myself focusing on his eyes, his extraordinary cheekbones, and the line of his long, straight nose. I only wished I could see the rest of his face better. I suspected his smile was attractive, but his top lip was shielded by facial hair.

"Your girls started work early this morning," he said in his gravelly drawl. "I collected some eggs."

It was only then that I realized he had several eggs cradled inside his large hands.

"My girls?" I asked, confused.

"The chickens."

"Oh. I didn't . . ." I shook my head. For some reason, it hadn't occurred to me that the danger birds might be laying eggs. I hadn't even thought to check.

For the first time, Cy wasn't wearing an oversized flannel shirt, but a T-shirt and faded jeans. It was a fitted gray T-shirt, and my word, he had some serious muscles. I'd previously noticed his wide shoulders, but now I could see the swell of his biceps and the ropy muscles in his forearms. His T-shirt clung to his trim waist, and his jeans hugged narrow hips.

Nice body, Bumpkin.

Lifting my cup, I took a slug of coffee to cover my surprise at the improvement a simple change of clothes had made.

Zeppelin jumped up at Cy, trying to get high enough to lick his face. Cy laughed, taking a step backward. "Almost dropped one." He nodded down at his hands. "Grab that top egg before it gets scrambled."

I wrinkled my nose, curling both hands around my half-empty coffee cup. "But they haven't been sterilized."

"Sterilized?"

"They've come from a chicken's butt. They must need cleaning."

His mouth tugged up as though I'd said something funny. "Just take the egg, then you can wash your hands."

With my nose still wrinkled, I reached for the egg. But I breathed in his scent at the same time, woodsy and fresh, and my gaze was focused on what I could see of his smile. My fingers landed on warm skin instead of a cool egg, and a spike of awareness shot through me. It was the same feeling I'd had when he'd touched my face as we were giving Zeppelin a bath.

Either Cy was giving off power surges like a faulty battery, or I was more attracted to him than I was willing to admit.

Feeling my cheeks start to heat, I snatched the egg and stepped back with it. He might be kind, and unexpectedly quick-witted, but he was the last person I should find attractive. A bumpkin drug dealer? No thanks.

"Is that coffee?" Lifting a hopeful eyebrow, Cy nodded at the cup I was holding.

"Well, it's too early for a margarita." To counteract any color that might have leaked into my cheeks, I put a little bite into the words.

"I'll take a cup." Without waiting for an invitation, he stepped inside, brushing past me. Cy had several inches on me, and the size of his shoulders and arms was impressive. As was the rear view of his faded jeans, which I couldn't help but admire while he walked toward the kitchen.

Very nice butt, Bumpkin.

Despite how wrong it was, I took my time walking down the hallway to admire the hug of his jeans and his lazy stride. He put his handful of eggs on the kitchen counter, and I set the one I was carrying next to them. After thoroughly washing my hands, I got out a mug and hit the button to make coffee come out of Carla's magic machine.

"Cream?" I asked. "Sugar?"

"I'll take it black."

Once I handed him the coffee, he leaned back against the kitchen counter and crossed one foot over the other. "How about you tell me who threatened you?" he suggested.

I gave him a flat look over the lip of my cup. "How 'bout I don't."

His gaze traveled over my face. He had to be registering my annoyance with the way he was trying to muscle into my business.

One of his shoulders lifted and then dropped in resigned acceptance. "Suit yourself." He took a sip. "Mmm. Good coffee."

"Right?" At least there was one thing we could agree on.

"How's your oven?" he asked.

"The setting you suggested worked fine." I motioned to the empty pizza box on the counter. "The last two nights, my pizza was edible. Made a pleasant change."

"You had the same meal two nights in a row? Should I tell you the settings to cook something else?"

"No need."

"No need?" he repeated. His brow creased with puzzlement. "You're not fixing to cook anything else?" Without waiting for an answer, he pulled the freezer open and motioned with his coffee to the stack of frozen pizza boxes I'd stuffed into it. "What's all this?"

"It's pizza, of course." I let out an exaggerated huff of breath. "Pizza belongs to a category of food called Not Grits. I assume that's why you don't recognize it."

Shutting the freezer, he turned to face me. "Pizza can't be all you're planning to eat?"

"Why not? Did you not see the Michelin star printed right there on the side of the box? Besides, I bought different flavors."

"There are vegetable gardens around the side of the house, and fresh herbs on the windowsill." He pointed his coffee toward the potted plants I'd assumed were for decoration. "At least you can make something fresh to have with the pizza."

"I don't cook," I informed him.

"Not at all?"

"Well, I can make Pop-Tarts."

"Homemade from scratch?"

"What?" I gave him a confused frown. "There's no such thing as home-made Pop-Tarts."

"Then how do you make them?"

"Put them in the toaster."

He set his coffee on the counter, as though there were no way he could demonstrate the depths of his incredulity other than by spreading both of his large hands. "Let me get this straight. You can't cook anything? Putting a Pop-Tart in the toaster is your closest equivalent?"

"What is it with everyone in this town and cooking? Anyone would think it was some kind of local law. Cook or get arrested. *Sheesh*!"

Crinkles appeared at the corners of his eyes. "Most folks like to eat at least some food that doesn't come in a box. It requires combining ingredients and applying heat."

"Well, I'm used to having dozens of restaurants and takeout places within a block of my apartment. It's not my fault that all you have around here is trees."

Leaning back against the counter, he slowly shook his head. His eyebrows were drawn down as though I'd told him something tragic, and he let out a sigh, though his eyes held a glint of amusement. "I can't let you eat that much frozen pizza, and I don't live far up the road. If you were willing to try to keep your rudeness contained, I'd let you come to my place for dinner—"

"Wait. I'm going to stop you right there." I held up one palm. "I'm not interested in a hookup, so you can forget about trying to put any moves on me."

Cy shook his head, his brow furrowed. "That's not what this is. My niece is staying with me. She's bored, and it would be good for her to have someone other than me to talk to."

He seemed almost offended by the idea he might have been hitting on me, and I studied him, trying to work out if he was for real. So far, he'd been kinder to me than any man I'd met in a long time, and experience had made it hard for me to believe he wasn't asking for anything in return.

Even if he was genuine, there were all those rumors about him. He didn't seem like a drug dealer, but my experience was limited. And where there was smoke there had to be fire, right? The last thing I needed was any more trouble.

"My niece is fifteen, visiting from Nashville," Cy added. "You need to eat, and frozen pizza isn't real food. So come for dinner, and I'll give you a no-moves guarantee."

Funnily enough, I believed him on the no-moves thing. But I still shook my head. "It's not a good idea for me to go to your house."

"What's wrong with my house?"

"For starters, I don't need any trouble with the law."

With a slow blink, he scratched his wild beard. "What in the devil are you talking about?"

"I heard you grow drugs."

His hand froze on his beard midscratch, then dropped as he drew his head back. The skin between his eyes pinched as though what I'd said had hurt him. For a moment, his expression was so pained, I regretted telling him.

"Who said that?" he asked.

"It was one of the bakery's customers."

He was silent for a moment, then gave a little nod as though to say it was to be expected. "I'm a Baxter," he said on a resigned exhale. "And to folks around here, that's the worst thing a person can be."

"Your family has a bad reputation, but you're really just misunderstood?" My tone made it clear that I didn't believe him. Eric wasn't the first unreliable man I'd dated, and I'd heard too many stories that turned out to be lies. It may have taken me longer than it should have, but maybe I'd finally stopped trusting too easily.

He shrugged. "Folks here only think they know me. I've been gone for years. They may have had the misfortune of knowing my daddy, but he was the one who grew weed, not me."

He seemed honest, not that I hadn't been mistaken about that kind of thing before. His gaze was level, his eyes clear, and his manner as confident as ever. Thing was, I wanted to believe him. I was probably just a fool, wanting to keep trusting the wrong people, but I couldn't seem to help it.

"So your house isn't likely to be raided by the police anytime soon?" I asked.

"I can't make any promises about that, seeing as I don't run the sheriff's department." He picked up his coffee cup to drain it, and when I didn't say anything, he added, "It's your choice. I'll make burgers tonight with my own homemade ketchup. Come or don't come, whichever you please."

Burgers did sound good, even without proper ketchup. A lot better than having pizza again. And I'd only need to stay long enough to eat.

Cy put his empty cup in the sink, then picked up Zeppelin's leash, getting ready to leave.

"Do you put pickles on your burgers?" I asked, watching him clip the leash to Zeppelin's collar.

"Why?" He straightened. "Don't you like them?"

"I more than like them. Pickles are my bottom line. Without them, there's no burger."

He shot me a sideways look, his lips quirking up. "Noted."

Despite how he was trying to hide them under all that facial hair, I noticed his teeth were white and even. "You have a nice smile," I mused aloud.

His eyebrows shot up. "Was that a *compliment*?"

It was only because he sounded so incredulous that I said, "I was only surprised not to see any chewing tobacco stains. And as far as I can tell, you don't have any teeth missing. At least, not the ones at the front."

Though he gave a rueful shake of his head, he looked amused. Hopefully he'd taken it as the joke I'd intended.

As he stepped onto the porch with Zeppelin on the leash, he said, "I'll be sure to give you extra pickles with your burger, and hope you can't talk while you're eating."

I grinned, and when his lips curled up in response, I was struck even harder by the symmetry of his features, and the glimpse of what had to be a devastating smile. Good thing he had so much scruffy facial hair. Without it, I'd probably be in serious trouble.

"Dinner would be nice," I heard myself say. "Thank you."

"My place is five minutes that way." He nodded up the road. "It's the one with the gravel driveway, and you'll see my truck parked out front. The driveway's rough, but Noah's pickup will handle it. Come around six."

When I shut the door behind him, I was still smiling. But that smile disappeared when my phone rang.

The screen said *Scary Drug Dealer*.

Yesterday, Spike had said he'd give me a day or two to get the money. Had Josephina left town yet? He couldn't be calling from her place, could he?

With my brain conjuring up all kinds of awful scenarios, mostly based on movies about scary thugs torturing people to get what they wanted, I answered my phone.

"You got my money yet?" Spike demanded.

"Not yet, but like I said, I'll talk to the bank and see if I can get a loan."

"Do it today. Get the money, or I'll come to Tennessee."

I let out a breath, grateful he hadn't mentioned Josie. "Spike, listen. I'm getting regular paychecks, so even if I can't get the loan, I can set you up with a payment plan in the meantime, until Eric gets back with the rest."

"A payment plan?" His voice rose. "Are you fucking kidding me? You think I sell encyclopedias?"

"What, drug dealers can't have payment plans?"

"Fuck," he said, but in a tired way, like I might be wearing him down. "Get the fucking money before I need to pay you a visit. Clock's ticking." He hung up.

I rubbed my eyes, my stomach churning. Though I'd talk to the bank, it was a long shot. The chance of getting a ten-thousand-dollar loan with no collateral was slim.

I dialed Eric's number. If I hassled him enough, maybe he'd pay what he owed just to get rid of me. The call connected after a couple of rings. Was that a good sign?

"Hello?" It was a woman's voice. In the background was a barrage of loud noise. The thumping beat of dance music didn't quite drown out the cacophony of voices. A shrill laugh, then a drunken shout. Clearly a party.

"Would you put Eric on?" I asked.

"Who's this?" the woman demanded, as though she had a right to know.

"Who are you?" I countered.

"Eric's my boyfriend," she said. "So tell me why you want to talk him."

I breathed out through my nose, controlling my fury. Honestly, I wasn't shocked. I was mostly angry with myself for not dumping Eric before he got me caught up in paying his debt.

"Put Eric on," I ordered, my tone icy. "Do it now."

She said something inaudible, and I heard Eric curse. A moment later, he came on the line.

"Hey, babe." The party noise in the background suddenly got muffled, as though he'd taken his phone into another room. "I don't know what that woman said to you, but I barely know her, so whatever she told you—"

"Eric." I cut him off. "If you don't pay Spike his money, I'm going to hunt you down and turn your testicles into dashboard ornaments. Are you listening to me?"

"Babe, that woman was goofing around, making trouble for fun. You know I love you."

"Shut up and listen to what I'm telling you. I don't care about that woman, or whatever it is you're doing over there. Spike threatened my *sister*. If he lays a single hand on her, I'm going straight to the police. I'll tell them all about how you threw a big party to make yourself look like a big shot and handed out cocaine like party favors. I'll tell them *everything*."

I should never have stuck with Eric after I'd found out about the wild three-day party he'd thrown after his band had played in Vegas. He'd always been a little insecure, thinking he needed to buy people's respect, but that stunt had gone beyond my understanding. When I'd found out, he'd groveled, begging me not to leave him. I shouldn't have listened.

"You can't go to the cops! Promise me, Mags, okay? If you talk to the police, Spike will kill you. He will. That guy is a serious dude."

"Then pay him!"

"I will, babe. You've just got to give me time."

"Thanks to you, I'm penniless, running from a drug dealer, camped out in rural Tennessee. I don't have time, Eric, and neither do you. Pay him or else. And you don't get to call me *babe*. Never again!"

"What does that mean?"

I let out a huff of breath. "What do you think it means?" Then I hung up on him.

It felt good to be the one to cut off the call for a change.

And if Eric thought our relationship was over, he was right. But if he wasn't sure if I was actually breaking up with him, he'd be more likely to do what I asked and pay Spike what he owed. Maybe it was wrong or cowardly of me not to tell him flat out that we were over, but who cared? All I wanted was to be able to stop worrying that the scary drug dealer might find a way to hurt Josie or someone else I cared about.

CHAPTER 11

CY

Brooklyn turned up at six o'clock that evening. Zeppelin was still at my place, and he raced me to the front door to greet her.

She was wearing black dungarees with the legs rolled up a little to show her ankles and thick-soled black shoes. On top was a white T-shirt that was so short, a sliver of bare skin showed around her middle, disappearing under the bib of her dungarees. A leather satchel worn crossways across her body finished the look.

"Nice outfit," I said. I was no fashion expert, but she looked like she could be a model on a runway. Only difference was, she was curvier and more beautiful. And a whole lot sexier. I could hardly keep from staring at that sliver of exposed skin around her midriff.

"It's ironic." She stepped into the hallway. "This is a New York version of a country look. I got these dungarees before I knew I'd be coming here, but now I fit right in."

"Practically a local," I agreed, thinking she was about as far from a local as she could be.

She bent to pet Zeppelin, who was bounding at her feet, excited to see her. Then she followed me into the living room, looking around with interest. When I'd invited her, it hadn't crossed my mind to worry about how rundown the house was. But now I was conscious of the faded paint and all the moving boxes piled up behind the couch.

The place was a dump. And with Brooklyn gazing around, it seemed even worse than before. Had that ancient water stain on the wall always been so noticeable?

"Something smells good," Brooklyn said.

I blinked. The woman who'd called me Deliverance seemed to have disappeared, and in her place was someone kinder. Instead of commenting on the house's obvious state of disrepair, Brooklyn had found something nice to say.

"You hungry?" I asked.

I wanted to say that I liked her hair the way she was wearing it, loose around her face in long waves, but she'd already accused me of . . . how had she put it? Wanting to put the moves on her? So I kept those thoughts to myself.

"I'm starving." She took off her satchel and put it next to the couch. With every movement, her midriff caught my eye again. Her olive skin was smooth and tempting.

Gemma's bedroom door opened. My niece emerged, a steady beat of rock music flowing after her. She took in Brooklyn's outfit and her expression of resentment turned into interest. "Hey," she said.

"This is my niece, Gemma," I said. "Gemma, this is Brooklyn."

Brooklyn gave me a rueful smile that—surprisingly—seemed to contain a hint of an apology. "Actually, my name is Mags."

The two exchanged hellos, then I asked, "Gemma, would you turn down your music? Dinner's about ready."

Gemma heaved a disgruntled sigh in my direction, then disappeared back into her bedroom. The music cut off abruptly before she re-emerged.

"You were listening to The Unforgiven?" Mags asked her. "I like that song."

My niece looked surprised. "You know who The Unforgiven are?"

"Sure. Their first album was the best. Their second, not so much."

"Wow. Yeah, that's right." Gemma flopped onto the couch, her expression more animated than I'd seen it in days. "Uncle Cy only listens to country and western music, so I thought his friends would be the same."

"Country music." Mags flared her nostrils. "There's a good reason so many of those songs are about women leaving."

Gemma laughed, her gaze flicking to me.

"Country music is soulful," I protested, moving into the kitchen to check the buns weren't burning. "Brooklyn, you can't tell me you like that awful guitar noise my niece listens to, with lyrics that make no sense? Some of them, you can't even make out the words." Opening the oven, I saw the buns were almost perfect. Lightly toasted, just how I liked them.

"Of course I like indie rock," Mags said. "I've been dating a musician."

I froze with the oven door ajar. Did that mean she currently had a boyfriend? The sentence wasn't clear. She could have said that she "used to date a musician" if their relationship was in the past. But saying she'd "been dating" implied it could be an ongoing state.

Not that I cared whether she had a boyfriend or not. There was no reason for me to be interested. And I wasn't.

"Does he play in a band?" asked Gemma. "Would I know who he was?"

I jerked around to face Mags so I wouldn't miss her reply.

Mags winced, then gave a reluctant-looking nod. "You might know him. The band's called Storm Front and he's the lead singer. Eric Storm."

"No way!" My niece's eyes went wide. "I've heard them. They're great! But I only know that song called 'City Pretty'."

"That single's the one that's had the airplay," said Mags. "He's written other songs, but that's his first hit."

"Wait." Gemma blinked rapidly. "What is Mags short for? You're not Magdalena, are you? The Magdalena from that line in the 'City Pretty' song?" She gave an incredulous laugh. "Holy shit!"

"Language," I said as I pulled the buns out of the oven.

My heart was beating extra heavily as though some part of me was disappointed she had a boyfriend. It was something that made no sense, seeing as she was off-limits anyway. And what did it matter if he was famous?

"Magdalena in the city, drinking coffee laced with whisky," Gemma sang. It was obviously from whatever song they were talking about.

"You have a really nice voice," Mags said.

Turning to the stove, I started putting together the burgers, doing it quietly so I could still hear them. I was trying to get past the fact that Mags was dating a rock star who'd written a song about her. Why did the idea irritate me so much?

Perhaps he was the man who'd threatened her over the phone. But that guy's name had been Spike.

"Tell me everything about Eric Storm!" exclaimed Gemma. "What's he like? When did you start dating him? You two are still together, right?"

Setting my homemade ketchup on the counter, I listened hard while silently applauding Gemma for asking the exact thing I wanted to know.

"That's a lot of questions." Stuffing her hands into the back pockets of her dungarees, Mags swiveled to face me. "Dinner looks like it's ready. You want some help taking it to the table?"

Damn. Why didn't she want to answer Gemma's questions?

"Sure," I said, giving no sign of my irrational frustration. "You take the plates, I'll grab the wine. And there's iced tea, whichever you prefer."

"I'll get the cutlery." Gemma surprised me by jumping off the couch and rushing to help. She was happy tonight, with her face alight and her eyes bright. Looking at her made me want to either smile or sigh with relief, seeing as I'd started to think her anger might have gotten fused in. And I had Mags to thank for the change.

We sat at the dining table, and both Mags and Gemma praised the burgers. Zeppelin hovered next to Gemma as she ate, and I caught her slipping some food to him under the table.

"If you want to feed her dog, you should check with Brooklyn first," I told her.

Mags shrugged. "Go ahead and feed him. He's not really my dog. He just turned up the other night, so I'm looking after him for a while."

"Why did you call him Zeppelin?" asked Gemma. "Did you name him after Led Zeppelin?"

Mags put down her fork, her eyebrows raised as though she was surprised. "You know Led Zeppelin, Gemma?"

"I only know 'Stairway to Heaven'. And everyone knows that song, don't they?"

"Not everyone. It came out before I was born, and long before you were born."

"Well, it was the first song I learned to play on my guitar."

"You play the guitar as well as sing?"

Gemma wrinkled her nose as she nodded. "I've had a few lessons. But my guitar was so old, it was warping, and I couldn't play it anymore. I've been saving up for a new one."

Mags threw both hands up as though overwhelmed by Gemma's genius. "You'll be playing your own rock shows soon."

"That's my *dream*!"

"When you're ready, I could put you in touch with some people."

"She's only fifteen," I said, startled.

Gemma's delight turned into a frown, and Mags shot me an apologetic look. I instantly regretted ruining the moment.

"Sixteen soon," Gemma muttered, giving me a glare that could breach a calf in the womb. Then she leaned closer to Mags, shutting me out of the conversation with her shoulder. "Tell me about the music scene in New York. I don't get to hear any good music here. Uncle Cy is into old white guys singing about how lonesome and brokenhearted they are. Bunch of whiners."

Mags snickered. Not that I minded. I was happy they were bonding if it meant Gemma was coming out of her shell. They could gang up on me all they wanted.

"Hey now, I like current music," I protested anyway. "Keith Urban is one of my favorites, and Claire McClure, of course. You know she's from Green Valley?"

"I've heard her name, but I don't think I've heard her music," Mags said.

"Have you heard of a band called MightNight?" Gemma asked Mags. "They're my favorite."

"They're good. Eric opened for them when they toured last year."

"You've *met* them?" My niece sprayed bits of burger out with her incredulous question, but she seemed too excited to notice.

"They're nice guys. If you like owning vinyl, I could ask the guitarist to send you an autographed album."

"He'd do that? That would be so cool!"

Mags nodded. "He owes me."

"Why does he owe you?" I asked.

She turned her lovely brown eyes to me. The lamp was behind her, creating a deceptively angelic halo around her dark hair.

"One afternoon before their show, the lead guitarist and some of their roadies decided to play drinking games. The roadies got too drunk to work, so I pitched in to help set up the stage." She rolled her eyes. "The guitarist was just as drunk as the roadies, but it was a sold-out show, so he couldn't go and sleep it off. He had to perform."

Gemma leaned in. "What happened?"

"He was staggering around so much, he almost fell off the stage. The other band members were trying to convince him to just stand still and play his guitar, but he wouldn't listen. So I put a stool on stage and ordered him to sit."

"He listened to you?"

She nodded. "Heaven knows why, but yeah. He did. After sitting down, he actually made it through several songs. Then for some drunken reason, he decided to start throwing his guitar pick into the crowd, and demanded I keep running on stage to give him more." She shook her head with a rueful smile. "And that, kids, is why you should always say no to tequila."

My niece laughed. "That's so funny! I wish I could have been there. Have you met any other bands?"

"Well, let's see . . ." Mags tapped her finger on her chin before reeling off some band names I mostly hadn't heard of.

Gemma had heard of them, though, and she responded enthusiastically, asking questions with wide, excited eyes. As Mags launched into another funny story about a concert that had gone wrong, Gemma listened with her lips slightly parted. Mags was clearly a big hit with my niece.

And with me.

My first impression of her had been negatively influenced by her insults. But now I was seeing a different side.

She had a rapid, quick-fire way of speaking, as though her thoughts were working double-time and her mouth was trying to keep up. She seemed street-smart, adaptable, and personable, and those were qualities I admired.

After leaving home at a young age, I'd managed to make a home for Ruth and myself. I'd not just survived but thrived outside of Green Valley, and gotten to know myself well in the process. I was smart, but I wasn't naturally good with people. Mags clearly was.

Watching Gemma gasp and laugh at her stories, I didn't want the night to end. In a short space of time, my niece had become animated and enthusiastic. The transformation was better than I could have wished for.

"You've seen so many bands play," Gemma said wistfully, after Mags had described a particularly wild concert. "I never get to see live music."

"Apparently, musicians play at the community center on Friday nights," Mags said, looking at me. "Joy and Amber from the bakery have been trying to talk me into going. It might just be rockabilly or bluegrass, but it could be worth a look. I might go next week."

"We should meet you there! Uncle Cy, can we go? Will you take me?" Gemma turned her eager gaze to me, and I hesitated, not knowing how to answer.

All I wanted was to keep that smile on my niece's face. But if the folks in town found out she was a Baxter, she'd be tainted by my family's bad name. I couldn't take her anywhere in public where she'd be seen with me.

Maybe Mags would be willing to take Gemma to the community center, but it wouldn't be fair to ask her right now when she'd feel obligated. Better to ask her later, when she'd be more free to say yes or no without Gemma's beseeching eyes willing her to agree.

"We'll see," I said. "Brooklyn, would you like more fries?"

"Thank you, I'm full." She pushed her empty plate away. "That was really good. Even the fake ketchup."

"Fake . . . ?" I cut off my indignant question with a rueful shake of my head when I realized she was joking.

She grinned, her eyes sparkling with clear hints of mischief, and I found myself grinning back. Then I realized my heart was beating faster and my body was charged up, as though my blood was restless in my veins. I wanted to touch her. To reach out and stroke a finger down her cheek like I had after giving Zeppelin a bath.

And I was struck by a bewildering—almost overwhelming—urge to kiss her.

Mags gazed back at me, and her eyes widened, her lips parting as though she could see what I was thinking and it took her by surprise.

Gemma got up, scraping her chair back. I jerked my gaze to her, trying to snap out of it.

"I'll take the plates out, Uncle Cy." Gemma reached for the empty dishes. She was smiling in a secretive kind of way, but that could have been from all the stories Mags had been telling. Hopefully she hadn't noticed the way I must have been looking at Mags.

I cleared my throat, pulling myself together. "Your momma's going to call you soon," I reminded Gemma.

"Oh. Yeah, of course." Gemma darted a furtive glance at Mags as she stacked the plates.

I could tell from her expression that she didn't want her new hero to know her momma was staying in a psychiatric institution. I wanted to tell her there was nothing wrong with where her mother was, and that she should be proud of Ruth for asking for the help she'd needed. But Gemma was still at an age where she embarrassed easily, so I didn't.

"Go and do your homework in your room, and you can talk to your momma in there," I suggested instead. "Leave the dishes tonight. I'll take care of them."

"Okay, thanks." The gratitude in her expression made me want to grin in triumph. Tonight had easily been the best time we'd spent together since she'd arrived. And I had Mags to thank.

Gemma took the plates she was carrying into the kitchen, then disappeared into her bedroom and shut the door. Mags got up, and the two of us cleared the rest of the table. Then I went to the small stereo in the living room to put on some music, smiling at Zeppelin as he flopped onto the rug and lowered his head onto his paws with a heavy sigh.

The haunting sound of a strong, clear female voice filled the air as I went to the sink to fill the frying pan with water. The music was so good, nobody could possibly dislike it.

"Who's singing?" asked Mags.

"Claire McClure. You said you hadn't heard her music."

Mags walked over to the sink. "I'll wash, you dry?"

"Let's leave them. I'll do them later. Would you like a nightcap?"

"Thanks, but I can't drink. I need to drive home." She put both hands on the counter and gazed out of the kitchen window.

I moved next to her to see what she was looking at. The only thing visible was the barn, its roof silhouetted against a night sky that was full of stars, with a large, bright moon.

The sky was beautiful, but I'd seen it a thousand times. I was more conscious of the woman beside me who took the word *beautiful* to an entirely new level. She wasn't tall, but she stood with her back straight and her chin lifted, the size of her personality exceeding her frame. There was something about the way her eyebrows were shaped in a natural quirk over her eyes that made her expression good-natured, even when she was being sarcastic. And the sliver of skin that peeped out from under her crop top kept drawing my gaze.

It was such a small glimpse of her midriff, it shouldn't be so tempting. Why was it so fascinating?

"It's quiet here," she said, clearly not talking about the music, seeing as Claire McClure's pure tones were still ringing from the stereo.

"That's what Gemma says."

"Where did you say Gemma was from?"

"Nashville. Home of country music and the Johnny Cash Museum." I shook my head in mock sadness. "How any niece of mine could disrespect the Nashville sound is beyond me."

"You have to admit, it *is* ridiculously quiet in this town. Everywhere except in the bakery, that is." Her gaze was fixed to something outside the window, her lovely face in profile. Her lush lips were slightly parted, and my gaze lingered over them. They looked soft.

"How long are you planning to stay?" I asked.

"I'm not sure yet. Jenn said I can work in the bakery for as long as I like, and Carla's not sure how long she'll need to be away. I'm hoping to head home in three or four weeks, but I'll wait until Carla and Noah get back."

"Do you have a job in New York?" I asked.

She turned to face me, leaning her hip against the kitchen counter. "I used to work in a fashion boutique, but I quit before I came here. I'd been at the same place for over five years and felt like I needed a change."

"A fashion boutique isn't much like a bakery."

"No, not much. I'm still getting used to how busy it is at the bakery, but I really like the people. Before I arrived, I was afraid we wouldn't have much in common, but everyone's been so welcoming."

"Maybe you're not so different to the folks around here." I leaned against the counter too, lifting my eyebrows and silently challenging her to argue.

She gave a little laugh. "I don't have a beard," she pointed out. "And I'd rather chew glass than wear a flannel shirt."

"What's wrong with flannel?"

"Nothing at all, so long as you're a lumberjack in a remote wilderness. If you don't own a mirror or interact with people, flannel is an acceptable fashion choice." Clapping her hand over her mouth, she rounded her eyes. "I can't believe I just said *flannel* and *fashion* in the same sentence." She gave an exaggerated shudder, making me smile. I was sure she was both joking and not joking. Inflating her real dislike of flannel for comic effect.

"No flannel then." I adjusted my features into a serious expression. "Got it." I was also joking but not joking. I had some flannel shirts I'd probably never wear again.

"Thank you for becoming a flannel-free zone. I appreciate your sacrifice. And in return, I'll attempt to wear shirts with a socially acceptable number of sleeves. At least when you're around." Her grin was small, crooked, and seriously cute.

"No need to wear anything extra on my account." It came out a little more suggestive than I'd intended, especially because I couldn't keep from glancing down at that enticing sliver of bare torso.

Her cheeks colored, and she turned toward the window as though to hide the fact she was blushing. Then she peered out at the darkness as though there were something to see.

"Is that a barn out there?" she asked after a moment. "Why is it so big?"

"It's the shed my daddy used for growing marijuana."

Her face jerked to mine, her expression startled. "Really?"

"He had a hydroponic setup. When I came back here after his death, nobody had been able to get past all the locks he had on the door. By the time I made it inside, his crop was so tall, it was trying to lift the roof off."

"Do you still grow it?"

"I already told you I didn't." The idea of treading the same path as the man I'd hated was unthinkable, and my tone was firm. "I converted the barn to grow mushrooms instead."

"Mushrooms?" She frowned as she said the word, making it sound like that was no better.

I stared at her for a moment, puzzled by her reaction. Then I realized what she must have thought and a pang of resentment shot through me. No matter what I did, folks always assumed the worst.

"Not those kinds of mushrooms." My tone was flat. "Legal ones."

"Sure." She sounded doubtful.

"You want to take a look?"

"No. That's okay."

She suddenly seemed distant. Maybe she didn't believe me. Or maybe growing mushrooms wasn't something she approved of. Perhaps mushrooms were like flannel shirts, not hip enough for her New York sensibilities. For all I knew, she might even dislike the music that was playing. Some big-city people might really be that strange.

Turning away from the window, she walked back into the living room. "I should go," she said. Only instead of going to the door, she sat back on the couch. "But first I have to listen to this song. As much as I hate to admit it, this singer is incredible. For bluegrass, this is really good."

Her admission about the music made me feel a little better. At least she didn't hate everything I liked.

"Careful, Brooklyn," I warned. "You might turn into a Southern belle if you don't watch out."

She screwed up her nose. "You haven't heard my opinion about cowboy boots yet."

"Maybe you haven't embraced cowboy boots because you haven't discovered how practical they are." I sat opposite her on the other couch, stretching my sneaker-clad feet in front of me. Just because I wasn't currently wearing a pair of boots didn't mean they weren't a good choice of footwear. Now that I'd converted her to bluegrass, she'd eventually come to see the value in the rest. Assuming she stuck around for long enough.

But her gaze had gone to the stack of boxes in the corner. "What's all that?" she asked.

I had to resist the urge to grimace at her question. The full answer could all too easily bring up things that were too raw and personal to talk about, so I kept my tone light and my answer succinct.

"Those boxes contain all my personal belongings."

She looked confused. "What do you mean?"

"Well, this is my daddy's house. After he died, I moved here to sell the place. I thought I'd only be here for a few weeks, but I decided to stay longer, so I called a company and arranged for the contents of my apartment to be packed up and shipped here. The movers carried everything in and put it there. I haven't gotten around to unpacking yet."

"How long have you been living here?"

I hesitated, considering whether to lie. The truth was disturbing. It didn't feel like fourteen months. While I was living it, time had dragged. But some-how, all those months had disappeared.

"A year," I said, rounding down.

"A *year*? And you still haven't gotten around to unpacking the boxes?"

I shrugged, uncomfortable. "Tell me about the person who's threatening you."

She tilted her head. "Are you changing the subject?"

"Yes."

My honest admission made her lips quirk up on one side in that cute, crooked smile.

"His name is Spike," she said. "He's a drug dealer. Eric owes him money, and Spike has decided I should be the one to pay his bill."

Eric was her boyfriend's name, and apparently he was someone who owed money to drug dealers. Hopefully, he was actually her ex-boyfriend, seeing as she hadn't made their current status entirely clear. The one thing that was crystal clear was that he didn't deserve her.

"Why can't your boyfriend pay him?" I asked, using the word deliberately to see if she'd clarify their status.

"Eric's on tour in Japan. He's far enough away that he feels safe. I'm a lot closer, and easier for Spike to torment."

I gave her a look that I hoped transmitted the extent of my stunned disbelief. "That's not fair."

"Yeah, and that's exactly what I told Spike. Funny, though, the scary drug dealer seemed not to care. It was almost as though he had no morals." She widened her eyes. "Weird, right?"

"Does this Spike guy know where you are?" Her description of him as a scary drug dealer was worrying.

"He knows I'm in Green Valley. He said he'd come here to find me, but I think he was just trying to scare me so I'd pay up faster."

I shook my head, my disbelief mounting. "And your boyfriend let him threaten you?" Her shrug told me what kind of man he must be. "Well, you'll stay here from now on," I told her. "There's a spare room. I'll get it set up for you."

"Thank you, but no. I'll be fine."

"I can't let you go home if you're going to be in danger."

"You can't *let* me go home?" She frowned. "What does that mean?"

"Just that you should stay."

"No thanks." It was clear by her tone she didn't like that I was pushing the issue. I considered backing down, but what if something happened and I could have prevented it?

"I'd feel a lot better knowing you weren't alone. The room just needs clearing out is all. Won't take long."

She got out of her seat, her mouth set into a stubborn line. "I promised my sister I'd look after her cat and chickens, and that's what I'm going to do." Then she picked up the satchel she'd left on the couch when she'd arrived. "It's getting late. Thank you for dinner."

Zeppelin jumped up as well, and the two of them headed for the door.

So much for trying to keep her safe. I should have known she'd react that way. Her obstinate side had been obvious the moment I'd met her. And though it should have been annoying, I had to respect her for it. I wouldn't want someone I hardly knew telling me what to do either.

I got up and followed her down the hallway. And though I was certain I was wasting my breath, I had to give it another try. "You shouldn't go home if there's a chance the drug dealer is going to come looking for you."

"Listen, I appreciate your concern, and that you invited me for dinner. It was nice of you, but I'm going to be fine. There's no need to worry."

As she opened the door, she stepped even closer to me in the narrow hallway. Her head only came up to my shoulder, and next to my bulk, she seemed slight. Maybe she had a large amount of determination and courage, but it seemed like it was wrapped in a fragile package. No matter what she said, I couldn't help wanting to keep her safe.

I had a sudden urge to put my arms around her and tell her not to leave. To kiss her until she agreed to stay. As we walked out together, her shoulder bumped against my arm, stirring up this urge to the point I had to put my hands in my pockets to keep them under control.

She had a long, determined stride, and when we reached the driveway, stones crunched crisply under her feet. Everything about her had attitude, even the way she walked. I couldn't help but imagine what it might be like to sleep with her. She'd probably want to call the shots in bed. I could picture her giving orders, making sure everything was exactly how she liked it. Kicking up a fuss if she didn't get her way.

Mmm. That was an enticing thought. Tussling with her in bed was an experience I'd very much like to have.

CHAPTER 12

MAGDALENA

*a*s Cy walked me to my car, the only light to illuminate where we were going shone dimly from his porch, so I had to peer at the uneven ground to be sure of my footing.

Zeppelin raced on ahead, and Cy walked beside me. My thoughts were in a whirl. When Cy had offered his spare room for me to stay in, I'd had a sudden, unwanted vision of the two of us in bed together. The image had seared through my mind, my body responding with a surge of heat in my lower belly that had radiated between my thighs. It had flustered me so much, I'd had to run for the door.

I'd been warned about him by more than one person. Was that why I was so attracted to him? It was a flaw in my personality. The worse a man would be for me, the stronger my attraction.

I cast a furtive glance up to Cy as he walked next to me. He seemed to feel my glance, because he looked down and met my gaze. His lips quirked up, and I had to admit, he didn't *seem* bad. So far, he'd been sweet and thoughtful. And I could only admire his calm, capable manner.

But what about the mushrooms? He said he wasn't growing the illegal kind, but I wasn't born yesterday. In the moonlight I'd spotted the enormous padlocks that secured the barn door. Why would he need to keep regular mushrooms so secure?

Besides, weren't mushrooms grown on enormous farms at scale then shipped all over the country? Surely Cy couldn't make money by growing a few in his barn? Not unless they were a front to disguise something illegal.

Zeppelin raced back to us, then snuffled around the ground while I fished in my bag for my car keys. Cy leaned back against the car, his hands in the pockets of his jeans and his face lifted to the sky. The porch light picked out the jut of his cheekbones above his beard.

All the nighttime noises that had freaked me out so much when I'd arrived were loud. Chirps, croaks, and the occasional screech or other weird call. But if Cy wasn't bothered by the noises, all the things making the sounds were probably harmless.

"Nice night," Cy said. "Venus is bright tonight. And there's Cassiopeia."

Drawing out my keys, I glanced up. The number of stars was breathtaking. "Which one is Venus?"

"That one." He pointed it out and I blinked in surprise at how big and bright it was.

"And the other star you mentioned?" I asked.

"Cassiopeia is a constellation. Turn away from the light and you'll be able to see five stars that zigzag across the sky." Putting his hands on my shoulders, he turned me so my back was to him, then pointed up so I could follow the line of his finger. "See them?"

"Yes," I said, though I had no idea if I was looking at the right ones. My heart sped up at the warmth and solidity of him at my back. One of his big, capable hands still rested on my shoulder, and I could smell his outdoorsy scent, with hints of pine and flowers. It was almost as though he'd grown from the earth, like one of the trees that surrounded his house.

"If you draw a line between the stars, does the pattern look like a queen on her throne?" His voice was low and close to my ear. The vibration of his chest sent pleasant shivers down my spine.

I squinted at the sky. "Not unless she's queen of the snakes."

His low chuckle made me clench my thighs. I'd thought the sound of his rumbly murmur was hot, but his chuckle seemed directly wired into my pleasure center.

"She was placed in the sky by Poseidon as a punishment for being vain," he said. "Now she's up there forever, combing her hair."

I clicked my tongue. "See what happens when a man gets too much power and lets it go to his head? Just goes to show how much better it would be if women ran the world. For starters, they'd let other women finish their personal grooming in peace."

He chuckled again, and the pleasant sensation it sparked in me was so overwhelming, I had to turn to face him. Standing this close, I was acutely aware of his size. His shoulders were almost twice the width of mine, and the top of my head barely reached his chin. And his biceps were so big, I'd have to use both hands if I wanted to circle them.

What was it about big men that was so appealing? Did it come from ancient caveman days when women needed to feel protected? If so, I couldn't be very highly evolved, because I found his size incredibly sexy.

"How do you know so much about the stars?" I asked.

His hand was on my shoulder and we stood close, our bodies almost touching, my face lifted to his. His gaze went from my eyes to my lips, and I stared at his bottom lip, imagining what it might feel like if I kissed him. His lower lip was enticing, but his upper lip was barely visible. Would it be scratchy?

He lowered his face, and my heart stopped.

Was he going to kiss me?

No, his lips weren't dropping to my mouth. They moved closer to my ear instead.

"I have an app on my phone," he whispered.

As he drew back to see my reaction, his lips twitched into a smirk.

"An app," I repeated with a laugh, though my pulse was jumping. "I thought you were going to tell me that all country bumpkins can navigate by the stars."

"I've never had to steer a ship, but I'm confident that I could."

He moved his hand from my shoulder to stroke my upper arm. Even though he was stroking over my T-shirt, not touching my skin, his touch sent pleasurable shivers through me.

"You're confident, huh?" His touch was so nice, I was losing track of what we were talking about. All I could think about was how close he was and how good he smelled.

"Very confident. Almost certain." His tone was soft and careless, as though he was paying as little attention as I was to the conversation.

His gaze caressed my lips.

He was definitely thinking about kissing me. Only he was taking his own sweet time about doing it. And I couldn't stand the anticipation.

"Are you going to kiss me?" I asked.

"Would you object?"

I swallowed. An aching feeling of want was spreading through my body, and I couldn't stop imagining how his lips might feel against mine.

Should I give in to my own bad judgement? Kiss a man I shouldn't, just because he happened to be unexpectedly sexy?

"I've never kissed someone with enough facial hair to have its own zip code," I murmured.

With a quirk of his lips, he ran his hand over his beard, taming its wildness for a moment before it sprang back into full chaos. "It's long now, I'll admit. I've gotten out of the habit of shaving, and I haven't trimmed it in a while."

"Do you have a chin under there? Your face doesn't end at your bottom lip?"

"Last I remember seeing it, I had a chin." His tone was as light as mine, but his gaze was serious. "Are you saying you don't want to kiss me because of my beard?"

"Your beard isn't the only thing standing in our way. There's also your ill-informed love of country and western music."

His laugh was a slow, warm rumble I could feel down to the soles of my feet. "Give it a chance, and you might just develop a liking for it."

"For beards or for bluegrass?"

"Oh, you're already a fan of bluegrass," he said, still smiling. "I converted you. And beards will be next. You know what they say. Once you go beard, you don't go back."

I let out a laugh that accidentally came out as a snort. "That's not what they say."

"It's what they *should* say." Lifting his hand to my hair, he took a few strands between his thumb and forefinger and gave them a gentle tug. His smile softened. "What's going on in that lovely head of yours? Are you thinking up more reasons not to kiss me?"

"How would I even find your lips in all that facial hair?" I sighed, because there were plenty of *excellent* reasons not to kiss him, and all I could think about was how much I wanted to do it anyway.

"It'll be fun," he said. "A treasure hunt."

"Your lips are treasure?"

"Of the best kind."

"Is there a prize if I find them?"

His smile grew. "One you'll like."

He lowered his face slowly, and he must have been able to read my eagerness because his lips quirked up again before his mouth found mine.

The contact sent a jolt of electricity coursing through my body. His beard was softer than it looked, while his kiss was firmer than I'd expected. He tasted of the red wine he'd had with dinner, and when he nipped my lip it felt so good that I let out a soft sound of surprise.

One of his hands went behind my head, caressing the nape of my neck and gathering strands of hair. The other hand splayed against the small of my back, holding me against him.

His beard brushed against my cheeks, but at first I barely registered it. My entire being was focused on other sensations, namely the warm caress of his tongue and the delicious tug of his big hand in my hair. Then I felt the hard jut of his erection pressing against my stomach, and an answering ache throbbed between my legs.

As Cy moved his head, his beard rasped against my face. The sudden roughness only intensified the hotness of the kiss. His lips were like velvet, but they were commanding. His bossy tongue controlled the kiss. Controlled me.

And I loved it.

A moment later, I realized I'd brought both hands up to tangle them in his beard so I could drag his face down harder against mine. He felt so masculine. Every part of him was big, strong, and hard. He was as solid as an oak tree, and he kissed like he ruled the world. No wonder I was so turned on.

When he pulled away, I was panting. I wanted more.

But he opened his eyes and smiled softly down at me, as though waiting for me to say something.

"That was . . ." I blew out my breath. "Unexpectedly amazing."

"Unexpectedly?"

I nodded. "You're the last person in the world I expected to kiss."

"The last person in the entire world." He gave another of his rumbly laughs, one of his hands still pleasantly heavy on the back of my neck, the other resting on my hip. "Bottom of your list. Scraping the barrel, huh?"

I tightened my fingers in his shirt. "Well, did you expect to be kissing me?"

He lifted a shoulder in a half shrug that was irritatingly nonchalant. "At least if I keep your mouth busy, you can't insult me."

"That was your plan?" I wrinkled my nose at him. "Then I guess it's perfect. I don't want romance, and it sounds like you don't either."

His hand went to my face, cupping it, his thumb brushing softly against my cheek. "Don't pull any punches, Brooklyn. Tell me how it's going to be." His tone was full of quiet humor.

"I like to be direct."

"I've noticed." He pulled me closer, the rumble of his voice going even lower. "So you don't want to kiss me again?"

"I wouldn't exactly say that. Not in those precise words." For some reason, it came out sounding breathless. I stared at his top lip, barely peeking out from that terrible beard. I shouldn't want to kiss him. But the needy thrum was throbbing relentlessly through my body and the low ache between my thighs demanded to be satisfied.

Fisting his shirt, I tugged him against me, reaching my face up to his.

This time, I sunk both hands into his beard, tangling my fingers in it. It felt wiry in my palms. Impossibly long. I used it to bring his face closer, to kiss him harder. I wanted his tongue, his mouth. His wonderfully big body. That giant, insistent erection I could feel, taunting me by pressing too high against my body instead of where I wanted it to be.

His big hands pressed into my back, tugging me into him. I tried to pull myself higher against him, wanting to climb him. I wanted him to lift me so I could wrap my legs around him. I needed friction.

When he let me go, I made an involuntary whimpering sound. The sound was embarrassingly needy. Hearing it allowed some of my good sense to come flooding back, and suddenly I wondered what the hell I was doing.

Kissing Cy hadn't been part of my plan.

All I wanted was to resolve my Spike problem and go home. Then I planned on being single for a very long time. If I ever wanted to date again, I'd go looking for a nice, safe banker or stockbroker. The exact opposite of a bad boy. I'd find someone clean-cut and well groomed, who wore three-piece suits all the time, even to bed. His name would be something like Alexander or Charles. Maybe Benedict. And he wouldn't be growing highly suspicious mushrooms in a padlocked barn.

Behind us, the porch light went on. Drawing back, Cy took his hand from my neck. I immediately missed its weight and the soft brush of his fingers against my sensitive skin.

He glanced at the house and frowned. Maybe Gemma was watching us from the window, and he didn't want her to know we'd been kissing.

My phone buzzed with a notification. Tugging it out of my bag, I saw a message from Eric. No, not a message. A picture. It was a photo of the crowd watching him play. There was a sea of people. He clearly expected it to impress me.

Great timing, Eric.

Cy's frown deepened as he stared down at the photo. "Is that from your boyfriend? Tell me you're not still dating that musician you talked about."

"Technically speaking, Eric and I are still together." I winced, tucking my phone away.

"I don't kiss women who have boyfriends."

"That's a good thing." I blew out a breath as I nodded. My head was still spinning and my knees were weak. Not to mention the serious situation happening in my panties, with aching parts of me begging for relief. "This picture is the perfect reminder of why I'd planned to stay away from men for a very long time. And I should go before your niece sees you kissing someone you hardly know." I rummaged in my bag. "Where are my car keys?"

"You pulled them out of your bag earlier, before we kissed. Then I heard you drop them."

"I did?" He must have scrambled my brain, as I had no memory of it at all.

He bent and scooped them off the ground, then handed them to me. "How much money does the drug dealer think you owe him?"

"Um." I sucked in another deep breath, still pulling my fractured thoughts together. "Ten thousand dollars."

"Hmm." If he was surprised at the amount, I couldn't tell. He stuck his hands in his pockets, his shoulders hitching up.

"And I already gave Spike all my savings," I admitted. "Ten thousand is just the amount Eric still owes." I shook my head. "You would not *believe* the cost of illegal drugs these days. It's criminal!" Then I gave a strained-sounding laugh. "Well, I don't have to tell *you* that, right?"

His eyebrows drew together. Now his frown looked both worried and puzzled. "What do you mean?"

"Never mind. It doesn't matter." I ran shaky fingers over my lips. They felt well-kissed, and I could still taste him. "I'll figure it out. If I can give Spike the money, all this goes away, and Eric can pay me back when he gets back from his tour."

"The drug dealer won't back off?" he asked.

"He's given no sign of wanting to."

"Then come back to my place tomorrow night with a suitcase. Stay with me while you're here, and if this Spike guy turns up, I'll have words with him."

He said it in a low, growly tone, and I wondered if by "words" he meant "fists". The thought he might be willing to stand up for me was strangely comforting, even if I'd never let him do it.

"Uh-uh." I shook my head. "Thanks anyway, but I'm not going to hide out at your place. I'm going back to Carla's."

He gave a frustrated grunt. "At least come back for dinner tomorrow night. I don't want to be sitting up here doing nothing, while you're down the road eating frozen pizza and waiting for a dangerous man to find you."

I sighed. How could I argue?

"I guess it would be rude to turn down another home-cooked meal," I said, conflicted. "And you're not going to kiss me again, right?"

"Not if you have a boyfriend."

"Forget about him. The important thing is, I shouldn't want to kiss you."

"Then it won't happen." He held up both hands to highlight the fact he was no longer touching me. "I won't press you."

"How gentlemanly."

"This is the South, sweetheart. You can expect me to be a gentleman." His gaze dropped to my lips and his voice deepened. "Unless you want me to act otherwise."

A fresh rush of arousal coursed through me, and it was so strong I could barely stop myself from moving back into him. But that would be reckless. This couldn't turn into anything, so there was no sense in driving us both crazy with wanting it.

"I'll keep that in mind," I said, opening my car door so Zeppelin could jump in. "Thanks for tonight. Dinner was nice."

"You're welcome, Mags."

"Hey, you finally got my name right, Cy. And it's twice as long as yours!"

He let out a rueful chuckle, and I shot him a teasing smile as I shut the car door.

As I drove away, he stood and watched me go. I kept my eyes on his dark silhouette, my heart jumping. I could still taste him on my lips. I could smell his scent, and imagine his big hands were still caressing my body, his tongue still claiming mine.

And I knew for a fact I was going to imagine it again *so hard* when I got home. The way I was feeling, I might even imagine it twice.

CY

The next morning, while I was showering and getting dressed, I kept thinking about kissing Mags. It had been a memorable evening. More than memorable. Last night, I'd barely made it into the shower before taking myself in hand. It took only a few swift strokes before I'd come hard, with the feel of her still on my lips and the press of her lush body vivid in my mind.

I'd wanted to kiss her a whole lot more. But seeing as she had other ideas, I'd just have to enjoy the memory.

Thinking about the evening made me smile to myself. And the smile lingered, even after I remembered I needed to put together some kind of lunch for Gemma. Monday would be her first official day of school, but today she'd get to look around, and hopefully make a friend or two. And she'd need to eat.

"You want chicken, cheese, and pickle sandwiches?" I asked her when I went into the kitchen.

She was sitting at the small dining table, a bowl of cereal in front of her. Staring down at her bowl, she screwed up her nose. "I don't want to go to school." Her tone was flat, but at least she didn't sound angry. She seemed resigned.

"You'll have sandwiches to look forward to at lunch break," I said, pulling the ingredients from the fridge.

"I heard you yell in your sleep again last night," Gemma told me.

"Did you? I can't remember waking up." Dammit, I was getting sick of having the same nightmare all the time. I would far rather have dreamed of Mags. Of good things, rather than bad ones. "Hope the shout didn't scare you," I added, turning to get a plate from the cupboard.

"I wasn't scared. But it sounded like you were." When I turned back to her, she was giving me a questioning gaze with her spoon resting on top of her cereal. "What exactly do you dream about?"

An image flashed into my mind of the nameless thing I'd probably spent last night running from, though I couldn't remember having the nightmare. At least my waking mind knew I wasn't a boy anymore, and that the creatures I dreamed of were really my father and his friends, twisted by my sleeping mind to look like monsters rather than men. My subconscious mind seemed to always return to the past. Usually to the time when I hadn't been able to defend my momma.

"I have bad dreams about my childhood," I said, spreading mayo onto slices of bread. "You know that. I already told you."

"Does my mother have the same nightmare?" She poked at the remains of her cereal.

"I guess she might."

Dropping her spoon, Gemma pushed her bowl away. "But Momma's always spent a lot of time in bed. Why would she do that if she has bad dreams?"

"I used to spend a lot of time in bed too, and it was because all the emotions I was feeling sucked the energy out of me. Your momma's probably the same."

Thinking back, it felt like I used to spend all my days and nights in bed, either dozing or just lying still, staring at nothing. My thoughts were a black maze with no beginning or end. My mind would tread the same worn paths over and over. And though I recognized it was happening, I couldn't stop it.

"Now your momma's getting some help, she might have more energy," I added.

"I hope so."

"And you'll need energy for school today. You'd better finish your cereal."

She stared gloomily down at the mostly full bowl she'd rejected. "I'm not hungry."

I thought about trying to convince her to eat a little more, and decided not to cause any friction.

"I'll get you a treat from the bakery today," I said. "It'll be here waiting for you when you get home."

Gemma's expression lightened. "You just want to go and see Mags at the bakery."

"I've put extra pickle on your sandwiches," I said, cutting them diagonally. "Lunchtime will be a highlight of your day."

"Mags is so cool." Gemma sighed. "Can you believe she knows all those famous musicians?"

"She seems to like the same music as you."

"Do you like her?" Gemma asked.

"Who, Mags?" I frowned down at the sandwiches, trying to act as though I barely remembered her and hadn't been thinking about her all morning. "She seems nice. Don't you like her?"

"Of course I do." Gemma grinned like we were sharing a secret. And it was so good to see her mood brighten that I beamed back at her.

"Are you almost ready to go to school?" I asked. "You know which bus to catch?"

"You can't drop me off?"

I shook my head, shooting her an apologetic look. "Like I told you, folks around here don't hold much respect for the Baxter name. I don't want them to see us together and start jumping to conclusions about you before they've had a chance to get to know you."

"Okay. I understand." She hesitated. "Can I ask you something, Uncle Cy?" By the way she started picking at the sleeve of the white shirt she was wearing, I could tell whatever she wanted to ask me was weighing on her.

"Of course." Putting down the knife, I flattened my palms on the counter and gave her my full attention.

"If Momma has a mental health disorder, and you have nightmares that make you shout at night, does that mean I'm going to get sick too?"

My stomach turned over, my mood plummeting. "No, Gem, it doesn't mean that." I gentled my voice. "The way your momma and me grew up had a lot to do with it. You didn't have a childhood like that."

"My father used to yell at Momma before we moved away from him. I remember hearing it."

I crossed to the table and sat in the chair across from her. "Do you want to talk about what you remember?"

"No." She studied her fingers, busy fiddling with the button on her shirt cuff. "I don't remember it well. But you said you were depressed before I arrived, and Momma's depressed. Is it something that's in my blood?"

"I don't think so. But if you're worried and want to talk to someone, you could see my therapist."

Her gaze jerked up. "You have a therapist?"

"Sure. I've been seeing her every week for the last month."

"Every week," she repeated, frowning. "You've been since I arrived?"

"I have an appointment every Tuesday at eleven. You didn't know?" I couldn't remember whether I'd mentioned it.

She dropped her gaze back to her sleeve. "Maybe I've been shut in my room a lot. But I hate being away from my friends. It's not fair that I have to spend so much time away from them. They're going to forget I exist."

"They'll be happy to see you when you get back," I said. "And in the meantime, you might make some friends here, too."

"I don't want friends here," she mumbled. "I don't want to be here at all."

"Well, I like having you here. And you know you can talk to me about anything, Gem, don't you? But if you don't want to talk to me, you can go and see my therapist. Or a different one. Whatever you like."

She lifted her gaze back to mine. "What if I don't want to go to school?"

"I know going to a new school must be scary, but give it a try. You'll meet people and make friends. Things will get better."

"All I want is to go home."

"Once your momma feels well enough, you can both go home." I stood and picked up her cereal bowl. "Come on, Gem. Give the new school a chance. Go with an open mind. Today will be an easy day, and you won't have to do any schoolwork until Monday."

She let out a loud huff of breath. "All right," she said in a reluctant tone.

"And when you get back, I'll have done some more to clean the house up and make it nicer, so you won't feel embarrassed in case you want to invite friends home."

She shot me a sideways look. "Or maybe you want to make it nicer in case Mags comes over again?" The suggestive way she said it made me wonder if she'd seen us kissing.

"Mags is coming for dinner again tonight," I said. "But it's not romantic. She's just a friend. And you liked talking to her, didn't you?"

"You liked talking to her too. It might be romantic."

"Mags already has a boyfriend," I reminded her.

"Yeah, an amazing boyfriend." Gemma sounded wistful. "Eric Storm is so hot."

"Are you ready to go to school? You don't want to miss the bus."

After walking Gemma to the bus stop and getting back home, the first thing I did was google Eric Storm. One look and my heart plummeted. In the first photo that came up, he was on stage, playing in front of an enthusiastic-looking crowd. He wore tight leather pants and a matching jacket, with nothing underneath. His washboard abs were on show as he strummed his low-slung guitar. He was clean-shaven, but not clean-cut. With his chiseled face and designer tattoos, he looked every inch a rock star.

CHAPTER 14

MAGDALENA

During my lunch hour on Friday, I went to see the bank manager to try and get Spike's money.

The local bank manager was a thin, balding man who looked as though he'd been born wearing a suit. When he shook my hand in a cold and unsmiling greeting, my palms were sweaty with nerves. The walls, floor, and desk in his office were drab shades of brown, and his beige suit blended into the surroundings in the most unfortunate way. His desk held nothing but a computer and some stacks of paper. He had no pictures, plants, or decorations. Not even a window.

Worst of all, there was no trace of humor in the man's face. No indication that he'd ever smiled, or even made a joke, let alone a mistake. And he definitely didn't look like the kind of guy who'd understand how I could have fallen for a charismatic rock star and then been left to clean up his mess.

It was hard to believe he'd give me a loan. But I had to try.

He motioned me to take a seat in his hard, unwelcoming visitor's chair. "How may I help you, Miss Solis?"

As I sat, I surreptitiously wiped my palms on the formal black pants I'd worn in order to make a good impression. "Did you get the loan application I emailed?"

"Ah. Yes." Instead of turning to his monitor, he took a printout of the form from a stack of paper and frowned down at it. "You're applying for a personal loan, but it says you've only been in your current employment for a week." His drawn-together brows showed both puzzlement and disapproval. "Is that correct?"

I shifted uncomfortably in the chair as nervous sweat trickled down my back. Being here felt disturbingly like visiting my mom and listening to her sigh over my lifestyle choices, or ask if I didn't think I could get a better-paying job.

"Well, yes," I admitted. "I've only just started at the bakery. But it's a steady job, and I'm staying at my sister's place so my outgoings are low. I can afford the loan repayments."

"How much collateral can you offer the bank?"

I swallowed. A few weeks ago, I'd had a little over fifteen thousand dollars in rainy-day savings. But it wasn't as though I could explain how I'd been scared enough to empty my account and give it all to a drug dealer.

"No collateral." Fresh sweat trickled down my back.

This was excruciating. Any minute he was going to shake his head sadly at me like Mom always did before reminding me how hard she and Dad had worked to give us girls a good education. I could almost imagine him asking why couldn't I find a *nice* boy instead of a tattooed guitarist, and when was I going to settle down?

". . . reason for wanting the loan?" he asked.

Damn. I'd been so busy beating myself up, I'd missed the start of his question. Wiping my palms on my pants again, I said, "The loan's to pay off a debt. But it's not my debt. It's someone else's."

"Someone *else's* debt?" His incredulous tone made my heart sink to new depths. He made it sound as though paying someone else's debt was the most irresponsible thing in the world.

And maybe he was right.

To most people, I'd seem irresponsible. I didn't have any money left in the bank, I still wasn't sure what kind of career I wanted, I'd done some pretty stupid things when I was a teenager, and I'd always dated guys who were bad for me. But that didn't mean I had to keep sweating into his uncomfortable chair, letting him make me feel like a loser.

"Tell me the truth." I lifted my chin, leveling my gaze at his eyes. "What chance do I have of being approved for this loan?"

He studied me for a moment before giving the sad shake of his head I'd been expecting. "I'm afraid the bank's policy is that low-collateral loans can't be offered—"

"Thank you for your time." I stood up, cutting him off. "I'll show myself out."

He didn't look surprised as I marched out. He certainly didn't try to stop me. And when the door shut behind me, it sounded like a nail was being driven into the coffin of my last chance to pay Spike off myself.

Now I really would be dependent on Eric to come to my rescue and pay what he owed. And if I'd learned anything over the last few weeks, it was that I couldn't count on Eric.

Driving away, I felt like bursting into tears. Eric wouldn't come through for me. Spike's threats would accelerate. I'd have to ask Josephina to stay out of town. And what about my parents? Would Spike threaten them next? Would I be forced to tell my mother I was in trouble? She already thought I was messing up my life. The last thing I wanted was to confirm it.

When I got back to the bakery, there were plenty of people sitting at the tables outside, but Wren was the only customer at the counter. She was talking to Amber, and they were smiling at each other as Amber bagged up her cookie order. Wren came in every day. A fact that was no surprise seeing how wistfully she looked at Amber, as though Wren thought she was sweeter than anything in the bakery's cabinet.

Those two were clearly perfect for each other. Wren was training to be a firefighter and loved cookies. Amber worked in a bakery and liked making her own candles. No wonder there were sparks between them. They had a lot in common. Unlike Cy and me.

"How did it go at the bank?" Amber asked me once Wren had gone.

"Not great," I admitted, tying on my apron. All I'd told her was that I was going to talk to the bank manager about my finances. Thankfully, she hadn't pushed me for any more details.

"I'm sorry, Mags." Her expression was sympathetic. "Is there anything I can do to help?"

"Thanks, but I'll figure something out." I searched for a change of subject. "Hey, has Wren asked you out yet?"

"Not yet." She made a sad face, pulling her mouth down.

"Why don't you just ask her?"

"I don't know. I don't want to scare her."

I snorted. "You couldn't scare Wren off if you dressed up as a ghost and said you were her boo."

Amber's forehead wrinkled. "Excuse me?"

"It's obvious she likes you! If you ask Wren on a date, she'll say yes. I'm sure of it."

She fiddled with the edge of her apron, running it through her fingers. "Wren's working tonight, but she mentioned she's going to next Friday's jam session at the community center. Maybe I should go too. But instead of making a big thing of it, I could just say I'll see her there."

"That's a good start."

She bit her lip. "Would you go with me, Mags?" Her expression was so nervous, I wanted to hug her.

"Of course I will!" Grinning, I bumped her shoulder. "I'd love a night out, and I can be your wingwoman. We'll have fun."

"Great. Thanks." She slumped against the counter with obvious relief.

"No need to thank me. I love getting dressed up and listening to live music. Even bluegrass."

"We don't need to get dressed up."

"But we should! Let's meet at my place to get ready. I have this vivid blue dress that would look amazing on you, and when Wren sees you, she won't know what hit her."

Her eyes lit up. "You'd lend me your dress?'

"Of course!" I rubbed my hands together, excited by the idea. "Should we ask Joy to come too? Now I'm thinking about it, both your love lives haven't been nearly exciting enough. It's about time for some action."

Amber wagged her eyebrows at me. "What about some action for you?"

The question was barely out of her mouth when Cy walked into the bakery.

As soon as his winter-blue eyes landed on me, tingles started in my stomach. And I had to admit, it was a nice feeling. I liked the way his smile creased his eyes. I didn't even mind the wildness of his beard anymore, except that it stopped me from seeing all of his face. Did he have dimples? I badly wanted to know. Combined with his high cheekbones, his long nose, and the hypnotic swoop of his dark eyelashes over his light eyes, a flash of dimples would knock me all the way out.

"Hey, Mags," he said in his low voice.

"Hey yourself." I found myself smiling back at him. "Where's Zeppelin?"

"Waiting in the car." He stuck his hands in the front pockets of his jeans, lifting both shoulders and nodding toward the cabinet. "I've come to get some cake so I can have it waiting for Gemma when she gets home from her first day at school."

"That's a nice thought. Chocolate?"

He nodded. "Chocolate's her favorite."

As I pulled the cake out of the cabinet and bagged it for him, I said, "She'll be okay, you know. First days are hard. But I'm sure she'll settle in quickly."

"I hope so." He leaned his hip against the counter, and I couldn't help but admire the way his wide chest filled out his T-shirt. The simplicity of the shirt put the focus onto his burly size by highlighting his muscles.

"We're having pot roast for dinner tonight. Gemma will be disappointed if you're not there to eat with us." His eyes heated as they roamed over my face. "And so will I."

Our kiss, in all of its full glory, replayed in my memory. My knees weakened, and my mouth went so dry, I had to swallow to be able to speak. "I like pot roast," I managed to croak.

"Good. I'll see you tonight." He gave me one last smile, held up the bag of cake with a nod of thanks, then left.

When I turned, Amber was gaping at me.

"What?" I asked.

She shook her head, her eyes wide. "Nothing. I'm a little surprised is all. You and Cy Baxter?"

I shrugged, trying to play it down. As much as I liked her and wanted to confide in her, she'd been one of the many who'd warned me against Cy. And after seeing the giant padlocks on his so-called mushroom-growing barn, I couldn't say she'd been wrong. Besides, it wasn't like I was actually dating Cy. Our kiss wouldn't be repeated.

"It's not like that," I said. "I'm just having dinner at his house. He lives near my place, and he's a good cook."

"Well, it was neighborly of him to invite you." Amber was a genuinely nice person, and she said it in a sincere way. But I could still hear a little reservation in her tone.

"Yeah, it was nice of him. Considering he's supposed to be a drug dealer and a suspected murderer." I grimaced. "That's probably why I'm attracted to him. Bad boys are magnets, and I'm like a little scrap of iron. They're magnets that have fallen into that dirty place behind the fridge where all the crap builds up, and even though I can feel them pulling me into the dirt, I can never seem to resist."

"So you admit you're attracted to him?"

"I know, it's unimaginable." I sighed. "I mean, he has so much facial hair, he looks like he escaped from Middle Earth. But he's been so nice to me. I mean, really kind and sweet. And then there are his eyes. Have you ever seen eyes so light, with such long, dark eyelashes?"

"He has striking eyes, that's for sure."

"And once you look past the beard, he has incredible cheekbones and a classical nose. Contagious smile. Amazing body. Plus, there's that rumbly voice. His voice does things to me it shouldn't."

"He's a good-looking man, there's no denying it." She scrunched her eyes doubtfully. "But there are all those rumors about him."

"I know," I said with a wince. "And at least some of the rumors must be true, because if I'm attracted to him, he's sure to be bad. It's a fault with the way I'm made. The worse they are, the more I like them. If a serial killer walked in, I'd probably find him irresistible."

"What does Cy do for money?"

I gave another shrug, fighting against the urge to tell her about his suspicious barn. "All I know for sure is that he has this quiet confidence I really like. He's good at cooking, and he's fun to talk to. He keeps showing up to care of me. But on the flip side, he lives in a rundown house, drives a pickup that belongs in a scrap heap, and looks like a . . ." I trailed off, not wanting to say the wrong thing.

"Like a hillbilly?" Amber shot me a questioning look.

I winced. "Is that an awful thing to say?"

She considered it a moment, then gave a solemn nod. "In this case, I'll allow it."

"But I still want to kiss him!" I blurted the truth, then groaned. "What's wrong with me, Amber? And how can I fix it?"

CHAPTER 15

CY

"Another delicious dinner," Mags said, as she finished the last mouthful of pot roast. "You're an excellent cook."

I put my knife and fork together on my own empty plate, pleased by her compliment. "Would you like some more?"

"Thanks, but I couldn't squeeze in another mouthful." She leaned back in the dining chair, one hand on her stomach.

"Gemma?" I asked.

"I'm full too. It was nice, Uncle Cy."

My niece seemed happy again tonight. Maybe the talk we'd had this morning had helped, or perhaps she was cheerful because her first day at school had gone well. Most likely it was both those things, plus the fact that Mags was here, the three of us enjoying another dinner together, and those two got along like they'd been separated at birth. Whatever the reason, I was just glad to see her smiling.

"Do you have anything else you need to organize for school?" I asked her.

"I have some books to order."

"Do you need help?" I asked. She shook her head, and I added, "Your momma's going to call soon."

Gemma cast a quick sideways look at Mags. "I'll take the call in my bedroom again, okay?"

"Sure."

After Gemma had disappeared to talk to her mother and shut her bedroom door behind her, Mags motioned to the corner of the living room where the stack of boxes used to be. I'd spent a good part of the day emptying them out, but she hadn't remarked on the change until now.

"The house looks bigger," she said.

I nodded. "It's about time I got started on the renovations."

She lowered her voice, pushing her empty plate away. "Do you mind if I ask about your sister?"

"I don't mind. But let's go outside. There's a place to sit out back." I didn't want Gemma to overhear me talk about her mother. "We could take some wine out with us," I suggested. "You could have a small glass and still be fine to drive."

"Thanks, but I'll stick with iced tea."

I got her a fresh glass of tea, then poured myself a glass of Shiraz. As she watched me pour it, she said, "It's funny you drink wine. You seem like you'd be a beer guy."

"I got a taste for red wine while I was in Paris."

She shot me a squinty look. "Paris, Texas?"

I replied by silently lifting my eyebrows.

Laughing, she shook her head. "Just when I think you're done surprising me." Then she headed out the back door, Zeppelin at her heels.

We took a seat on the outdoor chairs I'd had sent from Boston and had finally set out on the back porch. It looked out to the small yard and large barn. The sun had just gone down, and the stars would soon be coming out, though we'd need to turn the porch light off if we wanted to see them.

The night was warm, and the crickets were singing. Magdalena was wearing her hair in a ponytail, so I could admire her long neck. She wore smart black pants and a patterned blouse. Even after a long day in the bakery, she looked like she could be in a magazine.

Rock star or not, her boyfriend definitely didn't deserve her. No matter how famous, rich, or talented he might be, she was too good for him.

"My sister's name is Ruth," I said, watching Zeppelin sniffing around the grass near the barn. "We were real close growing up. She was only sixteen when our momma died. I was seventeen."

I mentioned my momma's death deliberately, knowing all too well what they said in town about my involvement. Mags had most likely heard the rumors about me, but to my surprise, her gaze stayed level.

"It must have been hard on both of you." Her tone was sympathetic.

I paused a moment longer, waiting for her to ask about the rumors. It wasn't a comfortable subject, but if she came out and asked me . . . well, maybe I'd tell her the things I'd only been able to tell my therapist.

Only she didn't. She just sipped her iced tea, her lovely brown eyes on mine.

"Our momma was a good woman," I said. "But our daddy was a mean old bastard, and our eldest brother used to be in and out of prison, until he finally earned himself a life sentence. We had another brother who got himself shot one night, breaking into a farmhouse. He died when I was six."

"Jeepers." She sat back, her composure gone. "I'm sorry."

"So you can see what our family was like. Why the Baxters have such a bad name."

She nodded wordlessly.

"I moved to Boston a few months after our momma died and took Ruth with me. It was rough trying to survive on a small income, but we were both happy to have left this place."

"I bet."

"Ruth fell pregnant not long after we left Green Valley. She married her boyfriend and went to Memphis, where his family were. And I had no idea he was abusive. Not until recently." I tightened my jaw, wishing I'd known better than to let my sister move so far away. "Most of her life, Ruth's been afraid of the men who should have been protecting her. No wonder she's struggling now."

"That's awful." Mags's expression was full of compassion.

I nodded, then sipped my wine, savoring the taste for a moment before I swallowed and continued.

"After splitting with her husband, Ruth raised Gemma in Nashville. I was still in Boston, so I didn't see either of them as often as I should have. Then, about a year and a half ago, our daddy died. Killed in a bar fight at the Dragon, so he died the way he lived. Drunk and violent." Zeppelin nosed up to me, and I petted his head but kept talking.

"Ruth has struggled with depression, but now she's getting some help. That's why Gemma's staying with me. I didn't want her to hear us talking about it because she's sensitive about her mother being in a mental health facility. But I'm proud of Ruth for taking that step." I blew out a breath, glad to have gotten my family history out into the open. "And now you know why people in town cross the street and spit when they hear the Baxter name."

She was frowning. "It's not fair for people to label you because of what your father and brothers used to do."

I shrugged, because of course that wasn't the whole story. But it was more than enough for one night. "Let's talk about something more cheerful."

"Okay." She lifted a leg onto her chair, dropping her knee to the side and tucking her foot under her thigh. It was a loose-limbed position I wouldn't even attempt, but she made it look natural. "What do you want to talk about?" she asked.

She was so limber, all I could think about were sexual positions. The entire Kama Sutra ran through my head. At least, the positions I could remember from my curious browsing through the book many years ago.

Did Mags have any idea how fucking sexy she was?

"Cy?" she asked.

I blinked. "Ah. How was work today?"

"Busy." Zeppelin moved next to her, and she stroked his ears. "And I'm developing a serious banana cake addiction. I'll have to take home a suitcase filled with cake when I leave."

The reminder she'd be leaving soon ripped all Kama Sutra thoughts from my mind.

"What will you do when you go back to New York?" I asked.

She bit her lip, looking uncertain. "I'm not sure. I like fashion. And I've realized that I really like food."

"Find a fashion store that sells food."

She grimaced. "At my age, I should know what I want to do with my life. Carla always knew she wanted to be a software developer. And Eric worked hard for years playing music and writing songs. Now he's a rock star, and I still haven't figured the career thing out."

"Don't be hard on yourself. Plenty of people have no idea what they want to do. And you have lots of time to try different things."

"I like helping people." She let out a laugh, her nose wrinkled. "Ugh, that sounds corny!"

"It sounds nice."

"Well, it's not like I'm performing life-saving surgery. I'm just serving food. But I like talking to customers."

"You brighten their day," I said. "They like you, and you give them good things to eat. That helps them."

She gave me a smile that was half disbelieving, half pleased. "Maybe." Then her smile fell away and she grew serious. "What about your job?"

"Growing mushrooms? This is the first time I've tried it, and I'm still learning. But so far, I like it a lot."

She studied me silently for a moment, then looked over at the barn. "You offered to show me your mushrooms. Does your offer still stand?" There was no trace of humor left in her tone.

"Of course. Wait here a minute while I get the keys to the barn." I went back in to grab them off the table by the door, then shut Zeppelin inside the house to keep him out of trouble, and led her over to the barn. Once there, I unlocked the big padlocks meant to deter any of my daddy's old customers who wanted to take a look inside to see whether any of his illegal crop still remained. Then I slid back the door, flicked on the overhead lights, and we stepped inside.

The hum of the humidity and temperature controller unit suddenly seemed loud. Despite its hard work, a pleasantly musty aroma of damp earth and fungi hung heavily in the air.

I'd partitioned the big barn into separate growing areas by hanging heavy plastic from the ceiling. Then I'd set up racks over my daddy's old marijuana beds and filled them with rows of grow bags, each bag filled with straw and mycelium, the thread-like roots of the mushrooms. In this part of the shed, the bags were filled with golden oyster mushrooms. The mushrooms exploded out of the bags in large, colorful colony structures, like a golden alien forest. They had lighter-colored stems that opened into vivid yellow caps.

"Whoa," whispered Mags, walking down the rows of mushrooms. Then, louder, she asked, "What are they?"

I slid the door shut behind us to keep the temperature and humidity steady. "Golden oyster mushrooms in here." Pulling aside the plastic curtain, I motioned to the area on the other side. "Enoki mushrooms through there."

She glanced to where the long, spindly white enoki mushrooms were growing, then turned back to the more spectacular golden oysters. "Mushrooms for eating?"

"Of course."

"I mean, you can put them in your food?"

She clearly hadn't seen these varieties of mushrooms before. But of course, she didn't cook. And she was probably used to the more common types: button, portobello, and maybe shiitake.

"That's what they're for," I said. "Golden oysters are slightly nutty, while enoki have a little crunch and are sweeter."

"The color is amazing! I had no idea there were mushrooms this bright."

"I've started growing pink oysters as well. But the golden oysters are ready to harvest."

Reaching out, she ran her fingers lightly over the caps of a cluster of mushrooms. "They're beautiful. Straight out of *Alice in Wonderland*. There should be a colorful caterpillar sitting on top of them, smoking a hookah."

The image she'd painted was clear in my mind. She was right. Now I'd think of it whenever I looked at them.

"They always spread out from the bag in a regular pattern," I said. "It's rhythmic. Like music." And because she'd come up with the caterpillar image, I expanded the analogy. "If they had a sound, I think it might be honky-tonk."

She laughed. "Musical mushrooms. That's very poetic."

I grinned back at her, pleased by her reaction. Though we'd seemed so different at first, we understood each other pretty well now. As though we clicked. I liked the way she thought, and it felt natural to say what I was thinking.

Some strands of her hair had come loose from her ponytail, and as she bent to smell a cluster of mushrooms, one strand fell forward. I wanted to brush it back, to run my fingers over the curve of her cheek with the same reverence she'd had when she touched the mushrooms. She was like music, too. Her face had a harmony I couldn't stop admiring.

"May I taste them?" she asked.

"Tomorrow night, I'll cook some as a side dish." I watched her face, wondering if she'd object to my assumption that she'd come to dinner again tomorrow.

She was busy gazing at the rows of bags. "This is what you grow," she said. "Mushrooms for eating."

"Just like I told you." I gave her a quizzical look, surprised by the way she was repeating it. "Did you not believe me?"

"I didn't think you grew *legal* mushrooms. I thought they'd be magic ones."

"I told you they weren't the illegal kind."

But my chest had tightened. It was obvious why she hadn't believed me. I'd never be able to shake the Baxter name.

"I've heard gossip about you," confirmed Mags. Then her brow creased as though she could read the heartache that gave me. "But fuck those people. They're wrong about you. And they don't get to label you."

I blinked, surprised by her sudden fierceness. "I'd rather not have sexual relations with them," I said. "But I appreciate the sentiment."

Her smile was slow, one side of her lips hitching higher. Its warmth loosened my chest.

"There are a lot of mushrooms here." She walked a little further down the row. "Who do you sell them to?"

"I've spoken to the owners of a few restaurants in Knoxville, and some of them placed orders. I need to drive back to talk to some more."

She turned to face me. "Why restrict yourself the restaurants in Knoxville? According to Joy and Amber, there are some nice places to eat in Green Valley."

I hesitated. But as reluctant as I was to keep talking about my reputation, I didn't want to lie. "You've heard what they say. Folks in Green Valley wouldn't buy anything from me. Nothing legal, anyway."

"There are a few nasty gossips, but most people are open-minded." She wrinkled her forehead. "Problem is, they've only heard one side of things. If you let them get to know you, they'll realize how wrong the rumors are, and how unfair they've been."

I shook my head. "I don't like the prejudice, but I understand it. All the generations of Baxters have been bad, as far back as anyone can remember. And once people have a firm idea about something, it's hard to change that."

"That's true." She bit her lip. "It's not even close to the same, but I've had a little experience of that with my family."

I frowned. "What do you mean?"

"It doesn't matter." She waved a hand. "It's nothing compared to what you've had to deal with." Tightening her lips, she walked along the row of mushrooms, examining them as she went. I got the impression she didn't want me to press her on her comment. And when she reached the end of the row, she turned and said, "It's humid in here."

"Let's go back to the porch," I suggested.

"How long have you been growing mushrooms?" she asked, walking back toward me.

"Not long. It took me a while to repurpose the barn. I'm about to do my first big harvest." I waited for her to reach me, then we strolled toward the door together.

"What were you doing for money before this?" she asked.

"When I lived in Boston, I worked in venture capital."

She stopped abruptly and stared at me with such a surprised look, I figured maybe she didn't know what venture capital was.

"I was employed by an investment firm," I explained. "My job was selecting start-up businesses to invest in."

"So you were in charge of a pile of money, and got to pick who to give it to?" Her eyebrows were creeping up. "How much money?"

"The fund invested close to a billion dollars."

"What the hell?" Taking a step backward, she held up both hands. "Now wait just one minute. You're seriously telling me that your job in Boston was choosing how to spend *a billion dollars*?"

I wasn't sure whether I should be offended or amused by how incredulous she was. "I chose how to invest the money, not spend it," I said. "But, yes. Essentially."

"How did you get a job like that?" she demanded.

"It's about calculating risk. Running the numbers. And I like math."

"You like math." Shaking her head, she drew her hands dramatically down the sides of her face. "A mathematician with an impressive corporate job. Next you're going to tell me your real name is actually Charles, and your closet is full of three-piece suits."

"My real name is Cy. And what part of all this is hard to believe?" I decided to be amused rather than offended. She had to be exaggerating her surprise, but I liked how impressed she seemed. It was good for my ego.

"It's not that it's hard to believe, it's that I had everything so wrong. Why didn't you tell me this before?"

"You didn't ask."

"But I thought you were a criminal!" She lifted both palms as though to stop me before I could protest. "And it wasn't only because of the rumors about you."

I frowned. "What else would make you think that?"

"You said you were growing mushrooms in your father's padlocked marijuana shed, you drive an ancient pickup, your beard could house an entire family of mice . . . and you were wearing flannel!" Her voice rose as though she was indignant. Like I'd mounted a deliberate campaign to trick her.

"I *am* growing mushrooms in my daddy's marijuana shed," I pointed out, running a defensive hand down my beard. "And I decided I may as well drive his old pickup around until it dies, seeing as the gravel driveway was damaging my paint job. My own car is in storage."

"Oh my God!" She huffed. "I can't believe this! You used to be a corporate whizz investing a billion dollars, and now you're a respectable business owner growing beautiful mushrooms. I was worried about kissing another bad boy, and it turns out you're good. And *I'm* the one paying off drug dealers and not going to the police when I know it's what a sensible, law-abiding person would do."

I took in what she was saying, and suddenly I wanted to laugh. "When you put it like that, I can see how you're a bad influence."

She gave me a level stare. "Very funny."

Walking toward the door, I pretended to scratch my beard so I could hide my smile. "Come on," I said. "You look hot." Her cheeks were tinged with pink. Though I had to admit, I liked them that way. She looked even prettier with red cheeks.

"It's the humidity. And the shock of realizing I'm such a bad role model."

"I'll get you a glass of water." Sliding the door shut behind us, I secured the heavy padlocks.

"Thanks," she said. "But I should get home."

"What about the drug dealer who's threatening you? I still think you should stay here. Take my bed and I'll sleep on the couch."

She shook her head. "I'll be fine at Carla's place."

"Is there anything I can say to get you to be less stubborn about that?"

"I'm not stubborn," she said. "I'm just not staying." Then she gave a stubborn lift of her chin as she shot me a stubborn look.

"Sure, you're not stubborn," I muttered, giving a frustrated shake of my head.

Truth was, I'd want her to stay even if she wasn't being threatened. I liked talking to her, and I especially liked how she made me smile. When she was around, my chest felt light.

There was only one thing I didn't like about her. One thing I *hated*. And that was that she had a boyfriend who was clearly an undeserving asshole. All my life, I'd seen men treat women badly. It made me sick to my stomach to know there was nothing I could do about it.

We stopped back inside so she could say goodbye to Gemma and collect Zeppelin. Then I walked her out to her car, keeping my hands in my pockets to avoid the temptation of wanting to touch her.

As we reached her car, she said, "Listen, I'm still struggling with the details. You had a corporate job in Boston, but you decided to ditch it and move back to the childhood home you hated, and now you grow mushrooms." She gave me a perplexed frown. "I've never been a math person, and I can't get it to add up."

I stopped beside her driver's door, my hands still in my pockets. "You said you wanted a change from your old job, and it was a little like that for me, too. When my daddy died and I inherited his house, I couldn't let it sit here collecting taxes. Figured I may as well take a break from Boston so I could renovate and sell it. But I found myself staying longer than I expected. The barn was just sitting there, and there's something about watching things grow that feels good." I shrugged. "It wasn't my original plan, but it seemed to work."

I purposely left out the long months after I arrived that I'd spent doing nothing at all. Logically, I knew depression was an illness and nothing to be ashamed of. But I couldn't help feeling like I'd let myself down. As much as I hated my father's toxic voice, it still whispered inside me, saying depression was something real men didn't suffer from. Though I could be proud of Ruth for how she was dealing with it, I was harder on myself.

Mags drew her eyebrows together, looking contrite. "I should have said it ages ago, but I'm sorry I called you Deliverance. It was mean. I was awful to you."

"I said some things too," I admitted.

She grinned, her apology dissolving into humor. "Hansel and Gretel? That was hilarious. Trying not to laugh almost killed me."

I smiled back at her as she opened her car door and got in. I'd never wanted anything as much as I wanted to kiss her again. It just about killed me that I couldn't.

CHAPTER 16

MAGDALENA

I had the weekend off work, and spent it lounging around the house reading a fantasy novel, sending increasingly angry messages to Eric, and worrying about Spike. On Saturday night I had dinner with Cy and Gemma, which included a generous helping of mushrooms. But on Sunday night, despite their protestations, I thought I should let Gemma concentrate on getting ready for school, and I stayed home with a frozen pizza instead.

Carla called me before work on Monday. And all I could say about her timing is that she should have known it'd be too early to call.

I leaned my phone against a mystery appliance that was sitting on the counter while I made the day's first cup of coffee. It was a video call, which meant my sister and I could see each other. She looked wide awake for such an early hour, especially seeing as she often suffered from crippling fatigue.

I felt like I'd dragged myself out of my coffin after some meddling wizard had brought my thousand-year-old skeleton back to life. I wouldn't officially be conscious until the caffeine hit my bloodstream.

"You broke up with Eric?" Carla asked. "Are you okay?"

Yawning, I nodded. I'd messaged her late the night before, after finally sending Eric a furious "we're over" message.

"I'm fine," I said. "It was a relief."

"Want to talk about it?"

"Sure. Sometime when it isn't practically the middle of the night."

"Sorry." She grinned, not looking sorry at all. "I was awake early and wanted to catch you before work."

I grunted. "Coffee now. Talk later."

Her grin fell away as she peered at the screen. "Hey, are my herbs dying?"

"Herbs?" I took a big gulp of coffee, closing my eyes for a moment so I could fully appreciate the vitality-restoring liquid. As it hit the back of my throat, I felt my long-dead heart start to beat again.

"On the windowsill." Carla motioned toward the screen.

I glanced behind me at my sister's potted plants. Now that she mentioned it, they were looking distinctly less alive than they had looked a few days ago.

"Have you been watering them?" Carla asked.

"Not yet." I sucked down more coffee. "I'll do it today."

"They need watering every day, brat. It was in the list of instructions I gave you."

"That wasn't a list, it was a novel. It had chapters." My snippy tone was due to not being at the bottom of the cup yet. In about ten minutes, I'd be a much nicer person. Like I said, she only had herself to blame.

"You didn't read my note?"

"I'm waiting for the audiobook to come out."

She let out a little sigh. "Oh, Mags."

My heart twisted at her disappointment. I was never quite able to live up to my family's expectations. And now that I'd ingested just enough caffeine to be able to experience emotions, I couldn't help but feel bad.

My guilt must have showed in my expression, because Carla's face softened. "Don't worry about the herbs, brat. I can plant some more." Her forehead creased. "Are you really okay? Not brokenhearted?"

"Not even a little."

"Okay." She looked doubtful, like she thought I might be hiding my sorrow. Carla had no idea about the whole Spike situation, or what a jerk Eric had been.

I also hadn't told her about Cy. She'd probably heard all the awful rumors about him, which made it a conversation I didn't want to have right now. Not while I still had coffee in my cup and my pajamas on, with less than an hour before I had to leave for work. Better to bring up Cy when I had time to explain how he'd been unfairly tainted by his family's bad name.

"How's your medical trial going?" I asked. My sister had chronic fatigue syndrome and was trying everything she could to improve her symptoms.

"My assessment is done. The next phase will start today."

"That's great! I really hope it helps."

"Thanks. So do I." She smiled at me. "How's Freud?"

"I'm about to feed him. Watch, and you'll witness the miracle of him getting out of bed." I put down my cup to grab a tin of cat food, then angled the phone so Carla could see her cat sidle expectantly into the kitchen. The cat might appear to sleep like . . . well, like he needed a wizard to resurrect his corpse, but the slightest clink of a tin of cat food on the counter would rouse him.

"Wait." My sister's tone was suddenly sharp. "What was that? Did a *dog* just come inside?"

I turned to see Zeppelin trotting into the kitchen, his tongue lolling. I'd opened the back door so he could go outside to pee before I made myself coffee, and apparently his hearing was as sharp as Freud's.

"Oh yeah." I angled the phone to focus back on me instead of the animals, leaning it back against the mystery appliance. "Don't worry, that's only a temporary dog."

"What's a temporary dog?" She didn't look pleased by the idea.

"He's only staying until I find his real owner. I would have asked you first to make sure it was okay, but he didn't call ahead to tell me he was coming."

As I spoke, I dished out cat food and dog food. Inside, I was berating myself. Sure, I'd been caught up with work, the Spike situation, and dinners with Cy, but I should have told her about Zeppelin. It had been thoughtless not to. And by letting her down, I'd let myself down.

"Okay," Carla said slowly, her tone doubtful. "Please could you make sure the dog can't get into the chicken run?"

"Actually, the dog's lock-picking skills are rusty. I've started training him to open doors, but he'll need a lot more practice." Putting the bowls down, I kept my fingers clear so they wouldn't get caught up in the enthusiastic gobbling.

Carla scrunched her nose. "Maybe I'm being overprotective, but is he house-trained, at least?"

I lifted my gaze as though thinking. "Well, mostly."

"Mostly?"

"So far he's only peed in your room. The good news is that I can't smell it from mine."

Her eyes widened in horror for a moment, then she realized I was teasing her and she shook her head with a reluctant smile. "Okay, you got me, brat. But there'd better not be any puddles when I get home."

"No puddles," I promised. And I'd make sure to replace her ripped-up cushions, too.

I always seemed to be trying to convince my sister to trust me. And given my history, I couldn't blame her if she didn't. It would be great if I could rewind time to undo the dumb things I'd done in the past, but it seemed those things would always be there, stuck in both of our memories. No matter what, I'd always be the same Mags who'd messed up. And I couldn't complain about it, seeing as I was the one who'd made the mistakes. And was still making them.

"I'd better get ready for work," I said, wanting to shower and dress before I made more coffee.

We said goodbye, and I'd just hung up when there was a knock on the door. Zeppelin barked, racing to the door with his tail wagging.

"Mags?" Cy's voice called through the door.

My heart gave an excited flip at the thought of seeing him, and a flush of anticipation radiated from low in my belly. I headed straight toward the door to let him in, then suddenly realized what I must look like. I was wearing a T-shirt and pajama pants, and I hadn't brushed my hair or teeth yet, seeing as I'd barely gotten out of bed when Carla had called.

"Just a moment," I called, darting into my bedroom to drag a brush through my hair while weighing up the getting dressed versus brushing my teeth question, seeing as I didn't have time to do both. Clean teeth were more important, I decided, racing into the bathroom for a lightning-fast scrub. And I added a squirt of perfume in case I smelled funky. I wasn't wearing a bra, but oh well. I'd just have to try not to bounce too much as I walked.

Zeppelin woofed impatiently at the door. When I opened it, he jumped up on Cy, excited to see him.

Cy took me in with a sweep of his eyes, his expression changing into one of appreciation. Maybe his cheeks even flushed a little. But honestly, I was too busy gazing at him in amazed silence to fully register what he thought of my braless T-shirt and pajama pants.

He looked . . . incredible. His beard wasn't unruly anymore. He'd trimmed and shaped it. It was still long, but a lot tidier. The strong line of his jaw was obvious, and his cheeks were sharper and more chiseled. His pillowy upper lip was visible, making me realize how serious a crime it had been to have hidden it before. His mouth was as arrestingly beautiful as his eyes.

Cy crouched to pet Zeppelin, while I stared at him in amazed silence.

"You've trimmed your beard." My tongue felt clumsy, like it had become a little too big for my mouth.

I wanted to touch his face. To trace the new lines and contours, and cup the hardness of his jaw between my hands. I wanted to kiss him and flick my tongue across his bare upper lip.

Cy looked up at me while sitting on his heels, rubbing Zeppelin's sides. He eyed my face for a moment, clearly reading my expression. Then his lips tugged up in a pleased half smile.

"It was about time," he said. "You like it?"

I swallowed to moisten my dry throat, searching for something to say that wasn't *Oh my God, do I ever*, or *Please do me now*.

"I like it a lot. You look great." I cleared my throat, pulling myself together and trying not to act like I was swooning. "But do all you country bumpkins get up so early? Couldn't you set the roosters to crow a little later?"

He rose to his feet. His newly snug beard made his jawline look even more delicious. And now I could see and admire the length of his throat. Add in the width of his shoulders, and his hotness had me melting faster than an ice cube in a microwave.

"You said to collect Zeppelin before you went to work," he said. "What time did you mean?"

I swallowed again, giving myself another mental shake. "Never mind. It's just that it's already been a morning." Standing back from the door, I motioned him inside.

"What do you mean? Did something happen?" He strode in, looking around sharply as though he was ready to tackle an intruder.

"My eldest sister called. Carla. The one who lives here."

Frowning, he swung to face me. "And that's a bad thing?"

"No, it's just . . ." I hesitated, wincing. It was silly. I felt like I was complaining about nothing.

"Just what?" he prompted.

"Well, you get arrested one or two measly times, and you get branded an irresponsible person for life." I led the way down the hall. "Not that my sister says anything about that, but sometimes I'm sure she's thinking about it."

"Okay, I need some context, so you need to start this story at the beginning. Context *and* coffee. Would you make me a coffee?"

"Happy to. Coffee is what I'm best at."

I got the machine going and used my well-practiced coffee-making skills to place a steaming hot mug in his hand, and a fresh one in my own hand.

Cy took a sip, then made a *mmm* sound of approval. "You make excellent coffee." He flicked his tongue out to lick a little froth off his mustache, and the sight was weirdly sexy. Probably because now I could see how nice his whole mouth was, and his tongue had already delivered such delicious kisses. Thinking about how it had felt sent a little shiver of lust down my spine.

Cy leaned back against the kitchen counter, his mug cradled in his big hands. "Now I'm all ears for your story. How did you get arrested?"

I slid onto the stool at the kitchen island. While we were talking, I could gaze at the newly exposed parts of his face without it getting weird. And with both elbows on the counter, I could cradle my coffee cup while disguising the fact I was braless.

"It's embarrassing," I said. "So shameful, I don't want to confess all the details. Basically, I was a rebel growing up. Short attention span, youngest child, easily bored, problem with authority." I waved a hand. "Pick an excuse that works for you, and we'll go with that."

"You were trouble." He didn't phrase it as a question, but as a slightly amusing statement, complete with a quirk of his lips as though he thought it was cute. Which it totally wasn't.

"According to my mother, I was nothing *but* trouble." I sighed. "And I attract other troublesome people. In high school, it was a bunch of friends who got their kicks through petty theft. More recently, I attracted a drug-taking rock star." I dropped my chin to give him a significant look. "And there's no need to mention that I thought you were a criminal, when it was really just me all along. I'm well aware."

"I didn't say a word." He covered his grin with his coffee cup.

"Well, luckily I don't have a record. I was a minor and got off with a warning, and it scared me straight." I wrinkled my nose. "The whole thing is silly, really. All this time I've felt like it's been hanging over me, but you've had to deal with so much worse."

He shrugged. "It doesn't matter what folks think of me, so long as they leave Gemma alone."

I frowned, because I hadn't considered how his reputation might affect her. "You don't think anyone would say anything mean to Gemma? They wouldn't, would they?"

"They would if they knew she was a Baxter. After my momma was killed, folks were awful to Ruth."

I stiffened at the thought. "And were they awful to you, too?" The idea that any of the people I was getting to know and like could bully Cy and his family wasn't a pleasant one.

"Some were, but I could handle it. Back then, Ruth was about Gemma's age. They shouldn't have treated her badly." Clenching his jaw, he gave a shake of his head. "I won't let Gemma be treated like that. That's why I've been trying not to be seen around town with her. So folks won't know we're related."

"You shouldn't have to hide." I leaned in, outraged on his behalf. "That's not fair! You've done nothing wrong."

"But I did." He frowned, his gaze turning thoughtful. "I did something that was very wrong."

"What did you do?"

He glanced at the clock on the wall. "To tell you the whole story would take a while. How long before you have to leave for work?"

I followed his gaze. "About half an hour."

"I'll tell you about it tonight. When you come for dinner." He drained the last of his coffee, then set his cup on the counter.

"Another dinner invitation?" I raised my eyebrows teasingly. "People will talk."

He was moving around to my side of the counter, to where I was perched on the stool. "We missed you last night. Gemma enjoys dinner a lot more when you're there." Stopping beside me, he lifted a hand to my hair to push back a strand and tuck it behind my ear. "And I like it when you're there."

His fingers trailed down the side of my face. The sensation made my cheeks feel hot and made my stomach flutter. I loved the way he touched me.

There were more questions I wanted to ask, but his touch was distracting. It made me want to forget about words altogether in favor of more touching.

"Do you have any idea how gorgeous you are? What you do to me?" His voice was a low rumble and his gaze was heated, dipping to my lips. I had a strong urge to sink both hands into his short beard. To feel its coarseness and use it to tug his face to mine.

Before I could move, he stepped back, and his expression changed. It hardened, his jaw visibly clenching. He put his hands in his pockets as he turned away from me.

"I need to go." He moved toward the hallway.

What? No!

"Wait!" I slid off my stool. "I need you to show me something."

He stopped, turning back slowly, as though reluctant to face me. His gaze dipped briefly to my breasts, then came back up, landing firmly on my eyes. "Show you what?"

I wanted him to show me how his hand would feel in my pajama pants. Or better still, how our two naked bodies would feel getting tangled in my bedsheets. My nipples were rock hard. He must have noticed. They were practically ripping their way through my T-shirt, fighting to get out.

I cleared my throat. "Come with me."

Instead of taking him to the bedroom, I led him to the laundry. Then I waved at the washing machine. Yesterday, I'd gotten as far as filling it with clothes and putting in the detergent.

"Could you show me how to work this thing?" I paired my demand with a challenging look, daring him to laugh at me.

"You've never used a washing machine?" His gaze flicked to my breasts again. My nipples seemed to be distracting him.

"Of course not," I said. "My maid has always done my washing."

"You have a maid?"

I pulled a "duh" face, secretly enjoying the way his IQ seemed to be dropping with every glance at my very erect nipples. "I know how to use the ones at the laundromat, but they don't have so many buttons. Put in the right coins, and they start on their own."

He stepped close to the machine and ran his hand across the display panel, scanning the options. "There are clothes in there?" He turned to meet my gaze. "And they're dirty?"

He seemed to linger on the word *dirty*, and it sent another jolt of desire into my core. Probably because I was already keyed up. And it wasn't my imagination that he was undressing me with his eyes. I could see him imagining stripping off my T-shirt and pajama pants and throwing them in.

I stepped close so I could put my hand on his chest, my palm pressing against the flat slab of his pectoral muscle. "Very dirty," I whispered.

His gaze swept to my lips, but he didn't move. It was as though he was torn. Arguing with himself, I guessed.

"You have a boyfriend." He ground the words out in a harsh tone, confirming my suspicions. I was practically throwing myself at him, and he was holding back because he was honorable. Every bit the gentleman he'd told me he was.

It made a nice change from Eric. In fact, I couldn't think of a single one of my exes who would have shown this much restraint. And it made me admire him even more.

"Not anymore," I said.

CHAPTER 17

CY

"Y ou don't have a boyfriend anymore?" I asked.

My mind was racing. My heart kicked into a higher gear. This was good news. No, it was the *best* news.

Mags gave a little shrug, her lips curving up. "Nope."

She was incredibly sexy in a pair of pajama pants and a tight T-shirt. Up until now, I'd been trying not to let my eyes linger on her chest, though I kept wanting to drink in the fact she wasn't wearing a bra. But now that she didn't have a boyfriend anymore, well, I was more than drinking. I was *guzzling*. I couldn't be more aware of the curves of her breasts and her nipples pressing hard against the thin fabric of her T-shirt.

"You broke up?" I asked the question dumbly, mainly because my thoughts were like a ball bouncing back and forth over a net. My mind kept hitting against the no-boyfriend thing, bouncing back to the no-bra thing, returning to no-boyfriend, and so on.

She quirked an eyebrow. "You need me to draw you a no-boyfriend picture? Because the picture would be a blank page with no boyfriend on it. Pretty easy to draw. I could whip it up in no time."

Maybe I should ask if she was okay, and pretend I was sorry about the end of her relationship. Only she didn't look upset, and I'd never been less sorry about anything. Bringing my hand to her face, I stroked her soft cheek with the back of my fingers.

Her eyes were dark and hazy, her gaze focused on my lips. But when she moved a little, her hip bumped against the washing machine. She blinked, then glanced backward at it.

"Aren't you going to show me how to turn that on?" she asked suggestively.

"Just press the button that says Start." I demonstrated by reaching around her to press it, and the machine started to fill with water.

"Wait. That's it?" Mags frowned at the panel of buttons. As she turned from me, the intoxicating scent of her perfume grew stronger. She smelled so good it was all I could do not to bury my nose in her hair. "What about all the rest of the buttons?"

"The machine defaults to a normal wash setting. The buttons are if you want to do something different."

"Oh." She turned her face back to me and rested her butt against the machine. "Well, that was almost too easy." Then she cocked her head, her lovely eyes roaming over my face. "I like your beard a lot better now that you've trimmed it. You look . . ."

She hesitated, so I took the opportunity to provide some acceptable options for the end of her sentence. "Debonair?" I suggested. "Ruthlessly handsome? Irresistible?"

"Tidy," she said. "But in a good way, not a boring, unattractive way."

"Hmm. I'm almost certain there's a compliment in there somewhere." I put my hand on her hip to tug her a little closer. Her breasts were calling to me, her nipples whispering a siren song, begging for my fingers and mouth. I'd been rock hard since the moment she'd opened the front door, and I kept defying the laws of physics to get harder and harder, when it should have been impossible.

"Now I can see your lips." Her hooded gaze was on my mouth.

"Don't restrict yourself to looking. Feel free to touch."

Putting both hands on my face, she stroked my freshly trimmed beard, following the line of the hair as though petting a cat. "I like the shape of your face," she murmured. "So sharp and strong."

Sliding my hands to her back, I captured her lips with mine. She kissed me hungrily, pushing her hands under my T-shirt. She felt incredible. So soft and pliant against me.

Moving my hand to her breast, I stroked its curve over her T-shirt. Then I circled the hard bullet of her nipple with my thumb, loving her weight in my palm. Even better was the little moan she made as I lightly pinched her nipple between my thumb and forefinger.

It wasn't enough. I needed to get underneath her T-shirt, to feel her skin. But at the same time as I moved my hand to the bottom of her shirt, she was dropping one hand to palm my hard cock over my jeans. And although my cock strained into her hand, the placement of her arm stopped her T-shirt from lifting. Not being able to touch her skin the way I wanted wasn't acceptable. I let out an involuntary sound of frustration, and she understand immediately what I needed. She let go for long enough to tug off her shirt.

Much better.

I bent my face to her breast, cupping it while I worshiped her with my tongue. There was nothing about her body I didn't love, and the shape and weight of her breasts was sheer perfection.

"Mmm," she moaned. "Touch me, Cy. I need you." Her voice was breathless with want. And I felt the same way. I'd been dreaming of this nonstop for days, and my desire was so strong I was on fire.

I pushed a rough hand under the elastic of her pajamas. They were loose, and she wore nothing underneath. Parting her, I slid my finger into her wet heat. She gasped into my mouth, digging her nails into my back. *Fuck.* She was so wet. So hot. Her fingernails dragged across my skin, and I loved it.

But I had to draw back.

"How long before you need to leave to get to work on time?" I demanded, my voice as rough as my hands.

She blinked, her eyes hazy. Her lips looked even more beautiful now they were kiss-swollen. It took her a moment to say anything, and then it was just an *um* sound, as though her thoughts were so scrambled she couldn't form words.

I loved scrambling her thoughts and driving her senseless. I wanted her to be unable to make any sounds except ones of pure pleasure.

With my lips on her neck, I trailed light kisses down her throat. "What time do you have to leave?" I repeated.

"Seven thirty," she whispered.

"So if we left you ten minutes to shower and dress, we only have twelve minutes to fool around."

She groaned. "Twelve minutes doesn't seem long enough."

I nipped her skin in agreement. "Not even close."

I was so hard, I had an almost overwhelming urge to forget about the time and bury myself inside her anyway. But I couldn't make love to her in twelve minutes. Not in the way I wanted, the way that would leave us both satisfied.

In that length of time, there was only one thing I could do, one pleasure I could allow myself. And for now at least, it would have to be enough.

I pushed her pajamas pants down her thighs, then put both hands around her waist. She let out a squeak of surprise as I lifted her onto the washing machine. It was still filling with water, and I sat her down on the glass lid, her knees spread.

She laughed a little at being up there, and my Lord, had I ever seen such a beautiful sight?

"You're gorgeous," I said and thought at the same time. Her hair was falling loose over her shoulders and her breasts jutted up as she put her hands behind her. Her eyes were bright, her lips rosy from my kisses.

"Aren't I a little high up here?" she asked, reaching for my jeans.

"Not for what I have in mind. Sweetheart, I want to taste you." I stepped back, evading her hands, then dropped to my knees. "We only just have long enough for that, and it's the best thing to do with that length of time."

As we couldn't make love, this wasn't just the next best thing, it was *necessary*. She needed my tongue, and I needed to revel in the best view in the world, enjoying the way she tasted and felt as I watched her come apart.

She bit her lip, watching me kiss my way up her soft thigh. Clearly not just willing, but eager. "What about you?" she asked.

"This is for me as much as it is for you." I rubbed my short beard gently over the sensitive skin on her inner thigh and her breath hitched. "That's it, beautiful," I murmured, using my hands to spread her further and letting my warm breath gust over her. "Lie back and enjoy."

Water stopped running into the washing machine, and the machine clicked into the agitation part of its cycle. The paddles inside it turned this way, then that way, swirling the clothes in the water. With each rotation, the machine shuddered.

Mags gasped with pleasure as I licked her, slowly exploring and savoring her.

"Oh my God," she moaned. "Cy, that's so good."

It wasn't just good, it was fucking amazing. I loved her taste and the way she smelled. I loved the way she looked with her head thrown back and her lips parted. I loved that she kept closing her eyes then flicking them open again, the sensations overwhelming her as she tried to watch me feast on her. And I loved that every time the machine shuddered, her spectacular breasts and her rounded, feminine stomach shook with tremors.

She moaned again. "I'm going to . . ." Her words were swallowed up in a groan as I pushed two fingers inside her. I lapped more quickly as she spread her legs wider, threading her fingers into my hair.

I wanted to tell her how gorgeous she looked, and how sexy she was. But she gave a little cry and then she was coming, her body shaking with the force of her release. She clenched around my fingers, and her thighs trembled. Her cries became loud, then slowly died down, the last one becoming a whimper.

Her eyes opened slowly. "Oh my God," she said on a gust of breath.

Rising, I lifted her off the washing machine and set her on her feet. She sagged against it, her arms around my waist, her cheek on my T-shirt, her naked body so tempting, it was all I could do not to carry her into the bedroom and throw her onto the bed.

"My legs are wobbly. That was amazing." Her eyes came up to mine. "But what about you?" She cupped me over my jeans.

My cock felt like it was trying to tear right through my jeans to force its way into her hand. I was so turned on that if she stroked me, I'd come quickly. But I just kissed the tip of her nose.

"We're out of time, beautiful," I told her. "It's seven twenty. If I don't leave now, you won't make it to work at all."

CHAPTER 18

MAGDALENA

To say I was in a good mood when I got to the bakery would be putting it mildly. I even out-smiled Joy and Amber. Mind you, neither was dating anyone right now, so they probably hadn't had the kind of smile-inducing morning I'd had. An orgasm that good would have made Ebenezer Scrooge break into a grin.

I was extra friendly to all the customers, greeting our regulars by name and remembering their usual orders. Joy was working in the kitchen with the other bakers, so it was just Amber and I on the counter. And when we finally got a short break without any customers in the store, Amber turned to me with a laugh.

"What's gotten into you this morning?" she asked. "Whatever it is, I want some! I've never seen you so happy."

Our conversation would get X-rated if I tried to describe exactly what had gotten into me, so I just gave her a little shrug. "I had a very pleasant morning." But I couldn't keep my smile from widening even further as I said it.

She raised her eyebrows, grabbing a cloth to wipe some crumbs from the countertop. "It must have been special. You're glowing."

"Am I?" I put both hands to my cheeks. They did feel a little warm.

"It's because of a man, isn't it? You have a dewy look." She squinted at me. "It doesn't have anything to do with Cy Baxter, does it?"

I didn't need to answer. The fact I couldn't stop smiling was answer enough.

She pushed her lips to the side. "Don't take this the wrong way, Mags, but are you sure getting involved with him is a good idea? I'm not usually one for gossip, but the rumors about him carrying on with his daddy's business have come from several different people. Can they all be wrong?"

"They *are* all wrong."

"He must be growing something, seeing as he's been buying straw—"

"It's not drugs. He's growing mushrooms. Gourmet ones."

She furrowed her brow, scrubbing at a sticky spot on the countertop. "Are you sure?"

"I saw them with my own eyes. He showed them to me last night, and he's going to sell them to all the restaurants around here."

"Oh." Her expression relaxed. "Well, if you've seen it, then it must be true. And it's not the first time wild rumors have been flying around that turned out to be wrong." She rolled her eyes. "Some folks like to believe the worst and spread it to anyone who'll listen."

"That's part of the problem. Cy's niece is fifteen, and she's just started going to school here. If people have the wrong idea about Cy, how will she be treated?"

"I'd hope she'd be treated well, no matter who she's related to."

"Cy doesn't think she will be. And I don't want to take the chance." I made my mind up as I said the words. "I'm going to start a campaign to fix his reputation."

"How will you do that?"

"By telling people they're wrong about him."

"Okay." She put the cleaning cloth back in its place under the counter and wiped her hands on her apron. "You'll talk to everyone in town?" It sounded like a sincere question, as though she believed it would really be possible.

"If I have to."

She nodded. "Well, you've been getting to know folks, and they seem to like you. If anyone can do it, I think you probably can."

I grinned at her, appreciating her vote of confidence. "Who are the key people to influence?"

"The biggest gossips are folks like Karen Smith and Bonnie Linton, but they're not well-liked around town." She paused for a moment thinking it over. "I'd say you need someone like Flo McClure on your side. She works at the sheriff's office and talks to everyone. Most folks like her."

"Okay. I don't think I've met her yet."

Amber snapped her fingers, her eyes lighting up. "Wait, what about Noah's momma? She's involved with all kinds of things around town, and on every committee you can think of. And she's a really nice lady. I'm sure she'd help spread the word."

"Great idea! I'm having lunch with her on Sunday."

The door opened and some customers came in. I nudged Amber, giving her a wide-eyed look. "Here we go," I murmured. Then I raised my voice. "Hello, Shelly," I said to the tall woman who approached the counter first. "And hi, Beau." I waved to the red-haired man just behind her.

Beau said a friendly hello, then gave me their order. As I was bagging their muffins, I asked. "Do you two know Cy Baxter?"

Shelly shook her head, glancing at Beau. "I don't believe so."

Beau's forehead creased. "I don't know Cy real well," he said. "But I knew his daddy. Ike Baxter was friendly with my daddy." The flare of his nostrils told me he didn't consider that to be an endorsement of Ike's character.

"Cy's a good person," I said. "Nothing like his father."

Beau gave a little shrug. "Like I say, I barely know him."

"Well, now that Cy's back in town, he's starting up his own agriculture business. He's growing gourmet mushrooms to sell to restaurants. Golden oyster mushrooms that are the color of daffodils, and tall white ones that look like alien pincushions."

"Golden oyster mushrooms?" Shelly looked interested. "They grow in clusters that make interesting organic shapes."

I nodded, remembering she was a sculptor. "Beautiful shapes. You should take a look at his operation some time. I'm sure Cy wouldn't mind showing you around." At least I was pretty sure he wouldn't mind. And if he made a few more friends, there'd be more people to spread the word that he was nothing like his father.

"I'd like to see them." Shelly looked at Beau.

Beau smiled back at her, his gaze warm. "Sure, honey. If we run into Cy, let's ask him."

After they'd gone, Amber bumped my shoulder with hers. "Great job," she murmured. "Beau's easy to win over, seeing as he's one of the nicest people in the entire world. But Shelly says exactly what she thinks. If she's willing to give Cy a chance, that's a good sign."

"Those two are just the start," I murmured back. Then I said a friendly hello to the next customer waiting in line, ready to start up a conversation and work Cy into it.

It proved to be a good day to start my campaign. We had a steady flow of customers, and I was able to talk about Cy to many of the people who came in. Lots of them had heard the rumors about him, but I managed to convince at least some of them that the gossip was wrong. Others seemed like they still had doubts, though I did the best I could. And I recruited Joy to help, so she and Amber could keep up the good work when I took a break from serving customers.

Around midday, Amber nudged me, nodding at the two women who'd just entered the bakery. "Here's the real test," she murmured. "It's Karen Smith and Bonnie Linton."

"Great. They like to talk, so they can help me spread the word about Cy."

She wrinkled her nose. "They only like to spread bad news."

"Follow my lead, okay Amber?" As the two women walked up to the counter, I gave them a wide smile. "How nice to see you both!" I exclaimed. "Mrs. Smith, you like the lemon cake, don't you? Mrs. Linton, the banana cake is particularly good today. Would you like a slice?"

The two women looked a little surprised by my effusive greeting. "We'll both have the banana cake," said Mrs. Smith.

"An excellent choice." As I dished it up, I turned my head to speak to Amber. "Did I tell you about Cy Baxter?"

Amber blinked at me. "What about him?" From the corner of my eye, I could see both Mrs. Linton and Mrs. Smith leaning in to listen.

"Cy was in here earlier," I said, "and I tried to get my courage up to ask him out on a date. But he looks so handsome now he's trimmed his beard, I'm afraid he won't be interested in me."

Mrs. Smith clucked her tongue. "Didn't I warn you stay away from that one?"

Mrs. Linton was shaking her head, her mouth turned down. "Those Baxters are no good."

"What?" I said, acting confused. Before they could say anything else, I let out a gasp. "Oh no, you haven't heard about Cy, have you?" I turned to Amber, my eyes opened wide. "They don't know about Cy."

Amber widened her eyes too, clearly enjoying herself. "Good Lord. Could it be that they really haven't heard?"

"Heard what?" demanded Mrs. Linton. Other customers had come into the bakery, but they looked as interested as the two gossips. In any case, nobody was suggesting we cut the chitchat and hurry things along.

"Well," I said, "you know that Cy was an important corporate businessman when he lived in Boston, right?"

"You don't say?" Mrs. Linton sounded like she didn't believe it.

"You really didn't know that?" I acted surprised. "But you must have heard he's started a successful business here, selling gourmet mushrooms to local businesses?"

Mrs. Smith sniffed. "I'm certain he's taken over his daddy's drug business. There's only one thing that man's growing."

I let out a laugh, turning to Amber. "That's funny."

She laughed even louder. "Hilarious! Oh my goodness. How could anyone think that?"

"Cy is the farthest thing from a drug dealer there could possibly be." I put my hand to my chest as though the idea had made me laugh so hard, I needed to catch my breath.

"He's highly respectable," Amber said, nodding. "An upstanding citizen."

Both Mrs. Smith and Mrs. Linton wore small frowns as I handed over their cakes.

"I've personally seen and tasted his mushrooms, and they're the best," I said. "He's sure to be as successful in Green Valley as he was in Boston." Hopefully I'd at least planted the seeds for some more charitable gossip than their usual fare. "Have a nice day, ladies."

As they turned to leave, Amber and I surreptitiously high-fived each other. We made a pretty good team.

And maybe this was going to work.

CHAPTER 19

CY

When Mags came over after work that night, she seemed to have had a good day. She looked pleased with herself and gave me a smug little smile when I inquired how things had gone at the bakery, though she didn't elaborate. I hoped it was our washing machine adventure that made her look so satisfied. Thinking about it had made me whistle all day as I mowed and weeded the grounds around the house.

After giving her and Gemma a chance to greet each other like the good friends they now were, I suggested to Gemma she should get her homework finished before dinner. Then I asked Mags to take a walk with me while I left the casserole simmering on the stove.

"Like . . . a hike?" Lifting one foot, Mags held it out for my inspection. "These are my favorite sneakers. They don't do mud."

She was wearing another of her runway outfits. This time, it was high-waisted black pants with a stretchy white top that made her breasts look sensational. It was a shame she wasn't wearing something more casual, but I needed to get her alone, and we should be able to stay clean.

"There's a path," I said. "No mud, I promise."

She was still squinting doubtfully, but I managed to coax her out of the back door.

I'd been thinking about her all day, mulling over how fascinating and fun she was. Last week, I'd watched her serving customers at the bakery and admired her ease with everyone she met. She had a way about her that people responded to.

She had all the qualities I admired, along with a kind of charisma, or magnetic energy, that made it hard for me to take my eyes off her. I could fall hard for her, and before that happened, I wanted to tell her everything about my past and make sure she knew who I was, good and bad.

So that's what I intended to do.

"Where are we going?" she asked.

"Down to the river." I whistled for Zeppelin. "Come on, boy."

The dog raced ahead of us, following the old stone path that meandered through the trees out back, cutting through the woods for five hundred feet or so before it ended at the river. Beside the water, there was a cleared area with some logs for sitting on. The river wasn't deep, but it was wide enough that Ruth and I had never managed to make a rock bridge that would allow us to go all the way across without getting wet.

"This is beautiful," Mags said, looking across to the tangle of tall trees on the far bank.

I nodded my agreement. Dragonflies buzzed softly by, and the water made a nice burbling sound. The trees provided just enough dappled shade to keep the clearing pleasantly cool. It was the kind of place you could sit and dream for hours.

"What are those flowers?" she asked, pointing to a large, leafy plant that crawled along a large part of the river bank. It was covered with clusters of blue flowers.

"That's wild blue phlox."

She wrinkled her nose. "Let me guess. You have an app on your phone that tells you the name of flowers, right?"

"Actually, they were Momma's favorites. They're one of the first flowers to bloom in springtime, and she used to say that when she saw them, she knew winter was truly over. She loved when they appeared. She always picked a bunch to put in the kitchen." I smiled to myself, remembering how happy she used to get when she had a jar full of blooms on the windowsill.

"They're stunning," Mags said.

"Momma used to call them her fresh-start flowers."

That particular memory made my heart ache to think about, so to distract us both, I bent to pick up a small, flat stone. Walking closer to the river, I skimmed the stone across the surface of the water. It jumped three times—no, four times—before disappearing.

Not my best effort by any stretch, but Mags said, "You're good at that."

"Ruth and I used to come down here all the time. We had stone skimming competitions. My best was six jumps."

She picked up a stone and weighed it in her hand. "How is Ruth doing?"

"Better, I think. I spoke to her today and she seemed a little brighter."

"I'm glad." Mags skimmed the stone. It jumped five times and she let out a triumphant, "Yes!" before spinning to face me, her eyes luminous with delight.

"Beginner's luck," I teased.

"You wish." She moved in close and pulled my face close for a kiss.

Her lips felt great and tasted sweet, as though she'd been enjoying delicious treats at the bakery. Her body was warm and pliant, moving against me as though she was hungry for me, and my body responded at once. I hardened against her, teasing her tongue with mine, and groaning as she ground against me. Sliding my hand to her bottom, I pulled her harder against me. She raked my back with her fingernails, her obvious eagerness ratcheting my arousal.

I wanted her. I needed to feel her.

But suddenly, I realized I was backing her against a tree, moving instinctively without conscious intent. And that wasn't what I'd brought her here for.

"Wait." I forced the words from my throat. "Stop."

"Why?" She sounded hoarse. "What's wrong?"

Letting her go, I backed away from her, running a hand through my hair and sucking in a deep breath. Somehow I needed to throw ice water over the parts of me that were on fire for her.

"I want to tell you something, and your lips are very distracting."

She pouted, her gaze still hazy. "So we can't kiss?"

"Afterward. If you still want to."

That seemed to startle her, because her eyes cleared. "What do you mean, if I still want to?"

"Please sit a moment." I waved to one of the giant logs my granddaddy had set in this clearing. Though they'd been here for years, they were sun bleached and hard, and no rot had set in. She settled on one, and I sat a short distance from her, far enough away that I wouldn't be tempted to stop talking so I could kiss her instead. I had to get out what I had to say, and couldn't leave the casserole simmering for long.

She sat, her face turned to me expectantly. "Okay?"

"Ruth and I were over there when my momma died." I pointed to the far side of the clearing. "See where the trees are thick, and behind them, there's an explosion of vines? There's a door there."

She jerked her head around. "Where?"

"See where I'm pointing? Follow the gnarled bit of that tree down and you can make out the door handle."

It took her a few more moments to spot it, but when she did, her eyes widened. "There. I see it! What is that?"

"It's a small hut my daddy built to store all the things he didn't want the police to find."

"Oh?" She squinted harder. "Well, it's a clever hiding place. We're sitting close, and I still wouldn't have noticed it."

"Ruth and I used to keep books and toys in there, for when we needed to stay out of the house for long stretches. Our daddy sold drugs to motorcycle gangs, and some of them would spend time at the house. Ruth and I used to hang out here until they left."

"I'm sorry you had to grow up with so much to fear." Moving closer, she reached out to take my hand, threading her fingers into mine. It was sweet of her, and I brought her fingers to my lips so I could kiss them. But then I lowered them again to keep talking. I had a lot to say, and I needed to get through it.

"The day my mother died, Ruth and I were over there when we heard our daddy hollering for us. When we went back to the house, Momma was lying by the porch steps."

She reached her free hand to cover our linked hands and squeeze, her eyes wide with sympathy. "How awful. I'm so sorry."

"We told the sheriff we saw our momma trip and hit her head. Nobody in town believed us. How could she die falling down a few porch steps? But we wouldn't change our story, and my daddy's friends swore he was with them at the time. The sheriff didn't have enough evidence to charge him."

"You lied to protect him?"

I nodded. "He said if he went to jail, the gangs he sold drugs to would blame us for their supply stopping. And they'd take it out on Ruth."

She sucked in a shocked breath, screwing her face up. "That's awful."

"He was an evil person, and I believed him. So I lied, even though it felt like I was letting my momma down." I frowned, remembering the awful weeks after her death. "And I also let down Sheriff James. He's the one I had to lie to, and he's a good man. He was kind to my sister when others weren't so nice."

"Is the sheriff still around? Maybe it's not too late to tell him the truth. It might make you feel better."

"Maybe."

It wasn't a bad idea. But I didn't want to mull it over now. The only person I'd told about my past was my therapist, and I'd done it bit by bit, over multiple sessions. It was a lot to hit Mags with all at once, but I had to do it before our relationship went any further. She needed to know all the things that had shaped me, and how many of the rumors about me were true.

"After that, I took Ruth to Boston and became another person. I worked nights and studied. When I graduated, I got a good job. I bought a house and an expensive car. I had short hair and no beard. I wore nice suits. Everything about me was different."

Her eyebrows were high. "No beard?" she repeated. "Nice suits?"

"I was clean-shaven." Despite the ordeal of having to tell her my sordid history, I found myself giving her a little smile. "Everything I tell you, and *that's* what you focus on?"

Her lips curved in response. "Shh. I'm trying to imagine it."

I rolled my eyes and she laughed. "Keep going," she urged. "Tell me how you ended up hairy."

"Well, as hard as I was working, I started feeling like everything was fake. Like it was all empty, and none of it mattered. You ever have that feeling?"

She nodded, her expression growing serious again. "I think I know what you mean."

"I was partying too much. Letting the city consume me. Out all night, barely sleeping, spending every minute busy so I wouldn't have time to think." I grimaced, remembering. "But then I got the call to say my daddy had died."

"How did that make you feel?"

It was the same question my therapist asked, and for a moment I felt like I was in her pastel-toned office instead of sitting on a log in the clearing that had been my childhood sanctuary.

"I knew I should feel elated that the murdering bastard was gone," I said. "I should be dancing on his grave. But there were other emotions too. Ones I didn't want to have, because how could any part of me mourn him?"

"He was your father. It's understandable."

"I hated him. But his death made me feel even more untethered." One hand was still clasped in hers, but I put the other on the log beside me, to feel the smoothness of the old wood that had been here since I was a boy.

"Did coming back to Green Valley make you feel any better?" she asked.

"It made everything worse. I had to face everything I'd been trying to forget." I focused on her warm brown eyes, taking comfort in the softness of her expression and the clasp of her hands. "Ruth isn't the only one who struggles with depression," I admitted. "Arriving back here was like sinking into all my bad memories. And I was overwhelmed. For a long time, I couldn't do anything. I didn't renovate the house like I'd intended. I only went out to stock up on food." I lifted one shoulder. "It's hard to describe what it was like. A dark kind of despair sucked everything out of me. And I did nothing at all for over a year."

I watched her as I said it, expecting her to be shocked. But her gaze stayed sympathetic and the pressure on my hand remained steady. The crease between her eyes was one of compassion, not judgement.

"Eventually I found a therapist and started on antidepressants," I said. "It took a while to find the right medication. Then there was some light in the darkness."

"I'm glad." She lifted my hand to her lips and kissed my knuckles.

"Coming back here was good for me, in the end. I've been finding some kind of peace. I still have nightmares, but haven't had a bad day for a while now."

"You've been healing."

I nodded. "If I'd stayed in the city I would have self-destructed. I guess I'm a country guy at heart."

She nodded, though I wasn't sure she could understand that, when she so obviously loved her life in New York.

The thought made me restless. Easing my hand from hers, I got to my feet. A smooth stone was lying a few steps away, and I bent to grab it, then weighed its polished surface in my hand.

"In Nashville, Ruth has been struggling with the same issues," I said. "The other morning, Gemma asked me if she was going to get sick too. I said no, but the truth is, I don't know."

Walking to the bank of the river where it curved inward so the water was calm and still, I skimmed the stone over the water with a practiced flick of my hand. It skipped on the surface once, twice, three times, then disappeared.

Mags came up behind me and put a hand on my arm. When I turned, she was looking at me with such warmth in her eyes, I had to swallow past a sudden lump in my throat.

"Thank you for telling me," she said.

"It's important you know everything."

"Because of what happened this morning?"

I kept my gaze level. "Because I'm falling for you."

After all the truths I'd confessed, it should have been an easy thing to admit to. But my breath caught in my throat as her lips parted and her eyes widened. My confession had caught her by surprise.

And maybe admitting it had been a mistake. She'd only just split up from her rock-star boyfriend, and she'd made her feelings about romance clear. In a few weeks, she'd head back to New York. I was fairly certain she wouldn't want a Tennessee relationship to complicate her life.

"I . . ." She swallowed, giving a little shake of her head. "I didn't expect that."

I gritted my teeth. It wasn't the reaction I'd hoped for, but I'd come this far. No sense in backpedaling now.

"How could I help falling for you?" I asked. "You're beautiful, and you make everything fun. I look forward to seeing you. And I haven't just been buying chocolate cake every day because Gemma likes it."

She frowned, and the doubt in her expression made my heart sink. "I like you, Cy. But I need some time to think. I didn't come here looking for another relationship, and I'm planning on leaving once I fix my Spike problem, so I have no idea how it could work between us in the long term."

I nodded, determined not to let my disappointment show. We were still getting to know each other. I was rushing things, expecting too much. *Feeling* too much.

She needed time, so I'd take a step back and give it to her. After all, I didn't know how things could work between us, either. On paper, we looked like an impossible equation. All I knew was that I wanted to solve it.

"Dinner will burn if we don't head back." Thrusting my hands in my pockets, I started walking toward the house.

She walked with me, her frown heavy. "Cy, I'm sorry."

"Nothing to be sorry about." I forced a smile. "Are you hungry?"

"Starving," she said, trying to smile back. "As usual."

CHAPTER 20

CY

couple of days later, I'd finished my mushroom harvest. The crop had been more successful than I could have imagined. I needed to keep busy, to keep my mind off Mags as much as I could. And it was time to get serious about expanding my business. I had to find some more customers.

The first farm-to-table restaurant I decided to visit that day was on the outskirts of Knoxville, far enough from Green Valley that the name Baxter wouldn't automatically get the door slammed in my face . . . I hoped.

I parked my rusty old pickup truck between a shiny Tesla and an even shinier Corvette in the parking lot. The restaurant was an upscale place, with a hand-painted chalkboard advertising the dinner special: duck egg carbonara with truffles. I'd timed my visit for midmorning hoping there'd be no diners, but a few of the tables were filled with people having either a late breakfast or an early lunch.

All the diners were smartly dressed, while I was in jeans and a polo shirt, carrying a tub of mushrooms, with my nails still a little dirty from the harvest. But when a young hostess in a short dress and heels appeared from the kitchen, she gave me a friendly smile.

"Table for one?" she asked.

"Thanks, but I'm here to speak to your chef."

She vanished back into the kitchen, and a lanky woman in chef's whites emerged, wiping her hands on a dishcloth. "Help you?"

Setting the mushroom tub on the nearest table, I pried off the lid. "You interested in golden oyster and enoki mushrooms?"

She came closer, eyebrows lifted as she gazed down at my crop. Plucking one of the golden oysters out of the tub, she brought it to her nose. "Beautiful color." She closed her eyes for a moment, breathing in, then flicked them back open. "You're a local grower?"

"That's right. My name's Cy Baxter." I spoke slowly and clearly, giving her time to react to my last name.

"Nice to meet you, Cy." She gave no flicker of recognition. "I'm Lucy. Can you give me a price list for your mushrooms?"

My muscles relaxed. "Sure. And I can leave these samples so you can see if they work for your menu. If you want to go ahead, I'll do a regular delivery."

"You'll leave these ones for free?"

"Yes, ma'am."

She gave me a smile. "Then I'll try out some recipes and see how our diners like them."

I left the restaurant feeling encouraged. There were nine more mushroom tubs in my pickup, and I'd planned my route around the restaurants I thought were most likely to be interested. Hopefully they'd all go as well as that one.

It wasn't until the fourth restaurant that I ran into trouble.

The restaurant was called the Crooked Creek Inn, and it was a rustic place, with rough wood floors, creamy linen tablecloths, and fresh wildflowers on each table.

Its owner was an older man with darkly burnished skin, salt-and-pepper hair, and an impressively large, silver mustache. He introduced himself as Mr. Johnson and seemed friendly enough at first. But when I told him my name, he pursed his lips, drawing back and setting his fists on his hips.

"Cy Baxter," he repeated slowly. "You're Ike Baxter's son."

"That's right," I said, keeping both my gaze and my tone level. "But my daddy's dead now, and good riddance."

"I knew your momma from church. Used to see you and your sister there, too."

I nodded. Momma had taken us to church every week, but after she died, Ruth and I hadn't gone back. We'd assumed the congregation wouldn't welcome us.

His eyes narrowed. "When your momma died, folks said she'd been beat to death."

Though it had happened many years ago, his matter-of-fact declaration landed deep into the center of my chest. For a second or two the pain felt fresh and raw all over again, before it settled back into its regular ache.

I forced a breath out of lungs that had momentarily stopped working.

"That's exactly what happened," I said, admitting it out loud for the first time. Finally, I could be honest. It was a relief.

"Your daddy should have gone to jail for it."

"Yes, sir, he should have. You'll get no argument from me."

"But you and your sister were the reason he didn't."

I folded my arms, reflecting his hard gaze back at him. "My sister was only sixteen. She was scared to death of my daddy's friends, and if you're fixing to blame her for anything, we'll be done here, and I won't bother you again."

Ruth was blameless, and anyone who said otherwise could kiss my grits.

Or, as Mags would say, they could fuck right off.

Incredibly, the thought of Mags cursing made me want to laugh. That was a first. Usually when one of the townsfolk was treating me or my sister with suspicion, laughing was the last thing I felt like doing.

"Hmm." Mr. Johnson's frown eased. "I'd forgotten how young she was. But if I remember rightly, weren't you grown up?"

"I was seventeen."

"Just seventeen?" He gave his head a little shake, but his accusatory tone softened. "You've been gone a long time. What are you doing in your daddy's rundown old house?"

"Growing mushrooms." I gestured to the tub I'd put on the table between us. "I've started with enoki and golden oysters, but I'll be adding other varieties. Might not be as profitable as my daddy's marijuana crop, but I figure it's better to grow mushrooms than ask for trouble."

He gave a little snort of amusement. "Never a truer word." Picking up the tub of mushrooms, he brought it to his nose to smell it, something that every chef I'd offered them to so far had done. "And I suppose your daddy finally got served some kind of justice, seeing as he died before his time."

I shrugged. "If the devil likes to barbecue, he has my daddy on his fork."

"Huh. Maybe he does." Mr. Johnson's lips quirked up. Putting down the mushrooms, he stroked one hand over his giant mustache. "Well, Cy Baxter, you and I might be able to do business after all."

Despite my resolution not to care about the folks of Green Valley thinking the worst of me, I felt a rush of relief that made it hard not to smile back at him. Instead I gave him a serious nod. "Then let's talk business."

By the time I walked out of there, I was on such a high, I decided there was something more pressing I needed to do than visiting the other restaurants on my list.

The fact I'd lied to the sheriff about my momma's death had always nagged at me. I couldn't change what had happened, but I could apologize.

The county sheriff's station wasn't a place I'd willingly been to before. To my daddy and brothers, it had been the enemy base camp, to be avoided at all costs. I'd had to go in for questioning after my momma died, but had never been back.

By the time I arrived and went inside, the back of my neck was damp, and my heart was beating too quickly. Still, I asked at the front desk if I could see Sheriff Jeffrey James and was eventually taken to his office where he was sitting behind his big desk.

"Cy Baxter." He stood to greet me. "It's been a while, but I heard you were back in town."

The sheriff looked older and grayer than the last time I'd seen him, and was probably pushing sixty. He was still a distinguished man, and his uniform fit him well. He motioned me into the chair on the other side of his desk before he sat back down.

"I thought it was about time we spoke about what happened all those years ago," I said, cutting right to it.

His eyebrows twitched up, and the spark of interest in his eyes told me he knew what I was talking about, with no clarification needed. "I'd like to hear what you have to say, son."

He'd called me son back then, too. I'd liked that about him. And on his desk, angled so I could just see it, was a photo of his family. The sheriff was standing next to his wife, and in front of him were Jackson and Jessica, his son and daughter. They were all smiling at the camera. The perfect family.

"You were right," I said in a rush. "My daddy killed my momma and I lied about it. If you decide to charge me for lying, or for giving a false statement, I won't fight it. But I want you to know the truth."

I sat back in my chair, feeling better about the confession than I'd expected. Being honest now was too late to do any good, but it still took some weight off.

"I knew what happened," the sheriff said in his calm, thoughtful way. "I've always regretted we couldn't do more." I'd never seen Sheriff James get riled up or upset, which was another thing I liked about him.

"My momma deserved better. And my daddy should have been punished."

He nodded. "Your sister hasn't come back to town with you, has she?"

"Ruth is in Nashville." I frowned, worried as to why he'd asked. "She was being threatened by my daddy's friends and was too afraid to tell the truth. You can charge me with lying but please leave her out of it."

He held up a hand, his eyes kind. "Now, don't get upset. I'm not thinking about charging her."

"Okay." I blew out a breath. "Good."

"Your daddy grew marijuana, didn't he? And he was the middleman for other drugs?"

"Yes, sir. He had a contact he used to meet in Huntsville. He'd collect the product and pass it on to the Iron Wraiths. He was real tight with Razor Dennings."

Razor was the head of the Wraiths, one of the local motorcycle gangs. Our daddy had described how Razor had earned his name by cutting people with a razor blade, carving into their skin. Ruth and I were terrified of him, and when he came around, we'd hide near the river.

"My daddy made it crystal clear what Razor would do to Ruth if we told the truth about momma's death," I said.

The sheriff rubbed his hand over his chin, his thoughtful gaze dropping to the photo of his family. Maybe he was comparing his family to mine.

"You know Razor went to prison a while ago, and he'll be behind bars for the rest of his life?" the sheriff asked.

I nodded. "It's finally safe to speak up."

"I could tell back then that y'all were afraid to tell the truth." He let out a sigh, meeting my gaze. "As much as I wanted to arrest your daddy, I could see you were in a tough place, needing to protect your sister. Thank you for telling me now."

"You're not going to charge me?" I held my breath, waiting for his answer.

"You were as much a victim of Ike Baxter as your momma was." He shook his head. "It wouldn't be right to hold you responsible for his crimes."

I let my breath out slowly. "Thank you, Sheriff."

"Your momma was well-liked, and after she died, there was a lot of talk. I understand why you decided to take your sister someplace else. But at your age, it can't have been easy."

The way he looked at me, it almost seemed like he could see everything I'd experienced, as though it was right there on my face. There was no hiding from Sheriff James.

"It wasn't easy," I admitted. "But we couldn't stay here. I took Ruth to Boston and we managed to get by."

"What were you doing in Boston?"

"Risk analysis for a venture capital company. But now I'm here, I've decided to grow mushrooms and sell them to local restaurants."

He lifted his eyebrows. "That's a pretty big change."

"Yes, sir. I worked behind a desk for a long time, but it always felt like there was something missing, and now I'm here, I'm finding there's something healing about getting my hands dirty and growing something real, instead of being online all the time." I glanced down at my fingernails. Sure enough, they needed a good scrub to get the last traces of this morning's harvest out.

"Well, I wish you success with your business."

Instead of getting up to leave, I hesitated. He was a good man. Though I hadn't intended to tell him about the trouble Mags was in, what could it hurt to have someone else looking out for her?

"Sheriff, there's something else I wanted to talk to you about. Have you met Magdalena Solis? She works at the Donner Bakery?"

"I don't believe I have."

"Well, she's new in town and she came here to escape someone who's been threatening her. A man called Spike. He's a drug dealer from New York, and he told her he was going to travel all the way here to hurt her unless she paid him a lot of money."

He leaned forward, steepling his hands on his desk. "Has she come in to report the threat?"

I shook my head. "She's too afraid of him. And she doesn't know I'm talking to you about it." I could only hope she wouldn't be angry that I hadn't spoken to her first.

His brow furrowed. "What exactly are you hoping I'll be able to do for her, son?"

"Just keep an eye and ear out, in case you hear about any strangers coming to town who might be here to cause trouble."

"I'll keep it in mind," he promised. "And you should encourage her to come in and see me. With an official complaint, we'll be able to do more."

"I will." Giving him a nod, I stood up. "Thank you for your time."

He stood too. Stepping around his desk toward me, he offered me his hand. I hadn't expected the gesture, so it took me a moment to accept.

As I shook his hand, he said, "Your momma would be proud of you, son."

My heart gave an extra beat, tripping over itself and hitting against my ribs. At the same time, a lump formed in my throat. I had to swallow to be able to answer him. "Thank you for saying that, sir. I appreciate it."

CHAPTER 21

MAGDALENA

*P*ulling one of my favorite dresses out of my closet, I handed it to Amber. "You have to wear this. It's perfect for you."

"You'd let me borrow it? It's gorgeous!" Amber held it up to her body and twirled.

"Put it on," Joy urged from where she was lounging on my bed. "You don't happen to have one of those for me, do you Mags?"

"I only worked in a fashion boutique for five years." I rolled my eyes at her. "Of course there's one for you."

Her wide smile was all the reward I needed. And when I helped choose a dress for her, and she looked just as perfect in it as I'd expected, she announced we were going to have the best night ever.

But secretly, I had doubts about how good a Friday night in Green Valley could be. I was used to spending my weekends watching indie rock bands play in hip venues. Would I be able to enjoy an evening at the Green Valley Community Center, followed by drinks at a place called Genie's Country Western Bar?

I mean, we were definitely going to be subjected to a *lot* of country music. And I was also worried because several of my customers had raved about the coleslaw that would apparently be part of the buffet at the community center, kindly advising me to get there early before it ran out.

It seemed like a bad sign that the highlight of our night out might be a salad.

"What are you going to wear, Mags?" Amber asked, browsing through my closet.

"The little black dress." I pulled it out. "It's a classic."

"Beautiful!" Joy grabbed my shoulders, studying my face. "You have such great hair. I'll style it for you. Cy's coming tonight, right? You have to look perfect."

"I hope he'll show," I said. "He sounded reluctant."

"Does he know about your campaign to fix his reputation?"

I shook my head. "I haven't told him."

"Most of the town must be on Team Cy by now," said Amber. "It seems like you've spoken to just about everyone." She turned to Joy. "Will you do my hair too?"

"Of course! Tonight you're finally going to move Wren past the friend zone. You have to look fabulous."

I grinned. It felt great to be hanging out with friends. And by the time Amber, Joy, and I arrived at the bustling community center, we looked like three fashionable New Yorkers in my best designer outfits. But we sure didn't walk into a venue like any I was used to.

The community center was actually an old school, complete with classrooms. Instead of being dimly lit, the lights were bright. Rather than a well-stocked bar, bristling with bottles, there was a buffet table with food. And it wasn't the rhythmic thumping of a drum beat or electric guitar sounds that drifted from one of the classrooms, but the distinctive twang of a banjo, fiddle, and other acoustic instruments. And a male singer was crooning. Yep, that had to be the sound of bluegrass.

In all honesty, I hadn't listened to much bluegrass before. In my head, it had been lumped together with other country music, just with more emphasis on fiddles and banjos, and a picking-at-the-strings sound. But I'd enjoyed the songs Cy had played. And against expectations, the music coming from the classroom made me want to start tapping my feet.

Maybe I *liked* bluegrass?

The realization was disturbing. I was also slightly disturbed by how many of the people in the crowded room I knew. Some of them smiled and waved at me. Julianne MacIntyre, a retired librarian who regularly stopped into the bakery for chocolate brownies, rushed over to complement the three of us on our dresses. I found myself chatting with her, and with Mr. McClure, the fire chief, and wondering how I could possibly be having a good time.

Could it be that I actually fit in here?

Once, the suggestion would have had me scoffing into my Negroni.

Now, it was . . . kind of *nice*?

Who even *was* I?

"Would you excuse us, Mr. McClure?" Joy linked her arm with mine, then Amber's. "We need to talk to someone." She tugged us both away. "There's Wren," she explained in a low tone. "Over in the corner, see?" Pulling her arm free from Amber, she gave her a gentle shove. "Go and say hello."

"But I don't . . ." Amber clamped her mouth shut midsentence as Wren turned and saw her.

Wren blinked, doing a double take. "Amber?" Her gaze traveled down Amber's body before she jerked it back to her eyes. "Wow. You look beautiful."

"Thanks, Wren." Amber's cheeks flushed, but she walked over to the other woman. "You look nice too."

Joy nudged me. "Look how sweet they are together," she whispered.

The dazed way Wren was staring at Amber made me smile. "Let's give them some privacy," I suggested to Joy.

"We can spy on them from the other side of the room," she agreed, leading the way.

But I'd barely taken a few steps before I spotted Cy through the crowd. He was talking to a distinguished-looking older man and a handsome younger man, neither of whom I knew.

"Joy." I caught her arm to stop her. "There's Cy. Who's he talking to?"

That's Sheriff James, and his son, Jackson, who's a deputy. Jackson doesn't come into the bakery because he has a strict diet, and I think Sheriff James must be too busy." Her eyes widened. "Look, the sheriff is shaking Cy's hand. And now Jackson is too."

I shot her a quizzical sideways look. "That's good?"

"Very good." She nodded emphatically. "The sheriff and his family are well respected. People will notice how friendly they are with Cy."

Cy turned his head and saw me. A slow smile spread over his face, and my heart flipped in my chest. I smiled back at him. He was wearing a long-sleeved shirt and fitted jeans, both of which looked spectacular on his burly body. His hair still went well past his collar, but he was easily the best-looking man in the room.

"I remember you mentioning how you weren't a fan of beards," Joy remarked.

"Maybe not. But I don't mind his." All I could think about was how amazing it had felt brushing against the bare skin of my thighs. And how it was rough when he kissed me, but in a good way. A way that sent little shivers of wanting straight into my core.

"Because you like what's underneath." She wagged her eyebrows at me. "And by underneath, I'm not talking about his face. I'm talking about under his clothes."

"Subtle," I told her with a laugh, my gaze still on Cy as he walked toward us.

After our big talk, he'd tapped the brakes on any more physical intimacy. He'd kissed me goodbye when I left his house the last few nights, but our kisses had been brief, and all our clothes had stayed on. Though I appreciated him giving me space, my sexual frustration was driving me crazy.

Still, the last thing I wanted was to hurt him, or myself. We were from different worlds, and I'd be going back to mine soon enough. So, though I was desperate for more than a few brief kisses, I intended to respect his boundaries, be honest with him, and let him decide what he was comfortable with.

She gave a theatrical sigh. "You're as smitten as Amber is. And I feel like a third wheel. I'll go and find someone else to talk to."

"Don't." I linked my arm through hers. "It's our girls' night. I won't run off with him, I promise."

"Hey," said Cy, his voice a low rumble. His gaze was soft on my face as though he wanted to kiss me. My heart fluttered. I wanted to kiss him back. But he turned to Joy and gave her a polite nod. "Hello, Joy."

"Cy." She smiled back at him, extracting her arm from mine. "I'm going to see if Cletus is playing his banjo tonight. I'll catch you two lovebirds later, okay?" She headed off in the direction of the classroom the bluegrass music was coming from.

"You look beautiful, Mags." Cy moved closer. Now I had his sole focus, my skin was getting a pleasurable goose-bumpy feeling. And when he ran his gentle fingers over my arm, I wished we were somewhere private. "Are you having a good night so far?"

"Strangely enough, I am. But Joy and Amber want to go to a country and western bar later, so I'm expecting things to get worse."

"Genie's?"

I nodded. "Is there only one bar in town?"

"There's the Wooden Plank and the Dragon. But both of those places can get rough, especially the Dragon. There's also the Pink Pony, if you're in the mood to watch women take their clothes off." His voice deepened, and his gaze went to my lips.

"Are you in that kind of mood?" I asked it in a flirty way, wishing we could be alone together.

He was still gently touching my arm, and his fingers were pleasantly rough on my skin. My nipples were hard, and probably visible through the dress I was wearing. I would have glanced down to check, only I couldn't tear my gaze from his eyes. I loved how light they were. They were mesmerizing. Like the clearest water in the Arctic, only instead of feeling cold, my skin caught fire everywhere he looked.

He bent his head so his mouth was close to my ear. "Only if the woman is you." His warm breath on my earlobe sent pleasurable shivers down my spine. And when he pulled back, his gaze was so full of heat, I had to swallow to moisten my suddenly dry mouth. I was all but overwhelmed by a rush of wanting to be alone with him. But I couldn't ditch Amber and Joy. That wouldn't be fair.

"Would you like to come to the bar with us?" I asked.

Cy blinked as though he was coming back to himself. "No, thanks." He took a small step back from me, looking around. "I never thought I'd come back here. Most of these people used to cross the street to avoid me."

"They don't look hostile." I scanned the room, ready to glare at anyone who so much as glanced at Cy the wrong way. But everyone was clustered in small groups, talking. I couldn't see anyone looking in our direction.

Cy's forehead creased. "It's strange. One or two folks stopped me on my way in, but it wasn't so they could tell me to leave or accuse me of anything. They stopped me to say hello." He turned his perplexed frown to me. "How is it that they're suddenly being friendly?"

I widened my eyes innocently, giving a shrug. "Maybe your family name doesn't matter as much as you thought."

"I don't get it." He scanned the room again, his brow still furrowed. "Anyway, it isn't as bad here as I expected, but I can't stick around. Gemma wanted to come but I told her she had to stay home." He grimaced. "She may never speak to me again."

"Why didn't you bring her?"

"It'd be a bad time for folks to realize we're related. She's making friends at school, and I don't want anything to mess with that."

"Being seen with you won't ruin her reputation. Next week, you should bring her."

He nodded, flicking his gaze around for a third time. It broke my heart to see him so wary, and made me even more glad I'd spoken to so many people about him.

"Do you have to leave so quickly?" I asked.

"You're having fun with your friends. Enjoy yourself, and I'll see you when you come for dinner tomorrow night."

"Okay." I had to admit, it was nice to hang out with other women. Even though I was longing to be with Cy tonight, I liked Joy and Amber a lot too. And it felt like I'd known them a lot longer than just a couple of weeks.

Putting both hands on Cy's cheeks, I pulled his face down to mine for a kiss. He kissed me back, but it was tentative and brief. Being here clearly made him uncomfortable. And it wasn't fair to try to keep him here if he wasn't ready for it.

"I'll see you tomorrow," I said.

"Count on it." He gave me a look that was so hot and wistful, it made my cheeks heat. Then he turned and strode for the door.

After he'd gone, I checked that Amber and Wren were still talking, then went to find Joy in the classroom where a group of musicians were playing. Chairs had been arranged in rows for the audience, and Joy was sitting in the front.

I slid onto a chair next to Joy and she shot me a smile.

"Where's Cy?" she asked.

"He decided not to stay. But I think my plan is working. He said people were being friendlier."

"That's great." As the song ended, her gaze went back to the band, and she clapped enthusiastically.

When they started playing the next song, I had to admit the band was good. And I recognized most of the musicians, as well as the people who were watching them play. Cletus was playing the banjo, and he was married to Jennifer, the bakery owner. And the man playing the French horn was the bakery's bread maker. He gave Joy and me a friendly smile when we caught his eye.

In fact, there were more people in the room I recognized than people I didn't. Funny how when I'd arrived, I'd felt so alone. Now I was practically a local.

Joy and I watched the band's entire set, then some different musicians played. They were playing something with a fast beat, and some of the crowd had started dancing, when I happened to look around, wondering where Amber and Wren might be.

A man came in through the door at the back of the room. He was wearing a leather jacket and black jeans, and his bleached white hair was very short. His face was familiar, but he wasn't from around here. No, he didn't belong in Green Valley.

My heart stopped.

I stared at him for a long moment in total disbelief. Surely it couldn't be?

Spike, the scary drug dealer.

It was definitely him. I'd met Spike in New York, when he first came looking for his money. He'd turned up at my apartment, and I'd been so scared by our brief meeting, I'd made the snap decision to escape to Carla's place.

And now Spike was here. He'd come after me. And he was clearly looking for me, his cold eyes scanning the room.

I slid all the way off my chair. Easily done, seeing as my bones had dissolved into jelly. Crouching underneath my seat, I tried to control the frantic pounding of my heart.

"Mags?" Joy stared at me with wide eyes. "What are you doing?"

"Don't bend down," I hissed. "And don't look down! Just act normal, okay?"

"What? Why?"

Squirming sideways, I peeked up between the seats. I could just see Spike's bleached, cropped hair. He was still looking around, and I held my breath. My heart was beating so loudly, it was a miracle he couldn't hear it. Thank goodness there was quite a crowd in this room, all gathered to listen to the band.

After a few moments, Spike turned and went back out of the room. I let out a relieved breath, but stayed where I was for the duration of a few more long, torturous minutes.

Finally, I risked standing up. There was no sign of bleached hair.

"I'm so sorry, Joy, I have to go," I told her.

"What? Why?

I hesitated a moment, then shook my head. I hadn't told anyone but Cy about Spike, and now wasn't the time for an explanation. Besides, I didn't want to drag Joy into it. Spike had already threatened my sister. The last thing I'd want would be for Joy to get hurt because of me.

"Sorry, Joy, I don't have time to explain now. Please apologize to Amber for me, and I'll call you tomorrow, okay?"

Without waiting for her reply, I rushed for the door. Hugging the wall, I checked through the doorway. No sign of Spike. The crowd was densely packed, especially near the buffet table. Heart thumping, I slipped out through the main doors and ran desperately for my pickup.

CHAPTER 22

CY

I was reading in bed when a soft knock came from the front door. I glanced at my phone. It was only nine o'clock, and early to be in bed, but I was planning to get up at the crack of dawn so I could start painting the walls in the living room.

Getting up, I pulled on a pair of sweatpants and tiptoed to the door shirtless, not wanting to disturb Gemma in case she was asleep. When I opened it, Mags was standing in the dark on my doorstep, still clad in the sexy black dress she'd been in when I'd seen her at the community center.

"Mags? Are you okay?" I kept my voice low as I drew her inside.

She looked gorgeous, but just one glance at her pale cheeks and stricken expression meant all I could focus on was what might have happened to her. Something was clearly very wrong.

"I saw Spike." She matched the low volume of my voice. "The scary drug dealer is here, looking for me. He was at the jam session."

My gut clenched. "Did he see you?" I demanded.

"No. I hid, then slipped out."

"Come in. You're shivering." Drawing her inside, I couldn't help but glance at Gemma's closed door. My first responsibility was to keep her safe, and by bringing Mags inside, I could be inviting trouble in too, putting Gemma in danger.

But no, I wouldn't let it come to that.

"You're cold. Sit down. I'll make you a hot cocoa." Fetching a blanket, I wrapped it around Mag's shoulders then gave her upper arms a vigorous rub. "Don't worry. You're safe now. I'll keep you safe."

I'd keep them both safe, her and Gemma. No matter what.

"I shouldn't be this cold," she said. "I was fine before."

"You've had a shock." I sat her down on the couch, then went to the kitchen to make hot cocoa. By the time I handed her a steaming mug, I was glad to see she'd stopped shivering and regained a little color.

"I didn't think he'd come all this way." She cupped her hands around the mug. "It's only ten thousand dollars. Why would he come here?"

"I won't let anything happen to you," I promised. "We'll go to the sheriff."

"What can the sheriff do, though? He can't arrest Spike for coming to Tennessee. It's not a crime."

"If the sheriff can't help, I'll meet with Spike and sort everything out."

If I had to, I'd pay the drug dealer ten thousand dollars to get him to leave Mags alone and keep him away from Gemma. But the idea of giving a man like him money left a bitter taste in my mouth.

I'd grown up around violence, and had the potential for it inside me, though I'd sworn never to use my fists in anger. Maybe it was time to consider breaking that vow.

I went to fetch the hot cocoa I'd made for myself, and when I walked back into the living room to join her on the couch, her gaze traveled down my body.

"Is that what you wear at night?" she asked. "Gray sweatpants and no shirt?"

I frowned, confused by her question, but at the same time relieved to hear a little bite return to her voice. "I don't wear clothes to bed. I put these pants on when you knocked. Why? What's wrong with them?" I squinted one eye at her. "You're not going to tell me sweatpants are the same as flannel, are you? At this rate, I won't have anything left in my closet."

"Gray sweatpants aren't at all like flannel." She lifted the cup to her lips and spoke around it, her gaze on my torso. "What's wrong with them is that there's nothing wrong with them."

I put my mug on the coffee table. "What are you saying?"

"You used to work behind a desk, right? So how come you look like that?" She waved her hand up and down my body. "Did you *live* at the gym? Do you take steroids? Did you get bitten by a radioactive rhino?"

Understanding came to me in a rush. "This house only has fireplaces for heating. In winter, it gets freezing, so I've been chopping a lot of wood."

The house's lack of heating had been a blessing in disguise last winter, as the choice between freezing to death or getting up regularly to put fresh wood on the fire had kept my mood from being totally swallowed up by the darkness. And all the exercise I'd gotten from the chopping had helped as well.

Now it was paying off in other ways. The compliment was nice to hear. It made me feel warmer than the hot cocoa had. But I didn't want to stand around shirtless if it was going to make her uncomfortable.

"I'll put on a shirt," I said, moving into the bedroom.

"Don't get dressed on my account," she called to me.

I grabbed a clean T-shirt anyway, and pulled it on.

When I came out of the bedroom, she said, "I don't want you to meet with Spike. He'll probably be armed."

"Who says I'm not?" I took a seat on the couch next to her.

She shook her head. "You're not going to confront him. You're not dying on my behalf, and you're not killing anyone either."

"Then we go to the sheriff."

She took a sip of her cocoa and swallowed with a frown. "At first I didn't call the cops because I promised Eric I wouldn't. But I've been trying to figure out what they can do for me. If I tell them he's here to intimidate me until I give him money, will that be enough to arrest him? If all they can do without proof is give him a warning, it'll only make him more dangerous."

"Sheriff James is a good man. Anything he can do, you can be sure he'll do it."

"But it's my family that could be in danger. What if I go to the police and he retaliates by hurting my sisters?"

She made a good point. But if Mags didn't go to the sheriff, I'd be forced to deal with Spike myself. And how could I do that without endangering Gem?

My eyes went back to Gemma's door, some primal part of my brain needing to make sure it was still closed and she was still safe.

Mags followed my gaze, and she made a sharp sound, her mouth twisting. "Shit. You're worried about Gemma, aren't you?" Putting her mug on the coffee table, she stood. "I didn't think of that. I'm so sorry. I shouldn't have come here."

"Yes, you should have." I stood too, putting my arm around her waist to stop her from rushing out. "Sit down. I can keep both you and Gem safe."

She was chewing on her lip. "But it's not fair to drag you into my mess."

"I'm glad you did." I was surprised to find the words coming out so forcefully, and even more surprised by the realization that I meant them so wholeheartedly, with no reservations. "Of course I'm worried about Gem. But I won't let you deal with this guy alone. We're in this together, no matter what."

Her cheeks flushed. "Thank you." She put her hand on my chest. "If Spike did anything to threaten Gemma, I'd never forgive myself. But thank you for saying that."

I drew her into a hug, squeezing her tight for a moment. With both my arms around her, she seemed so vulnerable, I could hardly bear it. Rage simmered in my gut, a primal anger that whispered the need to commit acts of violence against the man who'd threatened her. Part of me wanted nothing more than to tear his limbs off.

"Sit down." The anger made my words hard, so it came out sounding like an order. "Finish your cocoa."

She sat obediently, then picked up her mug and took a sip.

I sat next to her, thinking dark thoughts about my family's history of violence, and the uncomfortable realization that murderous urges were closer to my surface than I'd ever wanted to believe.

Mags's gaze was on my face while she sipped her cocoa. When she swallowed, she looked as though she wanted to say something. But after opening her mouth, she closed it again and gave a little sigh.

Finally she nodded to the living room walls. I'd spent the day sanding them and coating them with a stark white primer. "You've started painting." Her tone had become artificially bright.

I turned to glance at them. "That's just the primer. Gemma helped me picked a shade, so that'll go on next, after I've sanded the floors."

"Well, it looks better already." She drew the blanket tighter around her body. Her mug was poking out of her blanket cave and she had both of her hands wrapped around it.

"You're still cold?"

She gave a little shiver. "Must be the fright of seeing Spike. I'm still trying to calm down."

"First thing is to get warm." I stood and took the mug out of her hands. "Get into bed. Go on." I nodded toward my bedroom, cursing the fact I'd put some of my painting equipment into the spare room.

She blinked up at me. "Into bed?"

"You're sleeping here tonight, and I won't hear any arguments." I steered her into the bedroom. "Take my bed. I'll take the couch."

"But I can't stay here. When I went out tonight, I left Zeppelin at my place. Freud and the chickens would be fine without me for one night, but Zeppelin needs to go out to pee."

"I'll go and get Zeppelin. It'll only take me a few minutes." I was already grabbing my shoes. "While I'm gone, get into bed. Grab yourself a T-shirt or whatever you want to sleep in from out of my drawers."

I brushed off her protests, left quickly, and drove to her place while keeping my eyes peeled for anyone on the road. I thought about calling the station, but Sheriff James had been at the community center earlier, so he was off duty. He'd be home by now, probably in bed, and he was the only one I trusted to take me seriously. A Baxter asking for help from the sheriff's department was unheard of.

Mags would be safe at my place tonight, and we could go and see the sheriff first thing in the morning.

I let myself into her place, checked the cat was safely asleep on the bed, and collected Zeppelin, locking all the doors and windows behind me. Once I was back at my place, I rapped gently on the bedroom door. "Mags?" I called softly through the closed door.

"Come in."

On hearing her voice, Zeppelin wagged his tail and nosed at the door. As soon as I opened it, he rushed in, tail wagging. He jumped straight onto the bed and tried to lick Mags's face. She pushed him aside, smiling.

She was in bed with the blankets pulled up under her arms, and it looked like she was wearing one of my old T-shirts. Her long dark hair was splayed across the pillow. My heart beat faster to see her in my bed, and I could only wish she was there under better circumstances.

At least she was safe. That was the important thing.

"Feeling warmer?" I asked, staying at the door.

"Much warmer. Thank you, Cy."

"Do you need anything? Water? More cocoa?"

"Nothing, thanks."

"Then I'll say good night. Call out if you need—"

"You should sleep here tonight," she interrupted. "It's a big bed." She patted the space beside her. "Get in, Cy. The couch is far too small for you."

I shook my head. She'd had a bad fright and I wasn't about to take advantage of that. "I'll be fine."

She bit her lip. "Honestly, I'm still a little freaked out. I'd rather not be alone."

I hesitated, torn between wanting to comfort her, and wanting to do the right thing. "Zeppelin can sleep with you," I said. "I'll be right outside the door. Nobody will be able to get in."

"It's not the same. I'll still feel alone."

"Mags, you've had a scare. It wouldn't be right for me to get in bed with you when you're—"

"You're trying to be chivalrous," she interrupted. "And that's nice. But if you turn off your southern-gentleman setting, we'll both sleep better. There's plenty of room in here, and nothing has to happen." She held up both palms. "I promise I'll be good and keep my hands to myself." A lopsided smile peeked out. "Unless you want to be bad?"

CHAPTER 23

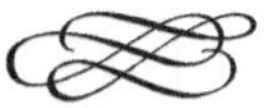

MAGDALENA

I woke with a start. It was early. The room had lightened a little, but it was still what I would call dark. Clearly too early to get up. Cy lay sleeping beside me, and Zeppelin was lying on my feet, snoring.

Cy was on his side, facing me, his chest rising and falling with each breath, and his lips slightly parted. He looked peaceful.

Last night, he'd agreed to share the bed with me, but to my disappointment, he'd only given me a chaste kiss good night, then rolled over and gone to sleep.

Now, at least, I had the chance to study his face while he slept. His cheek looked so smooth before it disappeared into his beard, I could barely resist the urge to trail my finger over it. Even without being able to see the beauty of his eyes, I was still struck by how handsome he was. His cheekbones were sharp, his face angular. His nose straight and strong. His features were classically perfect, even if his long hair was messy.

How had I not seen how handsome he was from the very first glance? Had I been blind? Or blinded by prejudice?

Truth was, now I'd gotten to know his caring, capable nature, that was what I mostly saw. The physical things—like how his eyes could be the color of ice water yet warm me to my core, or how mouthwateringly wide his shoulders were—those things were a bonus. A very nice bonus, sure. But the thing I most appreciated was how determined he was to protect me. Nobody had ever stepped up for me like that before.

And there was the way he made mushrooms seem fascinating. *Mushrooms!* I mean, how ridiculous to be interested in mushrooms, yet when he'd compared them to music, I'd been in awe of him. He was quietly clever, not a show-off like Eric. Cy had a whole lot more substance.

He was the type of man I could fall hard for, and honestly, I was more than halfway there already.

The blankets weren't far above waist level. And as Cy must have rolled over during the night, the T-shirt he'd worn to bed had twisted, pulling tight around his biceps and chest. Even relaxed in sleep, his muscles were impressive. His large, capable hand was curled below the pillow.

I tugged my feet out from underneath Zeppelin's solid weight, and the dog lifted his hand and thumped his tail on the bed a couple of times, probably hoping that I was about to get up to let him outside. But I had other ideas on my mind.

I moved closer to Cy, compelled by an overwhelming urge to breathe his air. By moving to the very edge of my pillow, our faces were only inches away. But it wasn't enough. I shifted my head onto the edge of his pillow so our noses were almost touching.

Cy's eyes fluttered open. My breath stopped at the sight of his pale irises, his eyes ringed with dark eyelashes. A slow smile lifted his mouth as his eyes focused on me. His hand uncurled and he shifted it up so his fingers brushed my chin.

"Morning," I said softly.

"It doesn't seem like morning yet. It's still dark." His voice was a sexy rumble, rough with sleep.

"Well, I was forced to wake you, seeing as you were snoring so loudly, you were scaring Zeppelin."

His lips quirked. "I don't snore. But I'm not going to argue seeing as you're such a nice sight to wake up to."

I inched my face a little closer. "You're not so bad either."

"Was that a compliment? Careful, Brooklyn. Don't get mushy."

"Never." I put my palm against his beard and kissed him softly.

He slid his arm over my back, pulling me against him. I snuggled into his warm bulk as he deepened the kiss.

He let out a low groan, and all at once the kiss became a whole lot hotter. Pulling me hard against his body, he nipped at my lips, then took my tongue with his, his mouth firm and demanding.

An overwhelming need for him surged in me as his erection pressed into me. He was barely contained inside the boxer briefs he'd worn to bed, and he felt like hardened steel. He shoved my T-shirt higher with urgent hands, as though his survival depended on caressing my bare skin.

I realized I was making embarrassing panting sounds, but I couldn't bring myself to care. I clawed at his T-shirt, desperate to have it out of the way, to be able to touch him everywhere. With an impatient grunt, he yanked his shirt off in one quick movement. Then he grabbed mine and pulled it off me, tugging it over my head as though it were on fire.

And oh God, it was so much better without all that fabric. Ever since I'd seen him shirtless, I'd been dying to run my hands over the hard ridges of his muscled body. He had a smattering of dark hair across his chest and I pushed my hand into it, loving the rough, manly feel of it. His burliness was such a turn on. I loved his hard slabs of muscle and washboard abs. He was all male and total perfection.

His hand went to my breast, cupping and pinching and soothing. Then his mouth was on my nipple. His tongue swirled over my peak, making me gasp with pleasure.

"I want you," Cy growled against my skin.

"Yes, yes," I moaned breathlessly, before a sliver of reason forced itself into my brain. "But what about Gemma?"

"She'll be asleep. We have to be quiet."

"Quiet. Yes. I can do that." He could have said we'd have to make a blood sacrifice, and my answer would have been the same. My need was overwhelming. The ache between my thighs was driving me beyond reason, making me mindless.

I pushed my hand into his boxer briefs and my hand closed around his erection. He made a sound of pleasure, a groan on an intake of breath, and I stroked down his length. He was thick and long. Silky smooth skin over iron. More perfection.

His cock was magnificent. And I was overwhelmed by a sudden urge to taste him. Sliding down his body, I yanked his boxer briefs down.

"Mags." He made as though to pull me back up, but I was determined. I wanted to feel him on my tongue. To take him into my mouth and give him the same pleasure he'd given me.

I pulled the blankets off as I traveled down, exposing us both to the chilly morning air. With one hand wrapped around the base of his cock, I licked its tip with the flat of my tongue. He groaned and I looked up at him. His eyes were hazy, his expression raw as he gazed back at me.

"Mags," he said softly. "I want to be inside you."

"You will be," I promised. "In a moment. First, I need to . . ." Instead of finishing the thought, I took him inside my mouth.

His fingers dug into my hair, and the tortured-sounding moan he let out made the ache between my legs more insistent. I slid my lips as far down his shaft as I could go, then pulled back up, swirling my tongue around the head of his cock as I went.

"Fuck," he hissed. His face contorted as though he was in agony, and a thrill shot down my spine. I loved seeing him so turned on. I wanted to keep going, to drive him to the edge of orgasm . . . But the tightness between my thighs was all but unbearable. I needed him inside me.

I sucked him into my mouth as far as I could take him twice more, then licked his length from base to tip as though I was licking an ice cream. When I finally moved back up his body, to kiss his lips, his breathing was shallow and his eyes dark.

He shoved my panties down as though he was desperate for me, spreading me and driving his fingers roughly into me. It was such a relief to feel them, I cried out with pleasure, but he covered my mouth with his, kissing away my cries.

"I'll get a condom," he said in a strangled tone, his mouth still on mine, his fingers plunging into me.

Up until now, I'd always used a condom and never considered going without. But I couldn't bear the thought of him moving away from me, even for a second.

"No need," I panted. I couldn't wait long enough even to explain that I was on birth control. I just rolled him on top of me, wrapping my legs around his hips.

He didn't argue, just fumbled for a moment, positioning himself at my entrance. Then he pushed inside me, filling me completely, and the sensation was so incredible, I thought I might die from the pleasure.

"Fuck, Mags." He bit my shoulder, my neck, driving his length in and out of me, punishing me with his size in the best possible way.

His teeth and tongue savaged and devoured my skin while I clawed at his shoulders, pulling him down onto me. I couldn't get enough. I wanted him closer. I wanted him deeper. I wanted all of him inside me as far as he could go.

Without pulling out, he scooped me up and flipped us both over so he was sitting on the bed, and I was straddling him. Then he put his arms around me, pulling me hard onto his cock. Helping me grind myself down onto him.

The position rubbed my most sensitive parts against his body, driving my pleasure higher. The sensation built rapidly, swirling and growing like the clouds above a forming tornado. When I felt his cock swell in me, I knew he was close too. The knowledge drove me over the edge, and I exploded in orgasm. I came so hard and so furiously, I was no longer flesh and blood, but for an endless moment, I was nothing but light and pleasure and pure sensation.

When I finally came back to myself, I was whimpering, my body jerking over his, rocking with the intensity of my climax. Cy made a sound that was half growl, half groan, and thrust upward, harder and faster, until he was coming too, his cock pulsing as he filled me.

Afterward, he kissed me gently, his eyes warm and cherishing. I lay on his chest and listened to the strong, steady beat of his heart. I felt close to him, surrounded by his warmth. Protected, safe, and loved.

But slowly, as my glorious mindlessness began to ebb, my anxious thoughts returned. Despite the sanctuary of Cy's bed, danger still lurked outside. Somewhere out there, Spike was looking for me. And no matter how firm Cy was about not turning me away, I'd thoughtlessly put Gemma in danger by coming to his house. If Spike managed to track me down, or discover my connection to Cy, he could threaten her.

As secure as I felt circled inside his arms, I felt guilty, too.

The hard truth was that I shouldn't have come here and put my problems on Cy's shoulders. And the only way to rectify my mistake would be to do what Cy wanted and go to the sheriff.

I could only pray that didn't make everything worse.

CHAPTER 24

MAGDALENA

Cy had fallen back asleep, but Zeppelin was up, standing next to the bed, whining softly. He clearly needed to go outside and pee.

The very last thing I wanted to do was move away from Cy's warm, comfortable body. But I had to take Zeppelin out. Then I should sneak away, back to my place. It wasn't just that I didn't want to put Gemma in danger. I also didn't want her to wake up and find me in bed with Cy. He hadn't expected me to turn up, or stay overnight, and we hadn't talked about whether he was comfortable with Gemma knowing about us. It wouldn't be fair to just assume he'd be okay with her discovering we'd slept together.

Slipping out of bed, I picked up the bra and black dress I'd worn the night before, and wriggled into them as quietly as possible. I discovered my panties on the floor beside the bed. Cy didn't stir as I dressed, grabbed the small handbag I'd used for my night out, then slipped out of the bedroom.

"Do your business quickly," I whispered to Zeppelin as I tiptoed through the living room and out of the back door. "Then we'll head home to feed Freud and the chickens."

A pair of sneakers that had to belong to Gemma were sitting beside the back door. I slipped them on instead of my high heels, hoping she wouldn't mind if I borrowed them briefly. By the time I had them in place, Zeppelin was running over the lawn on the other side of the barn, toward the trees.

Dammit, I'd forgotten his leash.

I ducked back inside to get it, then went after Zeppelin, enjoying the cool, fresh air as I walked. The morning was crisp, and beads of dew hung on the tops of the grass like tiny jewels. My bare arms and legs were chilly, but the trees in front of me had a quiet kind of majesty, drawing me toward them. There were some wildflowers along the edge of the tree line, and a bird caught my eye as it swooped, catching bugs.

Okay, so I could see why Carla liked Tennessee so much. It might be quiet, but the scenery was stunning.

Zeppelin was sniffing around happily, peeing on everything within leg-cocking distance. He caught the scent of something, barked, and raced off into the trees.

"Zeppelin," I whisper-shouted, not daring to call out too loudly. "Come back!" I walked swiftly after him into the woods, following the same path Cy had shown me. And I didn't need to walk for long before I emerged into the pretty clearing next to the river. Zeppelin was down by the water, sniffing his way along the bank.

In the morning light, the hidden shed Cy's father had built was just as hard to see as it had been when Cy had pointed it out. It was behind a thick grouping of trees which did a good job of hiding it. The door was covered with moss, and vines hung over it, further obscuring it.

Curiosity made me walk closer, picking my way across leaves and twigs to get there. It was so well camouflaged, it wasn't until I was standing in front of it that I could see the shape of the door. Judging by its covering of vines, it can't have been opened for a while.

Cy said he and his sister used to store their books and toys in the shed. Maybe some of them were still in there.

I took hold of the handle, expecting it to be locked, or for the door to be jammed shut. But when I tugged it, the old door creaked open, pulling free from the vines. Inside, it was so dark, I could only make out some lumpy shapes.

Extracting my phone from my bag, I switched on the flashlight. The beam of light revealed the shed was full of large plastic bundles. Dozens of them, stacked high.

Leaning closer, I peered at one of the bags. It was about a foot square and thickly wrapped with plastic that reflected the flashlight and made it hard to see what was inside. Judging from the rounded shape of the bundle, it had to be something organic.

A marijuana harvest?

That seemed the most likely explanation.

Did Cy know he had a shed full of weed? Surely he had to know. But why wouldn't he have turned it over to the police? Could he be storing it, planning to sell it?

My heart was hammering and I glanced behind me, a picture flashing through my mind of being caught with such a sizable stash. I could imagine the heavy hand of a policeman coming down on my shoulder, and my stuttered explanation being swept aside.

Swallowing hard, I shoved my phone back in my handbag and rushed to the water's edge to clip the leash to Zeppelin's collar.

I strode quickly back to Cy's place, tugging Zeppelin with me. To my relief, it was quiet. It was too early for Gemma to be awake, and when I crept in, the sound of Cy's deep breaths was reassuring. Thank goodness he was still asleep, because my stomach had filled with acid and my thoughts were heading into bad places.

I was sure Cy was honorable. And my gut told me he wouldn't lie to me.

But could I trust my gut?

After all, I'd ignored Eric's red flags, making excuses for his bad behavior and allowing it to get worse. Was I fundamentally broken? Did I want so badly for Cy to be the man I believed in that I was willing to overlook warning signs, just as I'd done with Eric?

If it hadn't been for my experience with Eric, I wouldn't hesitate to wake Cy up and simply ask him about the drugs. And if he told me he didn't know about them, I would have believed him without question. But now I wasn't so sure my judgement was sound.

I needed time to think. And I needed coffee. Lots of coffee.

Grabbing my bag and keys from where I'd left them, I snuck back out. I bundled Zeppelin into Noah's pickup as silently as I could. Then I drove away.

CHAPTER 25

CY

When I woke up, sunshine was streaming into the bedroom, and I felt fantastic. No nightmares last night, for a change. At least none that I could remember. And the way Mags had woken me early . . . well, that had been by far the best early wake up I'd ever experienced.

Rolling over, I stroked a hand over the empty space in the bed beside me. The sheets were cold, so Mags must have gotten up a while ago. I sat up and stretched, looking around. She wasn't in the bedroom.

Where was she? In the bathroom or the kitchen, perhaps? I couldn't hear any sounds.

Catching the urgency of my own thoughts, I smiled at myself. Though I'd been awake only minutes, already I missed Mags. I wanted more of her. A whole lot more.

Getting up, I pulled on pants and a shirt, and padded barefoot out to the kitchen. She wasn't there, or in the bathroom. She wasn't anywhere in the house, and neither was Zeppelin.

She must have taken Zeppelin for his early morning walk. Maybe I should make breakfast in the meantime and see if I could convince her to slip back into bed afterward. She'd want coffee first though, at least.

Cracking the back door open, I stuck my head into the crisp morning air to see if I could spot her or Zeppelin near the barn, or at the edge of the woods.

There was no sign of them.

Disquiet stirred in my gut.

Gemma wasn't up yet, but it wasn't exactly early. Zeppelin usually wanted to go out a lot earlier than this. She should have been back by now, and surely would have woken me before leaving.

What if Spike had found her? An image flashed through my head of rough hands grabbing her while she was outside and dragging her away.

I pulled on some shoes, then went out the back door, scanning my surroundings and debating whether to go into the woods first, or circle the house. Better to check around the house, I decided, heading down the side.

At the driveway, I stopped.

Mags's pickup was gone.

But why would she leave without waking me, or at least leaving a note?

My stomach churned, unease deepening into worry. With flames painted over it, the truck was distinctive. If Spike knew she was driving it, and had spotted it parked here . . .

Instead of letting my anxious thoughts get stuck down that path, I went back to the house for my keys, scribbled a quick note promising Gemma I'd be back soon, then jumped in my truck and floored it, heading to Mags's place as fast as the ancient pickup would take me.

When I rounded the corner and her house came into view, some of the tightness in my chest eased. Her pickup was parked out front. I pulled in behind it, rushed to her door and knocked loudly, calling her name.

She opened the door, and my muscles sagged.

"I thought something had happened," I said in a rush of relief. "Are you okay?"

Zeppelin came bouncing past her, out of the house. With a joyful bark, he jumped on my legs before racing back inside.

"Yes, I'm fine," she said, not moving from inside the doorway.

Despite her assurance, she didn't look or sound fine. The woman who'd fallen asleep wrapped in my arms was now frowning at me, her expression troubled. She didn't invite me in, but just stared at me as though searching for something in my face.

"What is it?" I asked. "What's wrong?"

She blew out a breath, running a hand over her hair as though she needed a moment to think. She'd changed into jeans and a long-sleeved top, and though she looked as lovely as ever, I couldn't focus on anything but the wariness in her eyes.

"It's not Spike?" I asked. "You didn't see him?" As I peered behind her, my chest tightened at the thought he could be hiding back there in the shadows.

But no, I couldn't detect any fear in her expression. If anything, she seemed upset with me. Something had given her that stiff posture and distant tone, and if it wasn't Spike, it had to be something I'd done.

Did she regret making love with me?

The idea was a knife in my heart. It hit me with such sharp, intense pain, I almost staggered.

"It's not Spike," she said, deepening my fear. Then she straightened, pulling her shoulders back and breathing in as though to brace herself against an invisible enemy. "Why is your father's secret shed full of drugs?"

Her question was sharp, and so unexpected that at first the words didn't seem to make sense.

"What?" I asked.

"Drugs," she repeated. "Bags and bags of weed."

"In my father's shed?"

"You didn't know?" She crossed her arms, her eyes narrow.

Her suspicious expression hit me just as hard as the idea she might regret what we'd done. I'd seen that look of mistrust all too often, but never on the face of anyone I cared for so much.

I was used to folks thinking the worst of me. But not Mags. Not after everything that had happened between us. I'd thought I could trust her not to treat me as though I was nothing more than a Baxter, no better than my daddy or brothers.

Though I was swallowing razor blades, I kept my gaze level, locked to her eyes. "I haven't looked inside the shed since I've been back in Green Valley."

I didn't expect her to believe me, and sure enough her expression stayed wary. "You've been here over a year," she said.

"What would I need in the shed? If my daddy still has his harvest stored in there, well that didn't occur to me." It was my turn to fold my arms across my chest. All I could do was tell the truth and try to shield my heart from the accusation in her stare. I couldn't make her believe me.

"You never looked?" Her tone was still blunt, but her expression softened.

"It was overgrown. Vines over the door." I clenched my jaw. "Well, you saw it."

Surely it was obvious nobody had opened that shed for longer than the time I'd been back. It hurt that she still doubted me. And that maybe the feelings I'd been having for her were more one-sided than I'd wanted to believe.

"I wasn't sure how fast those vines grow," she said.

"When I first moved into the house, some of my daddy's old buyers turned up, asking questions. As far as I know, nobody but my daddy knew about that shed. I told his buyers the barn had been ransacked before I arrived, when I'd pulled out his crop and burned it myself."

"And they believed you?" She uncrossed her arms, dropping her hands by her sides. Her frown had faded, and the suspicion was easing from her tone. But my throat was still tight, and my chest still felt like she'd landed a heavy blow.

"They seemed to. It helped that there's been all kinds of disruption inside the local motorcycle gang. The head of the gang was arrested, and they're more disjointed than they used to be." I lifted a shoulder. "Anyway, nobody's bothered me for months."

"I want to trust you." A raw edge bled into her tone. Her eyes creased as though she was hurting as much as I was, and she stretched out a hand as though she wanted to touch me but couldn't quite bridge the gap. "Eric made me doubt my own judgement. I hate feeling like I don't know what's true."

My heart twisted, and all I wanted to do was take her in my arms.

"I can prove it." Dropping my hands to my sides, I squeezed them into fists. "I'll go and tell Sheriff James about the drugs right now. I bet they're covered in a layer of dust. He'll see they can't have been touched since before my daddy died. He's a good man, and you can trust him."

"You'd do that?" She stepped into me, putting her arms around my waist. I didn't resist as she pulled our bodies together, mashing her face into my shoulder. "I'm sorry," she mumbled. "After everything, I just had to be sure."

I tightened my arms around her, hugging her closer. Then I smoothed her hair and kissed the top of her head. "I get it," I said. And I did. However badly it had hurt to see her mistrust me, I could tell those feelings had also pained her.

Putting my fingers under her chin, I lifted her face, meaning to kiss her. But when I caught sight of her eyes and saw the unshed tears glistening there, my heart cracked into pieces.

"It's okay," I whispered. "We're okay."

She swallowed, nodding, and I kissed her lips gently, reassuring her with soft touches. She felt so good pressed against me, the last traces of pain vanished, replaced with relief. Mags would be okay. She was in my arms, and Spike hadn't hurt her. Those were the only things that really mattered.

"I'm sorry," she said again, giving me a little smile. I was glad to see tears were no longer threatening.

I dropped my forehead to hers. "Don't be sorry, sweetheart. We'll go to Sheriff James together. I'll tell him about the drugs, and you can tell him about Spike."

"Thank you." She sighed, closing her eyes. "Funny that we need to talk to the sheriff about a drug dealer *and* a pile of drugs."

Her eyes flicked open, and she pulled back to look at me, her eyes widening. "Wait. I have an idea." She clutched my arms. "We have two problems, but they might cancel each other out. I mean, what if one problem could be the solution for the other?"

I raised questioning eyebrows, then all at once, I could tell what she was thinking. A drug dealer and a pile of drugs . . . putting them together, a possible solution did seem obvious. We had to be considering the same thing.

But that didn't mean resolving both problems would be easy. Or that it wouldn't be dangerous.

CHAPTER 26

CY

Several hours later, I stood next to my old pickup truck which was parked past the far side of town, about as far from where Mags was staying as it was possible to get. There weren't any houses around here. It was a small, dirt access road leading to one of the many walking trails around here, just a rarely used loop that cut into the woods a short distance.

Night had fallen, and there wasn't much of a moon. The silent road was dark, lined with nothing but trees on both sides. Not even a firefly to cast a glow.

Though I was nervous, I resisted the urge to pace back and forth, instead leaning back against the hood of the car, my legs crossed at the ankles. I put my hands in my pockets and pretended I did this kind of thing on the regular.

My pickup was full of drugs.

In fact, it was so full of drugs, it gave new meaning to the word *loaded*.

I glanced to the cab of my truck, wondering if I should mention the word-play to Mags. She'd probably think it was funny. Only I was still kind of mad she was with me at all. I'd argued hard to come alone. She didn't need to be here.

But hell, she was stubborn. And here she was.

At least I'd managed to extract a promise that she'd stay in the truck and keep quiet. She was scrunched around in the passenger seat so she could gaze out of the back window. And it was dark enough that I could barely see her silhouette, so maybe this Spike guy wouldn't even know she was here.

I heard the roar of a car engine approaching. A moment later, headlights shone into my eyes, making me squint and turn my face away. Music was playing inside the car, the *thump, thump* of the bass beat clearly audible as the car rolled close.

My heart rate kicked up. This was it. Showtime.

The car stopped when its front bumper was only a few feet from the back of my pickup. The engine died, and the loud music cut off. The headlights stayed on, making it all but impossible for me to see anything.

Both car doors opened. Squinting into the bright light, I caught the dark shape of a man unfolding himself from the driver's side. Another man was getting out of the passenger's side.

"Are you Spike?" I called.

"Who the fuck are you?" the driver growled. He had his hood up and I couldn't make out his features.

"A friend of Magdalena's." I nodded my head back, indicating the pickup's bed. "The truck's got what you want, like she told you. Y'all can take it all, just don't bother her again." Slowing down my speech, I exaggerated my accent. Mags had made disparaging assumptions about me based on where I lived and how I looked. Hopefully these New Yorkers would too. Better if they thought I was harmless.

"You armed?" the driver demanded. He was clearly in charge, so he had to be Spike.

"Nope." I held up both hands. "I ain't looking for trouble. What's in the truck is worth a whole lot more than she owes you. Ten times, at least." I had no idea of the street value of my daddy's stash, but Spike could judge for himself.

Both men walked to the back of my pickup and peered inside.

Then Spike stiffened. He stepped to the side, staring through the window, into the front of the pickup. "Who's in the truck?" He thrust a hand into the large pocket at the front of his sweatshirt. I was pretty sure he was armed and was holding his gun.

My heart rate kicked up. "Nobody."

I had a hunting rifle stashed under the seat of my truck and had instructed Mags to use it if she needed to protect herself. I could only pray it wouldn't come to that.

The passenger window opened, and Mags poked her head out. "It's just me," she said. "Magdalena." Her voice was high and nervous.

Spike sidled toward the window, his movements cautious. "Put your hands where I can see them."

"I'm not armed," she said. "And I told you I'd pay you back. This settles the debt, right?"

"This isn't money," he snarled.

I stepped toward him, trying to distract him and keep him away from Mags. "No, but it's better than money."

Spike swung toward me. Before he could say anything, his friend snapped, "Who asked you?"

"You want these drugs or not?" I spread my hands. "I don't have all night."

Both men stared at me a moment, eyes narrowed as though assessing whether I was a threat. Stepping closer to each other, they had a muttered conversation I couldn't hear. Then Spike raised his voice, addressing me.

"Why do you have all this?" he demanded. "What's really going on?"

"Nothing but what you see. I found these drugs in the woods. Magdalena's my friend, and I figured I could help her out, is all."

"You found this stuff?" He sounded disbelieving.

"I figure one of the local growers must have lost it. Finders keepers though, right?"

"It's a generous offer," Mags called from inside the truck, her voice still higher than normal.

The two men conferred a little longer in low tones. They still seemed unsure, but greed was a powerful motivator. With the drugs in front of them, how could they resist?

"Load the bags into our car," Spike snapped at me.

"Sure thing. But could y'all dip your headlights so they don't blind me? I'll be seeing stars for weeks."

Spike's friend dipped the lights so they weren't shining straight into my eyes, and Spike watched me warily as I carried the bags from the bed of my pickup, filling his trunk with them. There were so many bags of weed, I had to pile some onto his back seat. By the time I was done, their car was groaning with illegal product.

"Right." I brushed my hands together in a "job done" motion. "That's it."

"That isn't it," snarled Spike. He walked over to the passenger door and yanked the door open. "Get out here," he ordered Mags.

I tensed, balling my hands into fists, forcing myself not to rush between them. My heart slammed against my ribs. If he hurt her, I'd make him regret it. But I'd do everything I could not to let it come to that.

"You've got what you came for," I said, dropping the exaggerated accent. "Now leave." My tone was cold. My words sharp.

Spike yanked his gun out of his pocket and pointed it at the truck. "Get out."

Mags did what he ordered. She stood next to the truck, her hands in the air. She looked scared but defiant.

Spike leveled the gun at her. "You gave me trouble. Now I'll give you trouble."

My blood was pounding in my ears. It took everything I had not to rush the guy, but to walk slowly toward Mags, my hands raised. "I wouldn't do that," I said.

"Why? What you gonna do?" As I'd hoped, Spike swiveled to point his gun at me.

"You want to give her any trouble, you need to go through me." I kept walking.

Spike's friend was standing beside their car as though impatient to leave. He didn't seem to be armed, and was far enough away that I could ignore him and focus on Spike.

"You think you scare me?" Spike demanded.

"Not trying to scare you. I'm just saying how it is." I stopped in front of Mags, putting myself between her and Spike's gun and praying she stayed behind me. "Maybe you've killed before. And maybe you're willing to kill me to settle whatever grudge you think you might have with her. But are you sure nobody saw you drive into this small town? Are you willing to bet your freedom that none of the locals who've known each other for years aren't curious enough to remember what you look like, or the car you were driving?"

Spike was shorter than me, and slighter. I drew myself up to emphasize my size. If he fired, I wouldn't go down easily. I'd do my best to take him down with me.

"Maybe I won't kill you," he snarled. "But I can fuck you up."

I gave a deliberate shrug as though the threat didn't bother me. "You can try. Or you can take what you came for and leave. I put thousands of dollars' worth of drugs in your car. This doesn't need to get messy."

Spike strode up to me, shoving the gun barrel into my stomach. "If this is some kind of trick, I'll come back here and fuck you both up."

I pressed my lips together, saying nothing. As tempting as it was to grab the gun, I didn't move. This close, our height difference was even more obvious. I glared down at him through narrowed eyes, ignoring the painful press of the gun barrel into my gut.

Thankfully, I couldn't sense any movement from behind me. Mags seemed frozen.

"Come on," Spike's friend called. "Let's get out of here."

Spike hesitated a moment, then let out a grunt. "Stay here until we're long gone," he ordered. "If I see headlights behind me, you're both dead."

I still said nothing.

The gun barrel eased out of my gut. Spike walked backward for a few steps, keeping his eyes on me, then turned and strode to his car. The two men got in. When the engine started, loud music blasted from inside. While they turned the car around, I spun around to Mags.

"Are you okay?" I caught her arms.

She nodded, puffing out a breath. "Are you?"

"Get in the truck." When she did what I said, I shut the passenger door behind her, then strode around to get in the driver's side.

"Get down," I ordered. "As far down as you can."

She sunk into the front footwell, scrunching herself into a ball. "My hands are shaking."

"We'll be okay now. They're leaving." I peered through the back window to watch the car drive away, ready to drop and cover her body with mine the instant I heard a gunshot.

The car drove down the dirt access road, its red taillights bouncing as it made its way over the uneven surface. The main road was at least five hundred feet away, and thanks to all the ruts, they had to navigate toward it slowly.

It wasn't until the car's taillights reached the road that the patrol cars on the main road put their lights on. All at once, the dark, silent night turned into a blaze of flashing color and noise.

A voice rang out deafeningly loud over a patrol car's loudspeaker: "Stop your engine and put your hands on your head! You're under arrest."

I lowered myself closer to Mags, figuring it was the time for gunfire if there was going to be any. But the deputies had Spike's car surrounded, and he must have realized it would be pointless trying to get away. I watched as the two thugs got out of their car with their hands up.

"What's happening?" Mags demanded.

"They're being cuffed."

She rose out of the footwell to watch with me as the two men were frisked, loaded into the back of a patrol car, and finally driven away.

"You should stay there," I told Mags, opening my door. "It'll be less complicated that way."

I half expected her to argue, but she just nodded. It was hard to tell in the dark, but I thought she was still a little pale.

"You'll be okay?" I asked. "I'll be back as soon as I can."

"I'm fine. Hardly shaking anymore." She gave me a crooked smile.

I smiled back, then got out and walked down the access road. Two of the patrol cars were still there, the officers busy looking into the trunk and back seat of the car I'd loaded all the drugs into. Spotting Sheriff James, I strolled over to him and nodded a hello.

"Cy." He nodded back. "This is some haul."

"Yes, sir."

The sheriff gave me a wry smile. "Your daddy was a busy man."

"He must have been," I agreed.

One of the sheriff's deputies moved closer, his narrowed eyes moving over me. I recognized Jimmy Dale, a man I didn't know well, but who clearly thought he knew me.

"Are we arresting him, Sheriff?" Jimmy asked.

I tensed, but kept silent.

Maybe the folks around here would always look at me with suspicion. I'd never be completely okay with that, but as long as the people I cared about knew the truth, I could ignore the rest.

Sheriff James frowned at his deputy. "Why would we do that?" he asked.

Jimmy ran a hand over his chin. "Well, should we search his pickup?"

The sheriff didn't answer him. Instead he turned to me. "Thank you for telling us what was going on, Cy. We don't want drug dealers turning up in our town and threatening innocent folks, do we?"

"No, sir." I kept my gaze on him, not on Jimmy.

The sheriff nodded. "You have our gratitude, and if you want to head home now, you can go. We'll be here for a while, taking pictures for evidence before we impound the car. We'll need to take a formal statement, of course, if you don't mind coming into the station tomorrow?"

"I can do that, Sheriff."

He offered me his hand and I shook it. Jimmy had his lips pressed together and was looking sullen.

The sheriff clapped me on the back. "You're a good man, Cy."

"Thank you, sir." I couldn't resist shooting a smug look at Jimmy as I walked away.

CHAPTER 27

MAGDALENA

"Y ou're not so scary," I told the danger birds as I put grain into their feeder after work the following Thursday. The birds were kind of sweet, actually, with the way they clucked at each other. And the other day, I'd watched a YouTube video about different ways to cook eggs and scrambled some for breakfast.

Cy had also explained the different settings on my oven, and I'd successfully cooked a few different meals, not just for myself, but for him and Gemma too. In addition to frozen pizza, I could now cook frozen burritos, frozen curry, and frozen pot pie. Hell, I was practically a pioneer woman. Or a prepper. If an apocalypse struck, I might even be one of the survivors. Who would have guessed?

I'd only just gone back into the house when Eric called. I stared at his name on my screen while my phone rang, then I gave a satisfied smile as it went to voicemail.

He'd been calling a lot the last few days, not that I ever picked up. He'd left several groveling voicemails, telling me he missed me, and was sorry, and couldn't I give him another chance. I'd started deleting his messages without listening to them. Now Spike couldn't hurt me anymore, I never had to talk to Eric again. That was something to smile about.

"Zeppelin!" I called. He was sniffing around Carla's garden beds, but when I yelled his name, he came running.

I followed him back inside and into the living room, then flopped onto the couch. Today had been a busy day at the bakery, but I knew so many of our customers now, it felt like I'd spent all day chatting to friends. My feet didn't get sore anymore. And pretty soon, I'd head over to Cy's place to have dinner with him and Gemma. I might even end up in his bed again, even though I had to go to work in the morning, and that would mean getting very little sleep.

I grinned at the thought, a delicious shiver of anticipation running through me.

Zeppelin jumped onto the couch next to me and put his head on my lap. He looked up at me through his hairy bangs, and it was such a cute look I had to laugh. "I guess we're both getting comfortable here, huh?" I said out loud.

Ironically, the realization of how true that was made me feel a whole lot less comfortable.

I'd been messaging Carla every couple of days to check her treatment was going okay, but I hadn't spoken on the phone to her in ages, and I hadn't told her about Cy yet. It was way past time I gave her a call.

Carla took a while to answer my call, and when her face came on the screen, she was in a stark white room. She was propped up on a bed with pillows behind her.

"Hey, brat," she said with a smile. "How's everything?'

I frowned, studying as much of the room as I could see. Part of a machine was visible, and it looked like a heart monitor. "Are you in the hospital?"

"Just having some tests." She wrinkled her nose. "It's part of the trial. I have to get tested every few days. Noah's right here with me for moral support." She swiveled her phone to show me Noah in a chair. He waved and said hello, then Carla turned the phone back to herself.

"How are you feeling?" I asked, still worried.

"Good." Her smile seemed real. "I'm not getting my hopes up, but my energy's been a little better the last few days."

"That's great news!" I grinned at her, delight replacing my worry.

"I don't want to talk about it in case I jinx it. So tell me what's been happening there. Is Freud okay?"

"Freud sleeps and he eats. Occasionally, he farts. Do you know how much longer you'll be there and when you're coming home?"

Carla's eyebrows drew down. "You want to go back to New York? It's okay if you do, I can ask someone else to look after Freud until we get—"

"No, nerd." I heaved an exaggerated sigh. "I was just asking."

"We'll be here another couple of weeks. Seriously, do you hate it there?" She winced as though bracing herself for my answer.

"I don't actually. Hey, I had lunch with Noah's mother on Sunday. She's so nice."

Carla looked off to where Noah was sitting. "Honey, did you hear that? Mags had lunch with your mom."

A moment later, Noah appeared on the screen next to her, craning his head to get into the camera's field of vision. "How is my momma?"

"She's great! Such a lovely woman." I smiled, thinking of how we'd bonded. I'd told her all about Cy, and she'd promised to spread the word about him, and talk him up to everyone she knew.

"And by the way," I said. "I've started dating someone."

Carla's eyes widened, her eyebrows shooting up. "You have? Who?"

"His name's Cy Baxter."

"Baxter?" Noah frowned.

"You know him?" I asked.

Carla frowned too, but at Noah, not me. "Have I met him?" she asked. "I don't remember hearing his name."

Thanks to her illness, my sister didn't get out much. She had to be one of the few people in Green Valley who never heard any gossip.

Noah shook his head. "He left town years ago. I haven't seen him since I was a boy, and even back then, he always kept to himself. I'd heard he was back. His family doesn't have the best reputation."

"Cy's nothing like his father," I said. "He's a good person."

"Okay." Noah still sounded doubtful.

"Don't judge him until you know him," I said. Then I reconsidered that statement, thinking about my own past. "In fact, don't judge him at all. I'm telling you he's good, and you can believe me. He's the best."

"Well I'm happy for you." Carla nudged Noah.

"Sure," said Noah. "If you say he's a good person, I believe you." He gave me a nod, then moved back away from the camera, presumably going back to his chair.

"I wouldn't have pictured you with someone local," said Carla. "And I guess he doesn't wear flannel, considering all those things you said about hating that when you found out I was dating Noah?"

"Actually, Cy was wearing flannel when I met him," I admitted. "And you should have seen his beard." I gestured around my face, demonstrating how full it had been when we met, and exaggerating a little because it was funny to see how Carla's eyes were widening. "He's got hair past his collar, and I haven't checked, but I bet his closet is full of cowboy boots and cowboy hats."

"Wait, wait, wait!" Carla waved both hands, laughing. "You're dating a guy with every single one of the things you used to make fun of?"

I gave an exaggerated nod. "And he only listens to country and western music."

"That's so funny!"

"Yeah." I sighed. "Only it turned out that none of that stuff matters. Cy is special. He's way better than any guy I've ever dated, in every way possible. The problem is that I was only supposed to be here a few weeks. What happens when I leave?"

"He wouldn't go with you?"

"I doubt it. He's been building a business here, and renovating his house. He seems like he's getting settled."

She wrinkled her brow. "So what will you do?"

I shrugged helplessly. "I only wish I knew."

CHAPTER 28

CY

By the time Gemma got home from school, I'd finished putting the last coat of paint on the walls and hanging the drapes. "What do you think?" I asked her.

She gazed around the living room with a smile. "It's sick!"

I side-eyed her. "That's good?"

"Uncle Cy, it looks incredible! It hardly seems like the same house."

I grinned back at her, then swept my own satisfied gaze around. The new drapes went perfectly with the freshly painted walls. I'd sanded the old floorboards to get rid of the cigarette scars, then polished them until they had a rich shine, bringing out their natural beauty. A few plush rugs added extra warmth, and after carting away my daddy's old furniture, I'd brought all my good stuff in from where I'd stored it.

I'd also changed all the light fixtures and switches, and brought in some houseplants and other decorations. The large windows opened onto a view of the tidy lawn that stretched to the woods, with a glimpse of the river peeping through the trees.

I still had to paint the outside of the house, replace the old kitchen with a new one, and update the bathrooms, but I'd made a good start.

"I'm all done in your room, too," I told Gemma. "Go take a look at your new drapes."

She raced into the bedroom, Zeppelin bouncing at her heels. Her whoop of delight made me grin even wider. My back ached, and I had callouses from my hard work over the last few days, but as Gemma emerged from her room, her expression made it all worthwhile.

"It's so much better! Thank you." She threw herself at me, and I wrapped my arms around her, hugging her tight.

When Gemma drew back, her eyes were still full of excitement. "You think I could invite some friends over next week?" she asked.

"Of course."

I tried to play it cool and not grin too widely. But I was already anticipating telling Ruth how Gemma was settling in and making friends, knowing how pleased she'd be to hear it. Hopefully now Gemma was happier here, my sister might decide to move in as well for a while once she was discharged, so I could provide more support and make sure she was okay. It was well past time I got to know her again, like I'd been getting to know my niece.

And maybe if Ruth came back, she'd be able to make peace with the past, like I'd been doing. After our mother died, I couldn't leave fast enough. But now I was back, my memories of Momma had become more vivid, as though she was imprinted in this land. I remembered how she used to catch fish with us. How every spring, she'd pick the first blooms of blue flowers and make a bouquet. How she'd read us stories and sing us made-up songs.

I wanted my sister to remember those things too. The good times, not the bad.

But if both Ruth and Gemma came to stay, it'd be more important than ever that they could go out in public without being bullied or made to feel like they didn't belong.

I couldn't help but think about the way that Jimmy Dale had looked at me. He saw what he expected to see. Son of a murderer. Brother of a criminal. Then again, I hadn't done anything to change his opinion. Since coming back, I'd only been into town to buy food and other supplies.

Maybe it was time to make more of an effort. To change more than my house.

"You want a sandwich?" I asked Gemma, crossing to the fridge. "PB and J?"

"Sure. Thanks." She slid onto one of the kitchen stools to watch me pull out the fixings.

"I'll head into town tomorrow to get my hair cut," I told her as I put the bread slices onto plates. "It's about time I stopped hiding, and the barbershop is one of those places where people gossip."

She raised her eyebrows. "You want to know what people are saying about you?"

"I already know what they're saying. But I want them to start saying it to my face."

"So you can argue with them?"

I shrugged, spreading peanut butter onto the bread. "So I can turn it into a conversation."

"Good for you." She swiped some peanut butter off the edge of the bread and licked it off her finger. "And you'll get a nice haircut in the process. I wonder if Mags likes short hair?" When I lifted my gaze up to hers, she gave me an innocent, wide-eyed look, lifting one shoulder. "Just wondering, that's all."

Instead of commenting, I handed her the knife so she could lick the peanut butter off it. Then I got a fresh knife out to spread the jelly.

"Seeing as you're going into town, you should pick up some new clothes." Gemma got up to drop the knife into the sink, her tone suspiciously casual. "I mean, if you're planning on interacting with more people, you want to look nice, don't you?"

She was still wearing her too-innocent look, and I knew what she was thinking. Mags was into fashion. She always dressed well. Even I could tell she was stylish in an edgy, cool way. In other words, the opposite of me.

"I could take you clothes shopping," Gemma suggested, getting back onto her stool. "We could drive to Knoxville where there are more stores."

I finished making the sandwiches while I considered it. "You want me to take you to the jam session at the community center this week?" I asked.

"Yes!" She almost shouted the word. "Of course I do. I still can't believe you went without me!"

I slid her sandwich over to her. "Then we should both get something new to wear."

She gave a delighted squeal. "Really? Thanks, Uncle Cy! When should we go shopping?"

"If I write you a note, you think you can get out of school a little early tomorrow?"

"This is getting better and better!" She took a big bite of her sandwich and chewed, still grinning.

I loved seeing her so happy. It made me feel the same way. I took the stool next to her and pulled my own sandwich in front of me.

"In all the photos Mom has of you, you're clean-shaven," she said, swallowing her mouthful. "Would you ever shave your beard off?"

Surprised, I ran my hand over the bristles. "Having a beard means I don't need to shave every day."

"So you're lazy?"

"You think I should shave it off?"

She tilted her head to the side, studying me as though she'd never seen me before. "Actually, I kind of like it."

"Maybe I'll have the barber trim and shape it a little more." I found myself running my hand over it again and picked up my sandwich instead.

She nodded, her eyes alight. "A haircut, beard trim, and some new clothes. When she sees you, Mags will die!"

I laughed. "I'd prefer a non-fatal reaction."

She pursed her lips, adopting a serious tone. "I love you, Uncle Cy, but I need to tell you that Mags is a lot cooler than you are."

"I know she is." But it was the first time Gemma had ever told me she loved me, and my heart was expanding so quickly, I didn't care about anything else. "I love you too," I said. "Seriously, Gem. I hope you know how happy it makes me to spend time with you. I didn't see you anywhere near enough before, and I've really liked getting to know you better."

"Me too," she mumbled through a mouth full of sandwich. Then she swallowed. "But you know you're going to have to listen to more than just country music if you're dating Mags, right?"

"Will you do something for me?" I asked slowly. "I'd like to hear that song by her ex-boyfriend. The song you were talking about when you first met."

"Should I put it on now?" She reached for her phone and a few moments later, music started playing.

I wanted to hate the song, but I had to admit, her asshole ex had a good voice. The music was melodic, with a catchy beat. But he was singing about Mags. *My Mags*. About halfway through the song, I motioned to Gemma to turn it off.

"Your momma's going to call tonight," I said, because I didn't want to talk about the song.

"I know," she said. Then she asked, "Uncle Cy, is Momma going to be okay?"

"Sure," I said in my most reassuring voice. "She's sounding better on the phone, isn't she? They needed to get her medication right, and she's been talking to her therapist. She has some stuff to work through, seeing as she's been holding a lot of pain inside her for a long time."

"Pain from when you were kids, right? And because of my father?"

I nodded.

Gemma's mouth twisted. "I remember him from when I was little. He could be scary sometimes."

"That wasn't right. She deserved to be treated with respect, and so do you."

I hated that Gemma had been exposed to her father's ugliness. But she'd been young enough when Ruth had left Gemma's father, maybe his violence hadn't affected her too much. I hoped not.

"I was thinking of asking your momma if she wants to come and live here for a while when she gets out of the facility," I said. "Would that be okay with you?"

She nodded. "I still miss my friends in Nashville, but it's not so bad here. But what if Momma wants to stay in Green Valley permanently? I mean, you thought you were only coming for a few weeks and ended up staying."

"We have plenty of land. You two could live here, and I could build another house up by the river. It's pretty up there."

"I guess that would be okay." She ate another bite of her sandwich, looking thoughtful. "Uncle Cy, do you think Mags will stay in town?"

My heart clenched. "No," I said honestly. "I think she'll go back to New York."

Her mouth turned down. "But you want her to stay, don't you?"

I didn't answer, because I didn't need to. I was sure she could see how I felt about Mags from my face.

"You know what you should do?" Gemma's eyes lit up with enthusiasm. "You should walk into the community center on Friday night with a new haircut and your beard trimmed, wearing some nice new clothes. Like a male Cinderella! Then tell her how you feel about her and ask her to stay. I bet she'll say yes."

"Hmm." I ate the last of my sandwich, not able to feel nearly as much optimism as my niece. "Don't you have some homework to do?"

CHAPTER 29

MAGDALENA

It was my second Friday night out with Amber and Joy, and we started our evening at the community center again. The three of us had dressed up for our night out. Most people turned up wearing casual clothes. But not us.

"We're fabulous!" Amber exclaimed as we walked into the community center. She put a hand on her hip, pulling my favorite leather jacket open to show off more of the silky slip dress she was wearing underneath.

Joy grinned at her, then at me. "We sure are. You look gorgeous, Amber."

"You both do," I told them.

We were definitely attracting some admiring looks. And enough hellos to make me feel more like a local than ever. *And* I snagged a plate of food, with a generous helping of Julianne MacIntyre's locally famous coleslaw. Which, for the record, was delicious.

"Cletus is playing tonight," Joy said when we'd finished eating, hooking her head toward one of the rooms where the bands would be performing. "Want to go in and watch?"

"Sure." I dabbed my mouth to remove any coleslaw remnants. "Why not?"

We headed into one of the rooms where the musicians played. Nobody was playing just then, but their gear was mostly set up. The microphones were waiting on the low stage, though most of the instruments were still in their cases, leaning against the wall. Hardly anyone was in the room. Most were probably in line for the food and would come back once the music restarted.

We stopped in front of the stage. "Should we sit and wait?" I asked, gesturing to the rows of seats for the audience.

"Oh my Lord!" Amber stared at something over my shoulder, her eyes round with surprise. She grabbed my arm. "You're not going to believe who just walked in. He's so gorgeous!"

My heart leapt, and I broke into a grin. Cy had promised to meet me here, and Gemma had whispered that they were planning to drive into Knoxville to shop for clothes. She'd wagged her eyebrows at me, then stopped talking when Cy came back into the room, so I figured Cy had decided to buy something new for the occasion.

I couldn't wait to see him, and if my friends' exaggerated reactions were any indication, Cy must look great. Both Joy and Amber had wide eyes and parted lips. Amber was squeezing my arm, and Joy looked frozen in place.

A man cleared his throat right behind me and I grinned even wider, waiting for the low rumble of Cy's voice and for him to slide his arms around my waist.

"Hey, babe. Surprise!" It was a male voice, but it wasn't Cy's.

My heart plummeted.

Pulling my arm free from Joy's grip, I spun around.

"*Eric?!*" I yelped his name. "What are you doing here?"

My ex-boyfriend was wearing distressed black jeans and a ripped black T-shirt, printed with his own band's logo. And he was carrying his guitar case, as though he wanted to make extra sure everyone he met recognized him. He'd been famous for roughly two minutes, and he was clearly milking his new-found success for everything it could give him.

He ran his free hand over his tousled hair. "The whole tour thing was crazy, Mags. I partied way too hard." He shot me that sheepish little grin of his that used to make me melt. Now though, it was obvious he used it to dodge responsibility. He was nothing but an immature boy, expecting to do whatever he wanted and get away with it thanks to his pretty face and even prettier voice.

"What are you doing in Green Valley?" My tone was icy, and I narrowed my eyes into a glare. But his expression didn't change, and my hostility seemed to bounce right off him.

"I came for you," he said. "I need you, Mags."

"We broke up." I folded my arms. "It's over."

"Don't be like that." Eric put his guitar case down and reached for me, gripping my upper arms. "I can't get by without you. You're my muse, Mags. I haven't written a good song since 'City Pretty'. You inspire me, babe."

"You left me to deal with Spike alone, and now you think you need me?" I rolled my eyes. If he had as much talent as he did selfishness, he'd be number one on every chart.

"I'm sorry, okay? I let the whole touring and fame thing go to my head and went crazy for a while. I was a jerk to you, but that wasn't the real me, I promise. I can do better."

Stepping back, I pulled myself free from his grip. "Eric, I don't want to see you—"

"Wait." He waved both hands in a stop-talking gesture. "Before you say anything else, just listen to what I can offer. Let me save you, babe."

"Save me?"

"From this place." Nostrils flaring, he swept a disdainful glance around. People were starting to crowd into the room, murmuring to each other in low, excited tones. They'd obviously recognized Eric, and word seemed to be spreading fast.

"Hick towns are the worst," Eric said. "Like that movie where the guys go on that rafting trip and the hillbillies attack. What's it called?" He snapped his fingers. "*Deliverance*, right?"

My ears went hot, and I glanced behind me to make sure Joy and Amber hadn't heard. Thankfully, my friends had stepped back to give us some privacy, though they were still gaping at Eric as though he was about to unfurl a pair of wings.

Ask me, he was more likely to grow a pair of horns.

The people of Green Valley had been so sweet to me, so friendly and welcoming. How dare he insult them? Surely I hadn't sounded so awful when I'd first arrived?

"I know you gave up your apartment," he said. "But you can stay with me. You can move in, and I'll look after you. I'll make it all up to you."

"Oh my God!" gasped a familiar voice. Gemma pushed through the crowd and came skidding to a stop in front of us, her face alight with excitement. "You're Eric Storm!"

My heart stuttered. If Gemma was here, Cy must have brought her. I craned my neck but couldn't see him anywhere in the room. Though it had been almost empty when we walked in, now it was so full that people were struggling to squeeze through the door.

But where was Cy?

"I'm your biggest fan." Gemma gushed. "I love your music so much!"

"Then you're in luck." Eric gave her a self-important smile. "I'm about to sing for you."

Gemma's squeal of delight drowned out the protest I started to make. And anyway, Eric had already grabbed his guitar and was stepping onto the low stage, positioning himself behind the microphone. As he slung on his guitar, the crowd surged forward, pushing the chairs to the side and jostling for space in front of him.

"Testing," Eric said into the microphone. He strummed his guitar a few times. Then he grinned at the crowd, clearly feeding off their excitement. "I'm Eric Storm, lead singer of a little band called Storm Front, and I'm going to sing a song I wrote that was inspired by the love of my life, Magdalena Solis." He pointed through the crowd to me and I shrank back with a grimace. "It's called 'City Pretty'. Mags, this one's for you."

UGH.

He strummed his guitar and the familiar first notes of the song made several people in the crowd whoop and clap. Amber moved to one side of me, and Joy moved to the other.

"Can you believe this?" Amber breathed in my ear. "Are you going to forgive him?"

I couldn't be surprised at the question, seeing as I hadn't explained to Amber or Joy why I split up with Eric. They didn't know about Spike, how Eric had lied to me, or that I was certain he'd cheated on me. Looking back now, I could see there had been dozens of red flags throughout our relationship and I'd ignored them all. No wonder his bad behavior had gotten so much worse. I should have been calling him out on it from the start.

As Eric sang, some of the crowd started dancing. Others swayed and sang along. A few held up their phones, recording him. Gemma was up at the front with some kids her age who had to be friends from school.

In seconds, Eric had managed to focus everyone's attention on him, sideline the other musicians who were supposed to be playing, and turn our pleasant girls' night into a rock concert . . . not that any of the women thronging to the front of the crowd seemed to mind. Eric kept pointing to me as he sang, and some of those women glanced back at me with curiosity and envy in their faces.

There was something about watching a man on stage that made him seem at least three times as sexy as he'd otherwise be, and Eric was handsome to start with. Everyone was clearly expecting me to swoon at his feet. And Eric seemed to be expecting it too.

CHAPTER 30

CY

I stood inside the entrance to the large room feeling like I'd sunk under the surface of the ocean and swallowed a gallon of seawater on the way down. My stomach was heavy and churning. My chest was tight, and my lungs weren't taking in air like they should.

It wasn't that I felt like a fool in my new clothes, with shorter hair and a closely trimmed beard. It didn't matter how carefully I'd prepared for tonight, or that I was holding a gift for Mags—a bouquet of wild blue phlox flowers that I'd picked from beside the river, symbolic of the fresh start I'd hoped we'd get to have.

What mattered was that her old life had come calling for her, and as much as it galled me, I had to stand back, to let her choose what she wanted.

I couldn't see Mags through the throng of people, but I knew where she was, seeing as her ex-boyfriend had pointed her out and was singing to her. Gemma was dancing in front of the low stage, enraptured by the rock star.

Eric fucking Storm.

Maybe I couldn't hate his song, but I had no problem hating him.

Turning, I pushed my way back out of the room, growling rough apologies to the people who were still trying to get inside as I went.

Mags's ex-boyfriend obviously still loved her. And though I would have sworn she'd never take him back, he was putting on a damn good show. Making a big romantic gesture. If she chose him, nobody here would blame her.

Anger surged in my gut, spiked by frustration and fear of losing her.

Should I go back in there? I wanted to throw her over my shoulder and carry her out like a damn caveman. She was mine. *MINE.*

I paced down the hallway. There was a trash can, and I stopped for long enough to throw the bunch of pretty blue flowers away. I couldn't force her to choose me. She deserved some space, to figure out what she wanted. To decide *who* she wanted. Her ex was an asshole who didn't deserve her, but he was a rock star. All I had to offer was life in a small town, away from the city—and the music—she loved.

"Fuck!" I cursed louder than I meant to, and when I lifted my eyes, Karen Smith and Bonnie Linton were standing in front of me, their eyebrows crawling up to their hairlines with shock at my profanity.

Karen Smith drew herself up with a huff of distaste, her lips tightly pursed. "Just goes to show, you can dress up a Baxter, and he'll still be a Baxter."

"I was right about him all along." Bonnie Linton lifted her nose as though I smelled bad.

I needed some air. Heading out of the community center, I strode into the parking lot. At least there I could pace up and down in peace.

Or maybe I should leave. I could call Gemma and let her know I'd pick her up later.

"Uncle Cy!" My niece spotted me and came jogging over. "Are you okay?"

"Sure," I said through gritted teeth. "What are you doing out here? Has the rock star stopped playing?"

"He finished two songs, then announced he wasn't playing anymore and went to talk to Mags." She wrinkled her nose, her gaze sympathetic. "Do you think they might get back together?"

"That's up to her." I shoved my hands in my pockets. "Hey, what do you say we go to Nashville to visit your momma?"

She blinked at me. "What, now?"

I shrugged, fighting the urge to hustle her into the car and peel out of there, putting Mags's rock-star ex far behind us. "We could leave in the morning. Take off early."

Gemma scrunched her eyes up, squinting as though trying to figure out what my angle was. "Are you saying you want to run away?"

"Mags needs some time to decide what she wants. I figure I should give her some space, so it's better to get out of town for a few days. I don't want to push her."

"Uncle Cy, listen to me." Gemma grabbed my arms with both hands, her eyes wide and her tone earnest. "Listen carefully. You have to push her!"

I frowned. "What do you mean?"

"Mags needs to know how you feel about her. Have you told her yet?"

I shook my head. "She needs space so she can figure out how she feels without pressure—"

"Oh my God!" Gemma shook my arms. Or at least, she tried to, but because I was a whole lot taller and stronger, she didn't manage to move them much. "That's the stupidest thing I've ever heard! She doesn't need space. No offense, Uncle Cy, but you need to pull your head out of your butt right now or you might lose her." She gave an exasperated huff of breath. "I mean, you like her, don't you?"

"I'm crazy about her," I admitted. It felt good to say it out loud.

"Then go back inside and tell her." Gemma put her hands on her hips and glared at me so sternly, I gave my lips a rueful tug to the side.

Maybe my niece was right. Mags's ex-boyfriend was a good-looking asshole who thought singing her a song would make up for all the shit he'd put her through. She might not want to stick around in Green Valley, or to date me, but I had to go back in there and make sure she was okay. And if Eric fucking Storm happened to get pushy and give me a good excuse to sock him right in the nose, well, maybe I'd forget my vow of nonviolence and not try too hard to hold myself back.

"All right," I said. "And I love you, Gem. You know that right?"

She rolled her eyes, the gesture so much like Mags that it took me by surprise. "Get out of here," she ordered, pointing a firm finger at the door to the community center. "Stop wasting time and go get your woman!"

CHAPTER 31

MAGDALENA

Eric indicated that he was coming to the back of the room to talk to me, but it took him a while to get there. First, he had to acknowledge the adoration of the crowd. He posed for a few photos and signed some napkins, a couple of T-shirts, a shoulder, and the expanse of skin above one woman's breasts.

But now he was finally in front of me, wearing his self-satisfied, rock-star smile. It was a confident smile, with a touch of arrogance. A real panty-dropper.

Once, I would have been sucked in by that smile, willing to do just about anything so long as he kept it aimed on me. But I deserved better. I deserved respect. I deserved to be supported and valued, and even cherished.

To be treated the way Cy treated me.

"So, Mags," Eric said, putting his hand on my waist without asking for permission. "Should we get out of here? Let's pick up something to eat and go back to my hotel room to talk, okay babe?"

I glanced around. Everyone else in the room had backed up several feet to give us at least the illusion of privacy, Joy and Amber included. But plenty of people were still gazing avidly at Eric, and I couldn't blame them for that. He had plenty of charisma. It was a shame he'd let his fame go to his head.

"We're not doing that." I kept my voice sweet seeing as half the town was watching, but my heart was pounding. Eric had never been easy to say no to, and he was an expert at ignoring things he didn't want to hear.

"What, you're not hungry?" He smirked as though he found it funny.

"You owe me fifteen thousand dollars, Eric. The only place we're going together is to the bank."

"Sure, I'll pay you back." He put his other hand on the other side of my waist, smiling warmly down at me. "But it's Friday night and the bank is closed. I'll give you the money on Monday, when we're back in New York."

"I'm not going back to New York with you."

Leaning close, he lowered his voice to a murmur. "You'd rather stay in this hick town?"

"Take your hands off me, Eric." My tone was starting to get less sweet. As usual, he was ignoring what I wanted. How had I put up with his crap for so long?

"Babe, you should—"

"Get your hands off me!" I hissed it louder than I'd meant to, and several of the people standing closest jerked their faces to us, their eyes wide.

Suddenly, Joy was back on one side of me and Amber on the other.

"Everything okay?" asked Joy.

"Everything's fine," said Eric, his hands still on my waist. "Ladies, would you give us a little space?"

"Don't go anywhere," I told them. "Eric, get your hands off me right now."

"Fine!" With a heavy sigh, he snatched them off my waist and held up both palms. "Look, I'm not touching you, babe. I'm only trying to apologize. Why are you acting this way?"

"You can go back to New York now." I stared him straight in the eyes, my tone hard and final. "I'm not coming with you. And seeing as I have no faith that you'll ever pay me back the money you owe me, you can leave your guitar instead. I'll take it as payment, and we'll call it even, seeing as I happen to know someone who needs one."

I glanced around, but Gemma was nowhere in sight. She'd mentioned she couldn't play her old guitar and was saving for a new one. Eric had the best guitar money could buy. And when Gemma's friends found out she'd been given Eric Storm's guitar, she'd probably be the most popular girl in school.

Eric frowned. "Babe, come with me and—"

"I never want to see you again. We're over, Eric. For good. So goodbye."

His face twisted. My answer was finally sinking in. "You're making a big mistake," he snarled. "I could have any fucking woman I wanted."

"But you can't have me."

"You heard her, mister!" Joy folded her arms, lightly bumping her shoulder against mine.

"Yeah! You can't have her." Amber did the same on my other side.

All three of us glared at Eric. A united front. And I'd never been so happy to have friends by my side.

Eric's lip curled and for a moment he looked like he had no idea what to do. Then he spun on his heel and strode out, pushing through the remains of the crowd to get through the door.

I sagged. My heart was still thumping. "Thank you. Both of you, so much."

"Of course!" Joy put her arm around me.

"We've got you, girl." Amber looped her arms around both of us and squeezed us both. "I never liked his music anyway." It was a blatant lie, but I appreciated the sentiment.

When they let me go, I looked back toward the stage to make sure Eric's guitar was still there. Sure enough, it was right where he left it. At least one good thing had come from our crappy relationship.

I was about to let out a relieved breath, when Amber grabbed my arm, her grip tight. In the same moment, Joy made a surprised sound, jabbing me in the ribs with her elbow. Both my friends were staring at the door.

"Oh my God," Joy gasped. "He looks . . ."

"Hot!" exclaimed Amber.

I gave an impatient click of my tongue. Hadn't we been through this already? I didn't care *what* Eric looked like. What mattered was all the ugliness he had underneath.

I turned to say so, and the words died in my throat.

Cy was standing in the doorway. My heart fluttered when his eyes connected with mine. He'd had his hair styled in a textured crop cut, and his beard was short enough to really show off his angular cheekbones and square jaw. Why had he been letting his beard hide so much of his face when it was so nice to look at? Combined with his new clothes—dark-wash, slim-fit jeans and a crisp, white button-down—he looked more than hot. The right word was *spectacular*.

As he walked toward me, his eyes fixed on mine, and every muscle in my body went weak.

CHAPTER 32

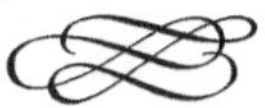

CY

Mags had dressed up for her evening out and was wearing a gold top that made her eyes glow even more than usual. And it revealed one smooth shoulder in a way that made me want to reveal a whole lot more.

"Is your ex-boyfriend still around?" I asked, stopping in front of her.

She gestured toward the door. "Um. He's gone . . ." She trailed off, and I wasn't sure what she meant, whether he was gone for good, or just in the next room. Either way, it didn't matter.

The only thing that mattered was that she knew the way I felt about her.

Problem was, everyone was staring at us. Karen Smith and Bonnie Linton were standing just a few feet away, their gazes judgmental. Her ex-boyfriend had just been singing to her. Everyone in this room would think less of her just for talking to me. I was a Baxter, after all.

Only that wasn't all I was. I'd always have my last name, but it didn't define me. I was a unique individual who deserved to be judged by the things I did, not by how I looked, what I wore, or who my family happened to be.

Turning from Mags, I stepped up onto the stage where the band equipment was set up, and moved in front of one of the microphones. I tapped it with one finger, like I'd seen people do, and from the sound the tap made I figured it must be on.

Everyone was looking quizzically at me, wondering what I was doing.

Maybe they expected me to start singing. I wasn't used to public speaking, and my throat was tight with nerves.

"I'm Cy Baxter," I said into the microphone, looking at all the familiar and curious faces around me. "Most of y'all know who my daddy was. He was an evil man, just like his daddy before him."

The room had gone deathly silent, and everyone in it seemed to be gaping at me.

Clearing my throat, I kept talking. "My daddy used to sell drugs, and my brother is in prison. But I'm not like them, and it's about time y'all stopped treating me that way. I'm using my daddy's barn to grow golden oyster and enoki mushrooms, and I'm selling them to local restaurants."

A man at the back of the room spoke up, his voice ringing out unexpectedly. "I've bought some of those mushrooms. They're good quality."

The man walked forward, emerging from the crowd. To my surprise, it was Mr. Johnson from the Crooked Creek Inn. He stroked his large, silver mustache, nodding around at everyone in the room. "Come for a meal at the Inn," he said. "Order something with mushrooms in it, and y'all won't be disappointed."

"Thank you, Mr. Johnson." I gave him a nod. "The reason I decided to come up here and announce all this is that my daddy's dead and my brother won't be coming back. The only Baxters who are left are me and my niece Gemma, and my sister Ruth, if she decides to come back from Nashville. And my niece and sister don't deserve to be tainted by my daddy's bad deeds. They've never done a thing wrong. They can't help being related to my daddy."

Some people were nodding, which was an encouraging sight. Magdalena smiled at me, which was even more encouraging. Her eyes were sparkling, and her expression seemed like she approved of what I was saying.

I smiled back at her. "Also," I said into the microphone, "I'm fixing to ask Magdalena if I can take her out for dinner somewhere nice. I hope she's going to say yes. And if she does, I don't want anyone giving her any trouble about it." I swept my gaze around the room once more. "If anyone has anything to say about me or my name, they should say it now, to me. Then they won't be tempted to treat Magdalena with anything less than politeness."

A woman's voice rang out from the back of the crowd. "I thought she was dating Eric Storm?"

I craned my neck trying to see who had shouted, but it didn't really matter. I answered anyway.

"I understand it might be confusing seeing as her ex-boyfriend was just here, singing to her," I admitted. "But whatever she decides, it's up to her. I've said everything I wanted to say." I stepped off the stage, walking back to Mags.

"You're going to ask me out?" Mags asked, raising her eyebrows. "That's definitely the most unique dinner invitation I've ever had."

I took her hand. "Well, what do you say, Brooklyn? Would you do me the honor of having dinner with me tomorrow night? Our first official date?"

A slow grin broke over her face. "Cy Baxter, I thought you'd never ask."

CHAPTER 33

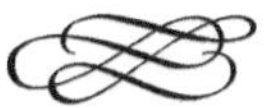

MAGDALENA

The next night, Cy took me to a restaurant called the Front Porch. It was a nice place, romantically lit, and the food was excellent. I recognized several of the other diners, of course, and they all nodded to Cy and smiled at me.

Cy's speech at the community center combined with my efforts to restore his reputation seemed to have worked. My heart warmed to see how surprised and pleased Cy was when people stopped by our table to say hello.

It warmed even more when I spotted Amber and Wren holding hands at a table in the corner, too busy smiling at each other to notice we were in the same restaurant.

After we'd finished our entrees, Cy took my hand across the table, his expression serious. "I need to tell you that I'm in love with you," he said. "And I want to find a way we can be together."

A small candle flickered on our table and in the candlelight, he looked more handsome than ever. The clear beauty of his eyes dissolved both my bones and my senses, and the feel of his fingers set my heart skipping.

I nodded, my chest so full of warmth and hope I felt breathless with it. "I want that too."

He gave me a relieved smile. "You'll be going back to New York soon, and I don't know if I can let myself get swallowed up in a big city again. But I've been looking at what kind of places are available outside of New York. Maybe in the Hudson Valley or the Catskill Mountains. If I sell my daddy's house and get a place there, it's not so far from the city that you couldn't live with me. Or if you aren't ready for that, you could join me for weekends."

I blinked at him, considering the option. Picturing him in a cabin in the woods. "It's beautiful in the Catskills," I said. But I couldn't help but wonder how he'd feel about being so far from his sister and Gemma.

He nodded. "I'd move to the city for you, Mags, if I had to. But being outside of it would be easier for me. I think I could be at peace there, the way I wouldn't be in the city."

"But you're building your business here," I said. "What would happen to it?"

He gave a careless shrug. "Doesn't matter. I could grow mushrooms in the place I move to, or I could find something else to do."

I stared at him in wonder, my heart full. He was willing to give up his business and move away from his family to make things work. He was so selfless and caring, I could only try to be worthy of him.

"How would you feel if I stayed in Green Valley?" I asked, squeezing his hand.

His lips parted. He stared at me speechlessly for a moment, then he swallowed. "If you . . . what?"

He was so surprised, I couldn't help but grin. "Tell you the truth, this place has grown on me." I gave a shrug. "I really like the friends I've made here. I'm getting to like bluegrass, and beards. Maybe even cowboy boots."

"What about flannel?"

"Let's not push it. There are lines I won't cross."

His grin was wide. I loved seeing him so happy. He looked even more gorgeous with such a wide smile, and the light shining from his eyes made my chest feel warm and light.

"Are you certain?" he asked.

"It turns out that I'm in love with you, too," I admitted. "So yes, I'm certain. When Noah and Carla return, I'll start looking for a place to rent."

"Move in with me." He didn't hesitate, and I gave him a relieved smile.

"Honestly, I was hoping you'd say that. Zeppelin too?"

"Of course!" He looked so pleased with the idea, I wanted to move in right away. If it wasn't for Freud and the chickens, I probably would.

"I thought I'd either stay working at the bakery, or start looking at other options," I said.

"A fashion store?"

"I'm not sure yet. Maybe I could open my own store. New York style turns a bit country. What do you think?"

He put his other hand over mine. "I think it's the best thing I've ever heard."

"City style turning country is the best thing you've ever heard?"

"I was talking about you being in love with me. *And* the mix of city and country. Seems like those two things must have been made for each other, they go together so well."

"So do you want some dessert?" I asked. "Or would you rather go and celebrate my brilliant idea?"

He leaned across the table to kiss me. "Let's go home," he whispered against my lips. "So we can combine city with country, and I can show you how much I love you."

EPILOGUE

MAGDALENA

Not long after getting back to Green Valley, Noah and Carla came to our place for dinner. The house was cozy now, much nicer than the first night I'd come over and Cy had cooked burgers. Cy, Gemma, and I had turned it into our home.

The evening Noah and Carla came for dinner, Gemma had gone to one of her friend's houses for a sleepover, so it was just the four of us there to enjoy one of Cy's delicious taco nights. And after dinner, we took Noah and Carla to the clearing beside the river where Cy had built a firepit. We lit a fire, laid down blankets and cushions, and roasted marshmallows over the dancing flames while Zeppelin bounded around, exploring the woods.

Cy and I were sharing a blanket. He leaned against some cushions with a log holding him up, while I snuggled against his chest. From where we sat, we could see past the fire, over the river, to where the trees stood out against the setting sun.

I glanced to a cluster of trees on this side of the river. "Over there is the shed where I found Cy's father's drugs," I told Carla and Noah. They screwed their heads around to peer toward it, searching for it in the gloom.

"You see the gnarled bit of that tree?" Cy pointed. "Underneath it, you should be able to make out the door handle."

"I see it!" my sister exclaimed. She was propped up on a pile of cushions while Noah was holding a stick with marshmallows, heating them in the fire.

"So do I," said Noah. "Is there anything in it?"

"Not anymore," I said. "It's empty, and a great hiding place if you have anything you want kept secret."

Noah's lips quirked up. "I don't have any secrets. This book is wide open." He pulled his marshmallows away from the flame to see whether they were getting soft, then moved them back to the heat.

"I still can't believe you set that drug dealer up," Carla said. "Are you going to tell Mom about it?"

"And add to my bad reputation?" I shrugged. "Why not?" Maybe it was because I felt so secure and content with Cy's arms around me, but I didn't want to have any more secrets, either. Like Cy, I wanted to own exactly who I was, with no lies or excuses.

Carla wrinkled her nose. "Mom can be hard on you, can't she?"

"She thinks I'm reckless," I said. "But that's because of things I did years ago. It's about time she changed her opinion."

"It's tempting to keep thinking of people the same way all the time." Cy's deep voice rumbled from his chest. "But we're complex, and we all change." Leaning against him, I could feel the vibrations when he spoke.

"People aren't fractions," Carla agreed. "When you reduce us to our simplest form, you limit our possibilities." She smiled as though getting to use math in normal conversation was a special treat. Cy nodded, letting his math-geek flag fly, and Noah looked at her like he thought she was smart and cute.

The conversation was in serious danger of tumbling off a dork cliff, and I was the only one who could rescue it.

"In other words, nerd," I said to my sister, "don't label people."

Carla laughed. "Well put, brat."

Cy chuckled into my ear, the sound as warm as his breath. The tickling sensation sent a pleasurable shiver down my spine.

"Anyway, I don't think you're reckless," Carla added. "Freud and the chickens survived your stay." She frowned. "Only I'm not sure why I have new cushions in my living room. You still haven't explained that."

"The new cushions were Zeppelin's idea. He didn't like the old ones."

Zeppelin must have grown tired of exploring the nearby trees, because he was lounging next to Cy and me, taking up most of our blanket, and keeping a close eye on the marshmallows. He lifted his head at the sound of his name and gave his tail a wag, sweeping it across the ground.

"I have to admit, I was in danger of being swayed by the rumors about you, Cy." Noah looked apologetic. "I should have known better than to listen to gossip."

"It's okay," Cy said. "Understandable. I'm glad you were willing to give me a chance."

He bent his head to brush his lips across the sensitive skin of my neck, sending more tingles into my core. As much as I enjoyed spending time with my sister and Noah, the sensation made me wish we were alone so I could ask him to do it some more.

Noah pulled his marshmallows away from the fire to peer at them again. Not a moment too soon. They were singed around the edges and turning into goo. He offered the stick to Carla, and she pulled one of the marshmallows loose with her teeth.

"Hot!" she gasped with her mouth full. "Too hot!"

"Good to know." Noah grinned. "Now I'll be sure and blow on my one before I eat it." He softened his teasing by leaning closer to kiss her.

Cy took their display of affection for an excuse to kiss the top of my head. One of his arms was draped over me, holding me against him. I loved the feeling of being enveloped by him, nestled into his bulk. It was especially nice to have the crackling, dancing flames in front of us and the river burbling beside us.

"Aren't you going to tell them your news?" Cy murmured into my ear.

Carla leaned back against her cushions. "What news?"

"We were at the community center last Friday night." I hesitated a moment, thinking of how Carla's illness kept her from going places. "Have you been to the jam session?" I asked.

She nodded. "Once."

"I used to go," said Noah. "Carla finds it overwhelming. The bright lights and noise."

"Too many people," my sister said with a grimace.

"Some incredible musicians play there," I said. "I got to talking to a band who want to record an album and book more shows. Long story short, they asked if I'd manage them."

Carla's eyes widened. "Can you manage a band? I mean, do you know how? Don't you need a legal background?"

"I talked to Sullivan about it, the guy who manages Eric's band. He's not a lawyer, but he works with one. He seems to think I'd be able to do it. He actually offered to mentor me."

"That sounds great," said Noah. "Congratulations."

"So great," agreed my sister. "I'm happy for you."

I grinned. "Thanks." It still didn't feel real, but the more I thought about it, the better I liked the idea. Sullivan had been enthusiastic, and I had a feeling it was going to be fun.

Cy kissed my neck. "You'll be good at it," he murmured. "I know you will."

I watched Noah as he ate a hot marshmallow before giving the last one to Carla. She took it warily, then bit into it.

"It's a bluegrass band," I said when it was in her mouth.

Carla choked. She coughed, then pounded her chest with her fist. "Bluegrass?"

"Wait until you hear them. When their album comes out, it's going to be huge."

"Does that mean you'll leave the bakery?" Noah asked.

"I'll stay at the bakery while I get things started. This only just happened, so I'm still wrapping my head around it. And I'm not sure whether I can make a full-time living from managing a band."

"Once you get going, more musicians will want you to manage them," Cy said. "It's the perfect job for you."

I turned my face to shoot him an appreciative smile. My biggest cheerleader. With him at my back, I could do anything.

His lips kicked up. "Tell Carla and Noah what else you spoke to Sullivan about."

"I was just about to." I rolled my eyes at him. He was quietly gleeful about the other news Sullivan had given me, whereas I couldn't help feeling sorry for my ex. I turned back to the others. "Eric's been kicked out of his band."

Carla and Noah exchanged a startled look. "How come?" Carla asked.

"Sullivan said Eric had been acting badly, getting high, fighting with his bandmates, and not turning up for shows. The band was on the point of breaking up, and they decided to replace him instead."

"*Can* they replace him?" she asked.

I nodded. "Apparently the new lead singer is really talented, and so far, the fallout from their fans hasn't been too bad. They're recording new songs and still filling venues. So yeah, it seems like they can."

Cy kissed my neck again. I didn't look back to check, but I had a feeling he looked smug. I was sad that Eric had thrown away all his hard work and talent. Hopefully, he'd get the help he needed and be able to resurrect his career once he was clean.

"After everything he did to you, he didn't deserve his success," said Carla. "Josie would call it karma."

"I hope Josie decides to visit us," I said. "I suggested it last time we spoke."

"That would be so great. Three sisters all together." Carla smiled, her eyes warm. "I'm happy you're staying in town, Mags. I love getting to spend time with you."

"And you're feeling better?" I asked.

"A little better, but I still need to manage my symptoms so I don't crash." She nudged Noah with her shoulder, wrinkling her nose. "Speaking of which, I'm sorry, but we shouldn't stay too long."

Noah nodded. "Let's get home." He turned to Cy. "Thanks for showing us your mushroom operation."

"Anytime." Cy sounded sincere, and I was glad he and Noah got on so well. I wanted to spend lots of time with my sister, especially if the four of us could hang out.

"We'll walk you to your car," Cy added, shifting as Noah and Carla got to their feet, so I had to lift myself off his chest.

"No need." Noah waved him back down. "You two look comfortable. Stay here. The path is easy enough."

I settled back against Cy's chest, all too happy to oblige. "We'll see you later," I told them.

"Count on it." Carla bent to plant a kiss on my cheek, then one on Cy's.

After they left, I gave a contented sigh. I was only in a T-shirt, but I had the warmth of the campfire on my front and Cy's warmth at my back. He draped his arm around me, stroking my upper arm with his fingers, his lips on my hair.

"This is nice," he murmured. "And the stars will come out soon."

"Will there be mosquitos?"

"The smoke will keep them away."

"My hair is going to stink of smoke."

"And your clothes." Cy nuzzled the back of my ear. "Unless you take them off."

I grinned. And though a delicious shiver was running through me, I acted surprised by his suggestion. "Take them off? Why would I do that here when we have a perfectly good bed in our bedroom."

"The house is such a long way away." His lips moved down to my neck, planting soft kisses against my ticklish skin. "To get you into bed would take at least five minutes. And I can't stand the thought your clothes might smell of smoke. I need to protect them." Putting his hand under my T-shirt, he pushed it up over my breast. Then his fingers delved underneath my bra, rubbing over my nipple.

I arched into his hand. "You're right," I said breathlessly. "Getting to the house would take too long."

He pulled my T-shirt off and moved over me, pushing me back so I was lying on the blanket. Then he smiled down at me. The softness of his eyes made the rest of his angular face more striking. His short beard fit him perfectly now, not hiding the squareness of his jaw, but enhancing it.

I smiled back. "My Cy," I whispered, the words coming out so unconsciously, it surprised me to hear them spoken aloud.

His smile widened. With his beard shaped back from his cheeks, I got to see a pair of perfect dimples appear. "My Mags," he whispered back. "I love you."

"I love you."

Our next kiss was slower. Our need was still there, but our urgency had transformed. Every touch was now a repeat of those words. Every touch a silent "I love you." It was in the movement of his lips against mine, and in the care with which his fingers stroked my bare torso.

Pulling back, he unlaced my sneakers one by one and tugged them off. Next he removed my jeans and underwear, pausing with each removal to kiss the skin he exposed.

"Are you cold?" he murmured.

"No, it feels good." The cool breeze whispering across my nipples only heightened my arousal, while the warmth of the fire on my bare thighs and the heat of Cy's big hands were pure pleasure.

He pulled off his own clothes quickly, then pulled me onto him. Over him.

I gazed down at him as I took him inside me. He clenched his teeth, hissing out a breath, then his chin lifted, his face tilting back. He groaned. "Mags." His eyes were dark, his hands cupping my breasts.

I groaned too, pushing down on him, wanting all of him. He was so big, so perfect, he filled both my body and my soul, giving me everything I needed. Everything I wanted.

Moving slowly, I rocked on him. He stroked my breasts and sides, then his fingers went between my legs. He knew just how to heighten my pleasure, to tip me over the edge.

He *knew* me.

Cy loved me.

The knowledge lifted me higher, as much as the practiced, expert strokes of his fingers did. As much as the thrust of him did, the way he drove so deeply inside of me. It was everything. *He* was everything.

As I cried out, shattering into a million shining pieces of sensation and pleasure, Cy pulsed inside me, groaning with me. He surged upward to wrap his strong arms around me, pulling me down onto his chest, both of us still orgasming together. His lips grazed mine, and his breath became my breath. Then he held me tight, the two of us so deeply connected, body and soul, it was as though we became one.

We snuggled together as the sky darkened and the stars grew bright. Zeppelin snored, the fire crackled, an owl hooted in the woods, and a deep, contented happiness settled into my bones.

After a long time, Cy spoke softly. "Mags, I've been thinking. You know Ruth is coming here soon?"

I nodded, my face against his chest, his chest hair rubbing softly against my cheek. "How could I not? Gemma's so excited. She can't wait to see her mom."

"The house will be crowded."

"I guess. But they aren't staying long. Unfortunately." I sighed. "We're both going to miss Gemma when they go back to Nashville."

"I want to ask Gem if she'll stay with us for the holidays. Would that be okay with you?"

"Of course!"

I lifted my head to smile up at him. He was lying on his back, one hand tucked behind his head, smiling back at me. In the firelight, he looked even more handsome, and another wave of contentment swept over me.

My Cy, I thought, managing not to say it aloud this time.

"I've been thinking about something else," he said. "What if I built a second house here, close to the river bank, with the trees all around? A house that's just for us, Mags. Designed by us. And we could leave the other one for Ruth and Gemma, if they decide to stay."

"Here?" I glanced beyond the fire. There were millions of stars visible. More stars than I'd ever seen in my life, brighter than I would have thought possible. The moon was full and so heavy it seemed to rest on top of the trees beyond the river. Its light sparkled on the water.

"This clearing was my sanctuary as a kid," he said. "This was the one place I could *be* a kid. Where I could forget about everything and be happy. And now you're that place for me." He stroked his fingers softly down my cheek. "I love the thought of the two of us living here together. But if you'd rather go somewhere else, or do something else, let's talk about it. I want to know what would make you happy."

I imagined what it might be like to make love with Cy in a cozy room with a big window overlooking the woods and the water. To wake up with the gentle sound of the river in my ears.

"I'd love to live here with you," I said. "It would make me happy, too."

"You wouldn't miss the city?"

"If I do, I can always visit my parents and Josephina. But I don't think I will miss it. My life already feels full. I have everything here that I didn't know I wanted. And as it turns out, it's just right."

Cy put both arms around me. He didn't say anything, but he didn't need to. His smile said it all.

ABOUT THE AUTHOR

Talia Hunter likes to include her three favorite things in her novels: toe-curling romance, snort-laughs, and heart-warming friendships. She recently moved to Australia's beautiful Gold Coast, where she's constantly amazed and not at all freaked out by the weird and wonderful critters. When she's not writing, you can usually find her with a glass of wine, a good book, at least one of her three cats, and a jumbo-sized can of bug spray.

Website: www.taliahunter.com
Facebook: https://www.facebook.com/taliahunter
Instagram: https://www.instagram.com/talia.hunter/
TikTok: @talia_hunter_romance
Goodreads: https://www.goodreads.com/taliahunter
Bookbub: https://www.bookbub.com/authors/talia-hunter

Find Smartypants Romance online:
Website: www.smartypantsromance.com
Facebook: https://www.facebook.com/smartypantsromance
Twitter: @smartypantsrom
Instagram: @smartypantsromance
Newsletter: https://smartypantsromance.com/newsletter/

ALSO BY TALIA HUNTER

The Grumpy Billionaire Romantic Comedy Series

The Billionaire and the Burglar (A Grumpy/Sunshine Romantic Comedy)

The Billionaire and the Booty Call (Grumpy Billionaire Romantic Comedy)

The Lennox Brothers Romantic Comedy Series

No Funny Business

No Laughing Matter

No Fooling Around

No Ordinary Christmas

The Lantana Island Series Contemporary Romance Series

Boss With Benefits

The Engagement Game

The Devil She Knew

ALSO BY SMARTYPANTS ROMANCE

<u>Green Valley Chronicles</u>
<u>The Love at First Sight Series</u>
<u>Baking Me Crazy by Karla Sorensen (#1)</u>
<u>Batter of Wits by Karla Sorensen (#2)</u>
<u>Steal My Magnolia by Karla Sorensen (#3)</u>
<u>Worth the Wait by Karla Sorensen (#4)</u>

<u>Fighting For Love Series</u>
<u>Stud Muffin by Jiffy Kate (#1)</u>
<u>Beef Cake by Jiffy Kate (#2)</u>
<u>Eye Candy by Jiffy Kate (#3)</u>
<u>Knock Out by Jiffy Kate (#4)</u>

<u>The Donner Bakery Series</u>
<u>No Whisk, No Reward by Ellie Kay (#1)</u>
<u>Dough You Love Me? By Stacy Travis (#2)</u>
<u>Tough Cookie by Talia Hunter (#3)</u>
<u>Muffin But Trouble by Talia Hunter (#4)</u>

<u>Oh Brother! Series</u>
<u>Crime and Periodicals by Nora Everly (#1)</u>
<u>Carpentry and Cocktails by Nora Everly (#2)</u>
Hotshot and Hospitality by Nora Everly (#3)
<u>Architecture and Artistry by Nora Everly (#4)</u>

<u>Small Town Silver Fox Series</u>
<u>Love in Due Time by L.B. Dunbar (#1)</u>
<u>Love in Deed by L.B. Dunbar (#2)</u>

__The Teachers' Lounge Series__

__Passing Notes by Nora Everly (#1)__

__Band Together by Piper Sheldon (#2)__

__Story of Us Collection__

My Story of Us: Zach by Chris Brinkley (#1)

My Story of Us: Thomas by Chris Brinkley (#2)

My Story of Us: Grayson by Chris Brinkley (#3)

__Seduction in the City__

__Cipher Security Series__

__Code of Conduct by April White (#1)__

__Code of Honor by April White (#2)__

__Code of Matrimony by April White (#2.5)__

__Code of Ethics by April White (#3)__

__Cipher Office Series__

__Weight Expectations by M.E. Carter (#1)__

__Sticking to the Script by Stella Weaver (#2)__

__Cutie and the Beast by M.E. Carter (#3)__

__Weights of Wrath by M.E. Carter (#4)__

__Common Threads Series__

__Mad About Ewe by Susannah Nix (#1)__

__Give Love a Chai by Nanxi Wen (#2)__

__Key Change by Heidi Hutchinson (#3)__

__Not Since Ewe by Susannah Nix (#4)__

__Lost Track by Heidi Hutchinson (#5)__

__Ewe Complete Me by Susannah Nix (#6)__

__Meet Your Matcha by Nanxi Wen (#7)__

__All Mixed Up by Heidi Hutchinson (#8)__

Bad Habit Book Club Series

Nun Too Soon by Lissa Sharpe (#1)

Educated Romance

Work For It Series

Street Smart by Aly Stiles (#1)

Heart Smart by Emma Lee Jayne (#2)

Book Smart by Amanda Pennington (#3)

Smart Mouth by Emma Lee Jayne (#4)

Play Smart by Aly Stiles (#5)

Look Smart by Aly Stiles (#6)

Smart Move by Amanda Pennington (#7)

Stage Smart by Aly Stiles (#8)

Lessons Learned Series

Under Pressure by Allie Winters (#1)

Not Fooling Anyone by Allie Winters (#2)

Can't Fight It by Allie Winters (#3)

The Vinyl Frontier by Lola West (#4)

Out of this World

London Ladies Embroidery Series

Neanderthal Seeks Duchess by Laney Hatcher (#1)

Well Acquainted by Laney Hatcher (#2)

Love Matched by Laney Hatcher (#3)

Wolf Brothers Series

Truth or Wolf by Anne Marsh (#1)

9 781959 097785